TWISTED FATE

by

Jonas Saul

PUBLISHED BY:

Imagine Press Inc.
Amazon Ebook ISBN: 978-1-519006-08-0
Paperback ISBN: 978-1-998047-90-1
Hardcover ISBN: 978-1-998047-89-5

Twisted Fate (Tales of Horror)

Aaron (Thirty-Nine)
Remains To Be Seen (Forty)

The Jake Wood Novels

The Immortal Gene (Book One)
The Immortal Target (Book Two)

Standalone Novels

'Til Death Do Us Part
The Drowning
The Woman in the Woods
The Threat
The Specter
The Mafia Trilogy
A Murder in Time
Frequency of the Dead

Co-Authored Novels

Collision Course (Written with Gary Ponzo)
There Will Be Blood (Written with Rania Stone)
The Soulless (Written with Rania Stone)

Short Story Collections

Twisted Fate (Tales of Horror)
Twists of Fate (Tales of Hope)

Hatred

WALTER SMATHEN STARED OUT the car window at the decrepit house and tried to calm his shaking hands. A rush of anger washed over him the minute his driver stopped in front of the rusted iron gate encircling the property.

He sat in the back seat of his Crown Victoria. His driver waited for instructions while Walter examined the abandoned house. It had to be over one hundred years old. He traced the foliage along the broken bricks. Two stories high, four columns stood proud in the front, supporting what was once a regal home, lost to tragedy more than twenty years ago. As Walter understood it, a business deal had gone awry. The Realtor said something about a mother and her two children being bludgeoned to death.

Walter had researched the house and read old news articles about the tragedy that night. The husband was still alive somewhere, but he'd lost his ability to function shortly after the murders and was committed to an institution. The murderer, an ex-business partner of the husband's, was never found. Some rumors say he's buried in the house. When Walter had asked how the husband escaped arrest, he was told the man used to be a police officer, and on the night of the murders, he was on duty with his partner. The alibi was solid.

A week ago, under the guise of full disclosure, Walter had asked his agent if he knew anything else.

"The house has sat empty since that night. I Googled what I could and asked around before showing you the place. Your plan to demolish this house and use the land to expand the mall's parking lot is the best thing that's come along for this area in a long time."

"I appreciate your attention to detail."

He'd rushed the closing and nailed a date a week later for the keys.

As rain slid down the window, Walter looked across the overgrown lawn at the old broken-down house. He tightened his grip on the door handle.

Why am I feeling such anger?

He hadn't felt such internal fury in so long that it seemed foreign to him.

A car's horn broke his reverie as the agent's Buick pulled up.

Walter's driver reached to open his door.

"Wait," Walter said, placing a hand on the back of the front seat. "It's okay. Stay in the car. I'll go in alone."

The driver eased back in his seat and nodded, catching Walter's eyes in the mirror.

Walter opened his door and crouched under an umbrella his Realtor held out just as he got to Walter's side. Together, they walked through the rusted gate and up to the front porch, where they found shelter between the columns.

"You have everything?" Walter asked.

"Yes, it's all here." Mike tapped an envelope held under his arm.

"Good. I want to take a look around first."

"I should caution you. I don't know how good the floors are, but the stairs broke down ten years ago. Walter, this house is in bad shape."

"I'm aware and will be careful. You can wait in the foyer. The demolition manager and a few of his men should be here anytime now. Make sure he gets those papers."

The front door resisted opening. He shoved it with his shoulder enough to force his way in. With the door open, a new sense of fear and anger tensed his stomach.

The soft light that fought through the curtained windows gave the house a haunted feel. But Walter didn't believe in such trivial things as haunted houses. He knew he was the only person in this house, alive or dead.

A wide staircase, broken and crumbled, led upstairs from the center of the foyer. There was just enough light to see open doors on the second floor.

He started for the large sitting room on the right, testing each step as if it wasn't something he could take back once committed to. The last homeowners attempted to create the image of a century home. Just inside the alcove, antique furniture sat in disarray, covered haphazardly by white blankets now turned brown, long lost to decay.

His chest tightened and wheezed as he inhaled. His attention was on the furnishings, he didn't notice the symptoms at first. He coughed and backed out of the room, careful to step where he'd made a path in the dust. He squeezed out the front door, sucked in a lung full of air, and coughed.

"You okay?" Mike asked.

Walter bobbed his head up and down. He put his hands on his knees and bent over, trying to get his breathing back under control.

"What happened in there?"

"Nothing. Too much dust. Wasn't … paying attention."

"Maybe we should wait out here for the demo guys."

Walter shook his head. "I want another look around."

"Suit yourself. Do you want an oxygen tank?"

Walter stood to his full height, cleared his throat, and frowned at Mike.

"Just kidding."

He turned back to the door and pushed his way in. This time he moved to the left of the foyer. Floorboards, withered by age and termites, cracked where he stepped. He stayed close to the wall and leaned into it for support.

Another room, larger than the foyer, opened before him with more pieces of furniture strewn about. Better light came through the large front windows.

Feelings of anger rose within him again. Violence thickened the air he breathed. He could taste it, touch it. As if the murders from two decades ago left tension in the air like a current of seething rage. He clenched his fists and leaned hard against the frame of the door.

Then his breath caught in his throat.

Before he could run from the house, a lone couch nestled in a corner near the back of the room caught his attention. Something about it drew his eyes.

He breathed deep, releasing the pent-up air trapped in his lungs.

The four legs of the couch were arched in a claw-like grip as if it held the floor in a solid embrace. The seat cushion appeared to be newer than the couch.

That's the one I want.

He'd have it delivered to his home office.

What is wrong with the air in this house?

He ran for the porch and panted as if he'd run a mile.

The rain had subsided. Walter checked his watch and decided to head home before his wife's next round of medications.

"Mike, tell the demo guys to remove the couch in the back corner of the room on the left. It's the only one without a furniture cover on it. I want it delivered to my home office later today. There's a cash bonus in it for them. Then instruct them to destroy the rest of this property on schedule."

He stepped off the porch and hurried through the wet grass to his car.

It took at least five miles of asphalt between Walter and the house before he began to feel better. His breathing resumed its normal rhythm, and he didn't feel as angry as he had earlier. He couldn't figure out what had angered him so much—he'd just been pissed off.

At sixty-two years old and as nearly financially free as he would ever be, anger was a mistress he rarely coupled with. There was no use for it. Lawyers handled all the shit that bothered him.

His wife had gotten sicker recently. She moped around the house and talked about dying, stuck in a *poor me* phase.

His son locked himself in his room when he should be out looking for a job. Lawyers didn't fix those kinds of problems unless he wanted to get a divorce.

Sure she's dying, but can't she do it with more dignity? People die every day.

***

Diabetes, in its final stages, is one hell of an awful disease. Walter had a private nurse for his wife, but the nurse had recently walked out. The new nurse didn't start until the weekend. With this only Wednesday, Walter would have to act as a nurse. Normally he wouldn't have minded caring for his wife, but not today.

"Where are you?" his wife shouted from somewhere in the house.

Two nights ago, she couldn't stay awake. Last night, she was an insomniac. Joan accelerated her symptoms because she skipped her insulin shots and ate the chocolate bars their son Alex snuck into her. No matter how often Walter warned him—not to mention the two diabetic comas his mother had experienced—Alex remained loyal to his mother.

Joan was nauseous and had vomited at least once a day this past week. She seemed to be confused about so many things.

He opened her bedroom door and stopped to watch her. How could he be thinking such inhumane thoughts? This was his wife, his Joan. She needed him. Yesterday, he sat and read to her. His patience had been limitless. But today, patience seemed distant, far away.

He placed the insulin needle on the tray beside her bed. She looked at him, smiled, and breathed out a long breath in an exaggerated sigh. Rancid was the best word to describe the air quality exhaled from her dying body.

"What took you so long?" Joan asked. "I've been waiting all day. The sheets need cleaning. I threw up over there and haven't eaten since this morning. Walter, get me some food. I'm sorry for my tone, but I'm used to the nurse being here. We do things a certain way."

"Joan, you know where I've been. I'll get you something to eat, but you'll have to watch how you talk to me."

Her eyes probed him. "What's wrong with how I talk?"

To avoid a fight, he started for the door.

"I asked you a question," Joan shouted after him.

Walter turned back to her. "We do not talk to each other this way. You're confused. Take your needle, and I'll be back with your lunch." He stepped into the hallway and slammed the door on her protests.

Halfway to the kitchen, his cell phone rang. He ran for his office and snapped it up.

"Hello."

"Walter? Oh man, this is bad."

"Mike? Is that you?"

"Yeah. The demolition guys and I are still at the house and ..."

"Do I hear a siren in the background?"

"Yes. Police and ambulance are here."

"What the hell happened?"

"Give me a sec. Let me go where it'll be a little quieter."

Mike breathed into the phone as he moved farther from the sirens. "There, can you hear me better?"

"Much. Now, tell me what happened."

"The demolition guys showed up just after you left. I walked them into the foyer and showed them the couch you wanted. One of the guys walked over to it and sat down. I told him how risky that was as the floor may not support him. He laughed at me and lay out on the couch."

"Mike, what has this got to do with emergency services?"

"I'm getting there."

"Get there faster," Walter said. He'd only left his wife's room minutes ago, and her screams reached his office.

"I told the guys to hurry up and move the couch so we could get on with the demolition specs. For some reason unknown to me, they looked seriously pissed off, especially the guy who had sat on the couch. They picked up the sofa and carried it outside to the front porch. Then the guy who had sat on the sofa ran back into the house. Let me tell you, he was mad about something. His co-worker yelled after him. We stepped into the foyer, but he was gone."

"Are you taking your time on purpose? Are you going to tell me why the cops are there?" Walter's patience had ebbed.

Joan banged something on the floor and shouted. Walter wondered how high her blood pressure was now. He almost shouted back at her but tightened his jaw to avoid hurling abusive slurs her way.

The nurse said to watch for diabetic acidosis. The last stages.

"The guy had climbed upstairs somehow. Then he fell. A piece of the old banister impaled him. He's dead, Walter, he's dead."

***

His nerves rattled; it took Walter ten minutes to prepare the sandwiches for his wife. He took them to her, doing his best to tune her out on the way up the stairs. The insulin needle lay on the nightstand table, unused. He knocked it off the table. It hit the floor and skidded under the closet door.

"What did you do that for?" Joan asked.

"You will eat your lunch in peace. Then you will sleep. If I hear another word from you, I will call the hospital and have you taken away. Understood?"

With a subtle tip of her head, Joan nodded her understanding. He knew the threat of the hospital would shut her up.

"Good."

He stormed out of the bedroom. His cell rang as he entered his office. By the time he got to the phone, he had cursed himself for being so abrupt with her. Some days were better than others, but today was his worst for some reason.

He snatched up the phone. "Hello."

"This is John Mackay. I'm with the Chicago Police Department. Are you the new owner of this house out here on Michigan near 55th?"

"Yes, I am."

"I was wondering if we could meet up so I could have a word with you."

***

Walter sat at his large banker's desk in his home office and tapped his pen. The demolition team had left the old house after their colleague's body had been taken away. They'd carried the couch into his office a half hour ago and collected the cash bonus.

He stared across the room at the couch that a dead man had sat on. It didn't match his office. He'd have to change a few things around so it would fit. Its shape didn't appear like a traditional sofa, so he'd looked it up online. It was a kind of chaise lounge with the back piece only on one side. The sitting area was long and designed for a person to extend their legs. A soft floral pattern covered the antique, which was something Walter would normally have detested, but this couch held meaning for him. He had no idea why, but it felt sentimental.

When the doorbell rang, he dropped the pen he'd been tapping.

"Fuck!" he smacked his desk and got up.

The doorbell rang again.

"I'm coming!" he shouted.

By the time he got to the door, he was ready to let the police in on a little secret. His wife was dying in the upstairs room, and right now, she was sleeping. So the next time they come to his house, could they not fuck with the doorbell.

He grabbed the knob, swung the door open, and stepped back in surprise.

Joan stood there, leaning against the door frame in her pajamas.

"What the *hell* is this?" he shouted.

"I noticed something about you," she said as she pointed her finger at him.

Walter scanned the street, looking for nosy neighbors. He grabbed Joan's arm and yanked her into the house.

"What did you notice, Joan?" He was surprised he had the willpower to keep most of the anger out of his voice.

"You always run when people ring the bell or call your phone, but you don't run for me when I call you."

"Actually, I do. I run for you every day. Otherwise, you would be in a hospital."

He helped her up the stairs. She leaned into him hard. He wanted to ask her how she'd made it to the front door on her own if she could barely walk.

"I wanted to ring the bell," Joan whispered. "I wanted to watch you run for me one more time before I die."

"You're not going to start that stuff about dying again, are you?" They were almost at the top of the stairs. "You know I come running when you call for me."

"That's only partly true. You run to me, not for me. Walter, don't kid yourself. It's been a long time since we were a *couple*."

They reached the top of the stairs, Joan leading the way now. She rolled around the corner with her shoulder on the wall for support. Walter stayed close behind, his hands near her lower back.

"You sound delusional," he said. "We *are* a couple. You have the best in-home nursing money can buy. You're not languishing in a hospital bed somewhere. You haven't got much to complain about, Joan."

She stopped so abruptly by his office door that Walter almost bumped into her.

"What's that?" she asked, pointing at the new couch.

"It's a chaise lounge. I just had it delivered. I retrieved it from the old house they're going to tear down for the parking lot expansion."

Joan lumbered across the hall and disappeared into his office. Walter followed, knowing the police officer would be there any minute.

"Joan, what are you up to? You need to get back to bed before you fall. You don't have the strength for this."

"There's something wrong with this thing."

There's something wrong with you.

"Everything is okay. You've just had a hard day without your nurse here. Now, come on, let's go back to your room." He took her hand and tried to coax her out of his office.

She snapped her hand back and moved toward the sofa.

"What are you doing?" he asked. Like a swarm of bees attacking a hive breaker, anger swelled in him. "Enough with this shit! I have people arriving at any moment for a meeting. You will go back to your room and sleep, or I will carry you."

Joan sneered. Then she dropped onto the couch. She tried to make it look accidental like she tripped, but Walter could tell it was deliberate. In the time it took him to respond, she had spread out the length of the couch, running her hands along the fabric.

"What the *fuck* are you doing?" He had forgotten how good it felt to get really angry. His fists clenched at the frustration she caused. The anger was so raw and unglued that he tasted blood. It took every ounce of his humanity not to strike her face. Then her body. And not stop until she was a bloody pulp.

The expression on her face changed. She rolled off the couch and hit the floor like a sack of lead balls with no bounce.

Her sobbing and weeping worked on relieving his anger. He unclenched his fists.

What's happening to me? Why am I so worked up today?

Normally her antics didn't rouse him past annoyed.

He lifted her waif of a body up over his shoulder and carried her out of his office, down the hall, and into her sour room. She didn't protest. She lay across his shoulder and cried.

He dropped her onto her bed and started for the door.

"Goodbye, Walter."

"Goodbye, Joan," he said, mimicking her words with sarcasm. He stopped at the bedroom door. "Do not come out of this room for anything. I'll bring your dinner, and I'll clean up this fucking mess after my meeting. Understood?"

Joan nodded. "I won't bother you again."

He slammed the door so hard the trim near the handle cracked, which pleased him. The crack was his mark, his stamp of anger.

Today is a good day to be angry.

He wouldn't excuse it. Emotions were meant to be felt.

"Hello?" A male voice.

He jumped a clear foot. His shout of surprise came out like a pissed-off cat's cry.

"You okay?" the man asked.

Walter looked over the railing and saw a cop standing just inside his front door. Evidently, he had forgotten to close the door after Joan's little fiasco with the doorbell.

"I knocked," the cop said, "but it was open. I heard a door slam pretty hard, so I stepped in. I'm Officer John Mackay. I called earlier."

Walter moved for the stairs. "Of course, come on in. May I get you a beverage?" He stepped off the top stair and waited for a reply.

"No, thanks. I just have a few questions for you, and then I'll be on my way."

"Come on up to my office. We'll talk in there."

Officer Mackay followed Walter into his office. Walter sat behind his desk while the cop sat in one of the two chairs facing the desk. The officer pulled out a pad and pen and began talking. It took ten minutes to get through most of the preliminary questions for the cop to establish that this was nothing more than a workplace accident.

"So I guess that's it?" Walter asked.

"For now. Since you own the property and were employing them, the Workplace and Safety Board will want to talk to you, too. You're going to have to wait on those demolition plans until our full investigation can wrap up. Shouldn't take longer than a week."

Walter stood from his chair. "That's fine. I completely understand. Now, if that's all, I must attend to my wife."

The cop put his pad away, got up, and headed for the hallway.

"That's some couch you have there."

"Thanks."

The officer slowed and stopped by the door. "Look at the legs on that thing. They look like claws or talons of some sort. Where would you get an antique like that?"

Was this a trick question?

The cop was just at the house where the couch came from. He talked to Mike and the demolition guys. He had to know the couch came from that house.

"I received it today. I try to find something to bring home in every piece of property I buy to demolish. Something to say that the life in the house isn't completely destroyed. This couch will live on long after the house is converted into a parking lot."

The cop nodded as if he knew something that Walter didn't. He could see the cop wanted to play the *I'm smarter than you are* card.

Let's evaluate pay grades, asshole. Then we'll see who's smarter.

They stepped into the hallway.

"Sad what happened, eh?" the cop asked.

"Very sad. Accidents can happen. People die every day."

A door banged against a wall somewhere.

"What now?" Walter said out loud.

He hustled past the cop and up to Joan's bedroom. She lay just inside the doorframe on the floor, face down.

"Okay, let's get you to bed." He struggled with her dead weight. His peripheral vision revealed the cop had followed him.

Joan seemed heavier than before. Walter set her down and caught his breath. He looked over at the bedside table. Strewn across the top beside the food tray was a small collection of needles with all their plungers pushed to the bottom.

He looked at his wife's arm. Blood had trickled from the inside of her elbow, where there were over a dozen puncture marks.

The cop talked into his radio, calling for an ambulance. Walter backed away from his wife's body as the cop checked for a pulse.

"People die every day, eh?" the cop said, repeating Walter's words from moments ago.

***

Walter needed a stiff drink. It was past nine in the evening. The last of the authorities had just left. As far as anyone could tell, Joan had killed herself.

His son had shown up about an hour after his mother had died. He locked himself in his room, where Walter could hear him crying.

What the hell's going on? Where did this day come from? Everything's so fucked up.

He poured more whiskey into his glass from the small bar in his office. He hated funerals, and now he had two to deal with. Send flowers to one and arrange the other. Nothing pissed him off more.

Wait a minute, he thought. *My wife just died. Why am I angry with her for the inconvenience? Shouldn't I be grieving? Perhaps it's because the Joan I'd married died many years ago.*

Her mental attitude toward the diabetic condition had deteriorated rapidly. With a better grasp of what challenges she had ahead of her and a will to overcome them, he would have had more respect for her. All she did was whine and complain like life owed her a chance. With a better diet and some exercise, his wife would be alive and in a healthier place.

Fuck her. She asked for this.

He tilted his whiskey glass back and shot the rest of it into his mouth. It raced down the back of his throat with a welcoming bite.

Would Alex ever stop bawling like a fucking baby?

The bottle of Canadian whiskey was empty now. He set his glass down and left the office en route to the cellar for another bottle. As he passed Alex's closed door, he stopped.

Damn, can that kid cry. Is this how twenty-year-olds grieve?

Walter banged on the door. "Alex, what's going on?"

The weeping continued unimpeded. Walter tried the door handle. It opened. He stepped in and stared at his son curled up on the bed.

"You gonna be okay?" he asked, not expecting an answer. At least not one he'd like.

Alex nodded and made a feeble attempt to wipe his eyes.

"Look, get yourself together and come to my office. I'm going downstairs. I'll meet you back there in a few minutes. We can talk."

Alex buried his face in his hands.

"Did you hear me?"

He moaned acknowledgment.

"I'll meet you in my office in five minutes." Walter walked away, leaving his son's door wide open.

He got to the basement, grabbed the bottle of whiskey, and headed back upstairs. He took a peek in on the way by Alex's bedroom door. The unmade bed was empty.

He walked over to the mini-bar in his office and stopped. Alex sat on the antique couch, scowling.

"What's going on with you?" Walter asked, amused that his son could show so much anger. "One minute, you're bawling like a baby, and now you look pissed off."

"It's all your fault!" Alex shouted.

Walter set the bottle down on the bar's shiny surface and scanned his son's face.

"You might want to watch what you say here. Your mother had diabetes. She was very sick. She had saved her needles and chose today to take them all at once. That had nothing to do with me. Are we clear?"

Alex didn't respond. He just sat there and glared at Walter.

"I *said*, are we clear?"

"Yeah, I'm clear, all right. You killed her."

"Okay, that's it. Call a friend, go to a hotel, but I want you the *fuck* out of my house right the *fuck* now!" Walter was conscious of his anger. He was aware of it on a cellular level. It was unfamiliar, but it was welcomed. It made him feel powerful and in control.

Alex got up from the couch and bumped Walter's shoulder as he passed him.

"Watch yourself, young man. I may be in my sixties, but I can fuck around like the best of them."

His son's footsteps pounded down the stairs, then the front door opened and shut with a slam. By the time he poured a glass of whiskey and took his first shot, tires screeched outside, and then the sound of metal crunched together.

He left the office and headed downstairs in a run. Too many people had pissed him off. His wife died today. His son was blaming him. And now one of his son's friends thinks he can show off and squeal his tires all over the fucking place.

He opened the front door and jumped out onto his porch, ready to scream at the offending driver.

He blinked and staggered, the whiskey already working on him. Two vehicles had hit each other. A black SUV had T-boned a smaller Nissan. A man was caught between the two vehicles.

Walter leaned on the doorframe for support. People across the street talked on cell phones. Probably calling for help, but it was too late. The guy was dead. His waist disappeared below the grill of the SUV. A running shoe lay about five feet back under the SUV, still attached to a leg.

Poor guy. Wrong place at the wrong time.

"People die every day," Walter mumbled to himself. He turned around and headed for the stairs. Someone behind him yelled. Someone else cried.

Why the hell does everyone have to be so fucking loud?

Halfway up the stairs, he teetered, the whiskey taking effect on his balance.

"Walter," someone said behind him. "Ahh, I think you better come and look at this."

He gripped the railing beside him as he looked down at Crawford, his neighbor, from two doors up.

Why the hell is my front door always left open?

"I already saw the accident," Walter said.

"I'm sorry, Walter. I really am."

What the fuck is Crawford talking about?

"You heard about Joan?" Walter asked.

Crawford frowned. "No."

"It's fine, Crawford. Maybe it's better she's gone. She doesn't have to suffer anymore. That's life. People die every day."

Crawford stepped back. "You okay, Walter?"

"Of course. Why wouldn't I be?"

More vehicles came to a stop in front of the house. The emergency lights splashed a myriad of colors across his windows and doorstep.

"Sure, people die every day, Walter. But this is Alex. He's your son." Crawford stepped backward out the door and disappeared.

Walter denied what he'd heard. It couldn't be. Alex was just here. They'd argued, and then he left the house.

Why the hell would he run out into the street directly in front of moving cars?

The walk down the stairs seemed long and arduous. Walter made it without falling. He got to the open door and looked at the carnage. A blue tarp had been placed over the man sandwiched between the two vehicles.

He got to his front steps, sat down, and waited for someone to confirm who was under the tarp. If no one came, then it wasn't Alex. Simple as that. He wouldn't believe it until then.

His stomach protested.

How much did I drink already?

He bowed his head and closed his eyes. He kept his breathing steady while holding his stomach, hoping the nausea would abate.

"Walter, you doing okay?"

He jumped, lifted his head, and banged his elbow on the porch railing. "Why the fuck is everyone scaring the shit out of me today?"

"Walter, maybe we should go inside and talk."

It was that fucking cop, Mackay.

"Okay. But we talk in my office. If you're going to tell me that that SUV hit my son, I know I will need a drink."

"Maybe you've had enough already."

Walter got to his feet, secured his balance, and glared at the cop. "You might be somebody on the street, but on my front lawn, I see a man trying to school me on drinking. From this moment on, while your visit to my property will be short, I'd watch what the fuck you say to me. I've had a terrible day, and I'm really fucking pissed about it."

Mackay didn't respond.

I give him credit for that.

They made it upstairs and stood across from each other in Walter's office. It seemed like only a few hours since Mackay had been there, and now another visit and another death. Walter wondered if he would need some kind of therapy. Or a lawyer.

"Have a seat, Mackay. You want a drink?"

"Not while on duty."

Walter poured a double and went to sit behind his desk but stopped halfway. He eyed the couch. The fucking couch that started everything.

"You okay, Walter?"

"Yeah. Just thought I'd try out my new couch."

He walked over and sat down.

The moment he touched the fabric, hatred coursed through him. A hate so vile that living another moment was contrary to its existence. The anger rose inside him like a red rocket firing salvos into his consciousness.

He downed his double whiskey in one long pull and glared at officer Mackay. He decided the fucking pig who had intruded in his home and his life had to die.

Fuck him and his badge. What the hell? Come into my house and want to interrogate me. Where's my lawyer? Where are my rights? Miranda, my ass. This guy was a fake, and killing him is the best thing for everybody.

Walter got up, opened the bottle of whiskey, and shot three huge gulps straight from the tip.

"Are you okay, Walter?" Mackay asked.

He turned and tossed the half-empty bottle into the corner of his office, where it rolled a few times, the rest of the alcohol spilling out.

"Just fucking fine, asshole."

"Calm down," the cop said, his hands in front of him. "You might want to watch how you're talking to me. I'm here on official business as an officer of the law."

"Fuck you, you fucking *pig*," Walter spat and lunged at him.

Mackay wasn't ready. Walter's two hundred-plus pounds smashed into the cop, and both of them dropped onto Walter's desk. The small of Mackay's back bent awkwardly and twisted from all the weight. He screamed in pain, and his ability to fight diminished.

They rolled off the desk and hit the floor. Walter dug his thumb into the center of the cop's throat and pressed. Mackay flailed at

Walter but was no match for Walter's hatred. It didn't take more than a minute for the cop to stop twitching.

"That halo over your head only needs to drop a few inches to become a noose, motherfucker," Walter said as he stood over the dead cop. He spat in Mackay's face.

The fact that this guy's body is even in my house makes me sick.

Walter vomited. It hit his desk and splashed onto his office chair. He vomited again, aiming for the cop's face, covering him with stomach contents laced with bile.

He couldn't believe how bad his body felt. What was wrong with him?

He half walked, half lurched to the corner, and picked up the empty bottle of whiskey. He searched for another drop, found none, then walked over to the couch.

What is it about this fucking couch?

People had died since he brought it into his somewhat normal life.

He tried to pry the main cushion back. It wouldn't budge. He didn't want to go all the way to the kitchen for a knife, so he grabbed a letter opener off his desk and cut along the edge of the cushion.

Why he was wrecking an antique in perfectly good condition was beyond him. All he knew, with some kind of certainty, was this thing had something to do with the day's troubles.

He got the side cut open and started working on the back.

People entered his house on the main level. He heard them talking among themselves.

"I'll be right down," he yelled.

His cutting hand worked harder as his vision blurred.

"Fucking whiskey," he mumbled.

He tossed the letter opener aside and stood with the help of the wall. As he lifted the cushion's edge, a voice stopped him.

"Step away from the couch and put your hands in the air."

A cop stood at the door, legs spread, a gun pointed at Walter.

"What the fuck do you want?"

"I said, step away and raise your hands."

"This is *my* fucking house. I do what I want to. Fuck you." Walter pulled up the cushion.

The gun's report deafened him. Something smacked him in the neck. He staggered away from the couch, let the cushion go, and bumped into the wall before falling. Blood covered his chest and arms. It flowed like an open hydrant in the street.

His anger ebbed along with his life. He closed his eyes, relieved it was over. In the last moment of consciousness, he tried to apologize, but all that came out of his mouth was his wife's name.

***

Shaking like a wet dog in December, Officer Johnson stood over the man's body.

What have I done?

He had only been on the force for eleven months, and now he'd just shot a man in cold blood.

Johnson looked at the sofa. What was the guy reaching for? He had probable cause. An officer was down, and this guy didn't listen to him twice. Then the guy reached to open a hidden compartment on the couch. How was he supposed to know whether the guy had weapons in there or not?

Johnson pulled the cushion back. His jaw went slack. His knees weakened, and he urinated in his uniform. He ran from the room and outside the house in seconds flat, only tripping once on the stairs.

He collected himself enough to radio in another crime scene. He called in the special investigations unit because an officer was down, and he'd fired his weapon.

Nothing would erase the image of the skeletal remains hidden inside that sofa from his memory. It was alive, he was sure of it. The skull had smiled at him, and a reddish light glowed behind its eyes.

Crazy as it was, he could still see the smile and the evil behind those eyes.

He deliberated a moment, then ran back into the house and raced upstairs. When he entered the office, both bodies were still lying as they were when he left.

He pulled out his gun and emptied it into the couch.

He went through the desk's drawers until he came upon a lighter. He paid little attention to the vomit spewed across the top of the desk and the chair.

With the lighter in hand, he ran over, placed it just below the edge of the couch, and flicked the switch.

The fabric caught quickly. Soon the end of the sofa was engulfed in flames. He swore he heard a high-pitched scream like that of a mouse being squished in a cat's teeth.

He ran downstairs and outside.

"I need an extinguisher," he yelled at the ambulance guy closest to him. A moment later, extinguisher in hand, he bolted for the house. Other officers entered behind him.

By the time they got to the office on the second floor, most of the room was engulfed in flames. Johnson stepped up close to the door and peered in. The couch was covered in righteous fire. He knew it was destroyed. Whatever that thing was, it was never coming back.

Someone pulled on his arm and told him to get out. He allowed them to pull him back to the stairs, where he turned around and walked out of the house, leaving the fire for the fire department to deal with.

His job was done. He felt it. After touching the couch, a piece of it possessed him, like being touched by Lucifer. He had felt the presence of hell. Instead of understanding life and creation, he felt death and how to cause it. Bestowed upon him was an understanding of the day's events and how whoever touched or sat on the couch was destined for a quick release from this life.

Burning it was the only answer. Destroying the deadly sofa was the only way.

He turned to his supervisor, who asked question after question.

"I don't know what happened. The guy reached for the sofa, opened a lid of some sort like he was going for a weapon, and I fired. After I shot him, he pulled out a lighter and set the couch on fire. That's when I ran for the extinguisher …"

The Elements

John Stevenson wondered if he would die out here as he watched the snowflakes fall. He took a sip of coffee from his mug as the snow accumulated on his property, burying the cabin deeper.

The cabin got colder by the hour, the ache in his leg increasing along with it.

The last piece of wood in the fireplace had been reduced to ash, with the rest of the firewood covered in snow outside on the front deck. John had figured he had enough wood to get him through until he left today. But now he may be stuck at the cabin another night.

He turned to the empty room and walked over to the sofa where he sat to consider his options. Being alone concerned him. After preparing the cabin to be closed, he'd gotten his backpack ready, checked the fireplace to ensure it was extinguished, and started for the door.

That was where the snow had stopped him.

He took the last sip of his coffee and set down the cup as the satellite phone rang.

He picked it up. "Hello?"

"May I speak with John Stevenson, please?"

"Who's calling?"

"I'm Doctor Morganson. Could you please come to Liberty Memorial Hospital as soon as you can? There's been an accident."

Images of his daughters, and his wife, flashed through his mind. He leaned back on the sofa, a hand on his forehead. He stared at the wooden roof, the thick beams holding the weight of the snow.

"What kind of accident?" he asked.

"I can give you more details when you get here. When should we expect you?"

He checked his watch. "It's two o'clock now. I could be there by six or a little later."

"That long? Isn't there any way you could come quicker, Mr. Stevenson? The police need your help."

The police?

"My help?" John leaned forward. "What're you talking about? What's happened?"

The doctor hesitated. John was about to ask if the doctor was still there when the man spoke.

"I can't tell you much over the phone, but the more you know, the better. You need to prepare yourself."

John rose from the couch and moved around the coffee table. There was something in the doctor's voice that told him to prepare to be decimated by the news.

He stopped pacing and glanced at the door. He should've left the cabin hours ago. He would've gotten to his car already. He was stuck deep in the mountains with one of the worst blizzards he'd ever seen, covering everything in a deep, thick white.

The last of his candles dripped wax as it burned by the door, casting a soft glow in that area. The snow continued to fall outside, the sky a blanket of gray and white. Inside the cabin, it was already getting dark. He thought of omens and wondered if the early dark was a premonition of things to come.

"It's your wife and child, sir," the doctor said. "They were in a terrible accident. I'm sorry."

"Are they okay?" he asked as he began pacing again. "Tell me that, at least. They're alive, right?"

"Your daughter will pull through. She was in a child seat. Her injuries are bruises and several scratches. I'm afraid it's your wife, sir."

"What happened to Tera?" He paused, then rephrased the question. "How bad?"

"We're still not sure."

"Look, I'm in a remote cabin over twenty miles from civilization." John's words rushed from his mouth like an auctioneer. "It's accessed by snowmobile only. I'm two hours from my car in the *best* conditions. From there, it'll take me a half hour to get to Liberty Memorial, depending on road conditions."

"Just hurry."

The line went dead. John set down the phone on the couch beside him and rubbed his face.

At least my daughters are fine.

Whatever happened to his wife would be healed over time. She was a fighter. She'd pull through.

Shit, what was that part about the police?

He grabbed his backpack, dropped the satellite phone in his jacket pocket, and limped across the wooden floor. He blew the candle out by the door with a soft puff of breath. The only illumination came through the main window from the glow of the fresh snow.

The backpack felt reasonably light as he threaded his arms through the straps and slipped it on his back. The wind buffeted him when he opened the door, and the bitter cold chilled his face. His eyes watered, blurring his vision. How could he do anything for his family from the cabin? How could he help his wife and his children?

"You can't," a voice whispered behind him.

He pivoted and ducked, his hands up in a defensive posture.

"Who's there?" he shouted.

The silence in the cabin taunted him, the shadows deepening in the corners. The breeze from outside rushed past him, cooling the sweat on the back of his neck.

"Hello?" he shouted.

It had to have been the wind. He was alone.

He turned back to the blizzard and stepped outside. The wind proved relentless. It hit him hard, a gust blowing snow into his face. He squeezed his eyes closed until it passed and then turned to secure the door with his key.

The trudge through the snow was long and hard with the ache in his bad leg. With each step, he thought about his family.

I'm coming for you.

His Ski-Doo was half submerged in snow. He pulled gloves out of his jacket pockets, slipped them on, and brushed off the Ski-Doo's seat. With a long exaggerated kick, he mounted the seat and was just about to fire it up when he saw an indentation in the snow to the right of the machine. The snow had melted in that specific area. He leaned down to get a closer look when the smell of gas hit him. A closer examination revealed the gas tank had leaked again. He sat upright and stared at the gauge.

Empty.

He shouted his wife's name and punched the top of the tank. Pain shot up his arm. He'd hit the tank at an angle, possibly breaking a knuckle. Upon inspection of the injury, he failed to see the source of the pain.

I have to get to the hospital. To my family.

He got off the Ski-Doo and started for the cabin's front door, retracing his previous boot holes in the snow, limping as the ache in his leg worsened. Through the front window, he detected someone inside the cabin, watching him—a woman in a long black dress, her face darkened in shadow, eyes rimmed a deep red. He reeled back at the sight of her, startled.

She floated away from the window and disappeared from view behind the wall by the front door.

"Hey!" John shouted, but the wind swallowed his voice. "What're you doing in my cabin?"

His hand aching, John fished out the cabin's key without dropping it in the snow, then unlocked the door.

He barged in and scanned the interior.

"I saw you," he shouted. "Come out, come out, wherever you are."

He turned sideways and listened. If someone were walking around his small, two-roomed cabin, he would hear them.

"Okay, you want me to come looking for you? Fine, have it your way."

He moved away from the door, turned to slam it shut, and, with what little light he still had, walked across to the fireplace where his ax leaned against the wall.

"Don't!" the voice shouted.

He stumbled on his feet, landing awkwardly on his bad leg. Balance lost for a brief second, he bumped the wall with his shoulder and smacked his sore hand into the ax's handle.

"Who the fuck's here?" he shouted. "Where are you?"

He lifted the ax. It seemed heavy in his left hand. If the opportunity came to use it, he would have to guide it with his sore right hand.

Although I wouldn't really use an ax on someone, would I?

Something thumped the roof. He looked up, staring at the wooden underside, not really seeing it in the darkening room.

I have to get that last candle working.

He moved away from the dead fireplace, his attention riveted on the other parts of the cabin. The intruder would show themselves again, and he would be ready this time.

The snow hadn't stopped in thirty-six hours, and he hadn't noticed any prints around the property when he got the last bit of wood yesterday. He hadn't heard any Ski-Doos approaching, either.

So who was here?

"Where'd the voices come from?" he asked out loud. He looked around the cabin, more slowly this time, scanning the already black corners. Someone could stand in any one of them, watching him, and he wouldn't be able to tell.

He thought of his parents. He remembered how they had died of hypothermia on a stormy winter night, just like this one. They had been lost in snowy conditions as they wandered. Twenty degrees below zero. The police had organized a group of volunteers. John had hurt his leg in a car accident while looking for his parents. He hadn't got there in time to help.

John moved along the wall to the kitchen, the ax dragging behind him. The drawer to the right of the sink held the wooden matches. He retrieved the box, walked back to the front door, and tried to light the candle.

The small amount of light did nothing. He had no more than an hour before this last candle would blow out.

The satellite phone rang.

Startled, he yanked it from his jacket pocket, stumbled on his bad leg, and lost his balance. He hit the floor hard, trying to save the phone. The pain in his hand went from a dull throb to an instant pounding.

Even though he saw his breath in the chilly cabin, his forehead was clammy with sweat. It felt like his eyes were bulging from their sockets.

What a mess I've become.

He lifted the phone as it rang again.

"Hello," he said through breaths.

"Hello. John?" a male voice asked.

"Yes, who's this?"

"It's Brian, Tera's brother."

John attempted to get to his feet but was met with difficulty. The phone had slipped below his ear when he'd cupped it between his shoulder and jaw.

"I'm sorry. Could you repeat that?" John asked.

"Brian, you know, your wife's brother."

"Right, Brian. What's up?"

"Liberty Memorial just called me. They said there had been an accident."

"They called me, too. I'm trying to make my way there now."

"As you know, I'm in Britain. It'll take me until at least tomorrow to get a flight out. Do you think you could handle Suzy on your own?"

"Of course I can." John paused and stared vacantly at the front door of the cabin. The flickering candle drew his eye. "Wait, what do you mean by *handle* her?" As he asked the question, something else came to him. The doctor had said his daughter would pull through. The doctor had not said *daughters*.

"They didn't tell you?"

"The doctor told me my daughter would be okay and to hurry to the hospital because the police needed my help. That was it." John struggled to his feet and made it to the sofa, where he dropped hard and leaned heavily on the backpack that still clung to his back.

"Tera had an emergency telephone card in her purse. Your name was first on the list, mine second. Doctor Morganson just called me five minutes ago to see if I had a picture of Suzy."

"Why would they want her picture?"

"Officers at the hospital were notified there was another daughter, and when they called the officers still at the scene of the accident, they saw small footprints leaving the area. The prints walked straight into a clump of trees where they were lost. They're organizing a search party as we speak. John, I'm sorry, but Suzy is out there somewhere, alone and cold. Her jacket was found in Tera's car. John, she could be hurt, and it's below freezing. You have to hurry."

John's head spun. How could things get any worse? His wife and one daughter were in the hospital. His other daughter was alone in the dark somewhere, freezing.

Just like my parents ten years ago—alone and freezing.

He would have to tell Brian of his predicament. He moved the phone from his left ear and switched it to his right. In his shock at the news, he had forgotten how bad his hand was. When he opened his fingers to take the satellite phone, the pain flared, causing him to fumble the handset. The phone fell from his grasp, hit the wooden floor, and split into pieces.

John stared at his salvation, scattered in at least five plastic chunks at his feet. He was now a prisoner in his own cabin. No means of transportation out. No way to communicate with the outside world. He was on his last candle and didn't have enough wood to sustain any kind of warmth overnight. His hand was likely broken, and his daughter was wandering in a snowstorm somewhere miles away, lost in the dark.

He kicked a couple of pieces of the phone away and walked over to the window, leaving the ax leaning against the sofa. The light was fading for another day. In a short time, his world would be absolutely black.

He cursed the snow for taking his parents from him. He cursed it for hurting his wife, who now lay in a hospital bed without him by her side. But most of all, he cursed it because it stopped him from doing his job as a father and husband.

Maybe I could bundle up and start walking.

The ache in his bad leg told him he wouldn't get very far.

He counted three whole days since he had taken his pills. Usually, when he came up to the cabin to lock down and write uninterrupted, he chose not to take the pills. Some of his best work was done when he felt closer to his schizophrenia.

John smacked his left hand against the window pane.

Why the hell didn't I get that reserve snowmobile?

He had always talked about it. Even after the gas leak on the machine outside was fixed a month ago, he'd told his wife he would get a reserve one, just in case.

He walked away from the window and turned on the radio. White noise came out of the speakers. He adjusted the dial left and right until a station came in. The sound was laden with static. After a little more fiddling, he turned it off and stood back to his full height.

"Don't."

He ignored the voice that taunted him from somewhere in the cabin. It had to be in his head. Just to be sure, he surveyed the room again.

Something banged outside, making him jump.

That's how they're doing this. They slipped out of the cabin as I entered it. Bastards. I'll show them not to fuck with me.

He hobbled over to the couch to retrieve the ax. When he got to the front door, he eased out of the backpack and placed it on the floor. With both gloves back on, he hefted the ax up to rest on his shoulder. Then he opened the cabin door.

The snow had already begun the task of covering his previous tracks. The little light he had left was just enough to look around for other prints, but the snow remained undisturbed elsewhere.

Wind buffeted his face, feeling colder than before.

He eased out and stepped into the thickest part. The soft, powdery snow covered his knee, rising to mid-thigh.

Another bang sounded to his right, and he turned, gripping the ax, ready to take on the intruders. The shed door sat ajar a few inches, moving back and forth in the wind. It slammed shut before drifting open once more.

The shed.

The shed had spare gas.

Why he didn't think of it before baffled him. He took large strides to wade through the snow, limping and stomping until he got to the shed's door. He laid the ax against the outer wall and examined the situation.

The door opened outward, but the snow was too high to allow much movement. John leaned down and dug the drifted snow out of the way, digging a small path so he could open the door enough to squeeze inside the shed. Only his left hand was of any use, though. The cold seeped through his glove with ease. All feeling disappeared within minutes. He stood and balanced on his good leg, leaned against the side of the shed, and waited until he got his breathing under control.

A glance back at the cabin's window and the woman was back. Her features were drawn, pale, frightened.

"You should come out and help me instead of just watching all the time," he yelled at her.

He turned back to the shed's door, grabbed the edge, and swung it back and forth, trying to get enough room to squeeze through.

The cabin had no electricity. He used candles and a generator for light, wood for heat. There was always enough gas and wood to get through a weekend, but extra gas was stored in the shed for exactly this sort of situation. He chastised himself for not remembering.

He got the door open enough to squeeze through but then stopped. The shed was as black as an enclosed coffin. The only flashlight John had was in the cabin. He would have to make his way around the shed by feel.

The spare gas would be under the work table.

He welcomed the reprieve from the wind as he felt his way along the walls. Objects bumped his hand—it was still too numb to feel anything—so he had no idea what most of them were.

He located the table by bumping into it with his thigh. Carefully, he leaned over and felt around under the table so as not to knock his head. The cold seared his legs as his pants rode up and clung to his skin.

Someone moaned behind him. He jumped and smacked the back of his head on the underside of the table.

"Who's there?"

Someone was in the shed with him, but they didn't make any more noise.

Get the gas. Fill the snowmobile. Then get the fuck out of here. That's what I'm going to do.

He reached down to where the spare gas container should be and clamped his left hand onto the handle. When he lifted it, the weight was wrong somehow. It should be heavier. He brought it close to his ear and shook it, listening to the contents.

Empty.

A month ago, when the snowmobile's gas tank had leaked, he'd used the last of the reserve to get him down to the mechanic.

He hadn't replaced the missing fuel.

Damn it.

He turned in the dark and listened as he thought he heard the sound of distant engines. It seemed far off, but the sound was there just the same. He hustled in the dark to where he thought the shed's door would be but missed it. In his hurry to leave the shed, he collided with the wall that held tools on a peg board. To make matters worse, his aching hand hit a sharp tool, his nose the wall. His eyes watered, and his hand redoubled its throbbing.

Through glazed eyes, he glimpsed the luminescence of the new snow outside. He quickly slipped out of the shed and stopped to listen for the engines again.

Nothing. No sound at all. He wondered if being off his meds was a good idea. His wife needed him. His daughters needed him. He needed to get out of there. But how? He couldn't think properly anymore.

Am I going to die up here?

He trudged through the snow, using the tracks left by his previous steps, and entered the cabin again. The cold had seeped in when he left the door open, and there wasn't a fire in the fireplace to counter it. Shivering, his hand and nose aching, he looked around for the woman who had been watching him through the window.

A crackling sound came from the radio, pulling his attention to it.

Did I leave it on?

The radio announced there had been a multi-vehicle accident on the highway. A pileup. Seven people were hurt, with four succumbing to their injuries at Liberty Memorial.

The news rambled on, but John's world had stopped. He was stuck there, a virtual prisoner of the elements. The elements that took his parents. The same elements were stealing his family away at that very moment, and there was nothing he could do about it.

The sound of engines again.

What's going on?

He cocked his ear. The sound faded.

He wobbled over to the couch, where he lay down, his head on the armrest. A case of the shivers overtook him. He wondered why he hadn't grabbed a few pieces of wood and brushed the snow off them. He could've started a fire by now. Anything to stave off the hypothermia that would eventually take him.

How would he go on after this? How could he live after losing his wife and his two little girls? Where was Suzy now? Still wandering or already freezing to death?

John cried, his tears warm but cooling rapidly as they drifted down his face. Too many events mirrored the night his parents died. They'd been lost, wandering, people out looking for them.

Who was the woman in the window? Why am I here? Who am I?

The sound of engines again.

His mind slipped.

The sat phone rang.

Startled, he jolted sideways, eyes wide.

"Am I hearing things?" he asked out loud.

On the third ring, he convinced himself that it wasn't an illusion. He moved to get off the couch and fell to the floor in a heap of cold, non-functioning limbs.

The phone stopped its incessant drill.

I thought I dropped the phone. It had broken.

He was sure he heard engines as the sounds grew louder and closer. Consciousness became harder to maintain.

John forced himself up, leaning his back against the couch. He waited. The engines stopped somewhere in front of the cabin. A moment later, the door to the cabin slammed inward.

A policeman entered, followed by a paramedic. The third person was a ghost. John couldn't believe it.

Tera, his wife. She ran to him.

"Oh, John, what have you done?" she asked. She held his face in her hands. "I told you to take your pills. You were supposed to be home two days ago on Sunday. It's Wednesday morning, John."

She was gently moved aside as the paramedic started examining him.

John had enough strength to stay awake a little longer. He knew his hallucinations could be strong, but never like this. This one, while alone in the cabin, could've killed him.

The woman taunting him earlier stood by the door now. She wasn't in the window anymore, and as far as John could tell, no one else saw her. Tera turned to see what he was looking at.

In a wave of lucidity, he realized that the woman by the door was a younger version of his mother.

She opened her mouth and whispered, "You're mine. I'm waiting for you, John. There's nothing you can do to stop it."

She reared her head back and laughed a horrid, guttural cackle, her lower jaw becoming grotesquely unhitched while she laughed.

John shouted and tried to get up. The paramedic eased him back down.

"Did you hear what she just said?" he asked.

Tera exchanged a glance with the cop, then the paramedic. She looked back at him.

"John, I'm the only woman in the room. I didn't say anything."

"We have to stop her," he shouted. "We have to stop her."

He looked for the woman, but she was gone. In her place was his father, shaking his head.

"Goodbye, John."

His father's face devolved into something unexplainable. John screamed and arched his back as he tried to get away.

When he turned around, the sofa was drenched in blood. It dripped off the center cushion, falling into a small puddle beside his head. The blood had pooled where the cushions were torn.

What the hell happened here?

He turned back around. The paramedic was gone. The policeman had disappeared. His parents were nowhere in sight. But Tera was there. She lay across the open doorway on her stomach, straddling the threshold of the cabin, her back a mess of blood and hair.

John gasped and brought a hand to his mouth.

"Baby?" he whispered. "What happened to you? Where is everybody?"

He crawled across the floor to her. The pain and the cold were momentarily forgotten. When he moved the hair out of her face, he discovered Tera's eyes open, lifeless, empty.

He didn't have to check her pulse to know she was dead.

John looked down the length of her body and saw the ax embedded in her back.

"What?" He crawled away quickly and bumped into the wall. "How? Why?"

His body shuddered.

"How could this be?" he asked.

"It just is."

He spun around so fast that he lost his balance and rolled onto his shoulder. When he looked up, no one was there.

The candle still burned by the door. It was the only light source in the cabin, and the light it gave off was so dim he could barely see, but it was enough to know he was alone with his dead wife.

Is someone else here? Did they kill my Tera? Did I kill my Tera?

He looked back at her. She was still dead.

"No, no, no …"

He looked down at his leg. The pain had increased to the point where he wondered if he could walk on it.

Blood seeped through a hole in his jeans.

"What the hell's going on?"

He inspected his injury. He'd never seen a bullet wound before, but as far as he could tell, he had one in his leg.

"Who shot me?"

"Don't," the voice whispered.

This time the word was more of a plea like someone begging.

He didn't bother to look for the source. Even if he spun around, he wouldn't see anything. Whoever walked through his cabin could hide too fast for him to bother looking.

He attempted to get to his feet.

If Tera's here and I'm here, then who's taking care of our girls?

He made it to his knees, but the leg with the bullet wound wouldn't support his weight.

"When did I get shot? Nothing is making sense." He shook his head, frustrated without answers.

Up on his knees, he stared at the inert form of his wife and saw a small revolver in her left hand.

"*You* shot me? Why, honey?"

Something flashed through his mind.

He shook his head to dislodge the memory.

"No way. I did not kill my daughters. Not me. I could never do that."

"Don't, please, Daddy, don't."

He spun around. The speaker was his mother again. She stood in the corner of the cabin, a soft light coming from somewhere inside her body.

"Don't," she repeated.

"Why are you here? Get out. This is my family. You're dead."

"You're dead, too."

"Not yet."

John used the back of the couch to stand. He leaned heavily on his good leg and hopped toward the bathroom. He needed bandages as his leg still bled.

"Don't," the thing behind him said.

It was taunting him, trying to bait him into losing his mind.

He hit the bathroom door, half fell, half ran inside, using the sink to catch himself. He didn't recognize the face in the mirror.

"Hello, pretty," he said. "Aren't you in some kind of trouble now?"

When he turned for the medicine cabinet, he slipped on the carpet and fell before catching himself. John hit the floor awkwardly and bent his wrist back.

"Fuck," he swore at the intense pain. "What else can go wrong here? My wife's dead, and I don't know if that's real or I'm seeing things."

A sticky-cold substance covered his back. He leaned up and turned to look at what made him slip and fall.

Blood.

He followed the blood to its source. It appeared to be coming from the bathtub.

His leg was completely numb now, but he had to see what was in the tub. He dragged himself across the bathroom floor, the small mat coming along under his weight. He got to the edge of the tub and lifted himself up.

"Don't do it," the voice said.

"Fuck you," he shouted back.

He glanced in the tub. His daughters appeared to be sleeping.

In a flash, it all came back to him. The fight. The ax and the gun. Everyone screaming. His wife yelling the word *don't* over and over.

Distraught, he eased back to the bathroom floor and dragged himself out and across the cabin. As he neared the door, he saw the woman and the man standing on either side. The woman wagged a finger at him as if he'd been a naughty boy.

He kept dragging himself, leaving a trail of blood in his wake. When he got to his wife's body, he pushed her aside and pulled himself out onto the snow.

John crawled and dragged himself away from the cabin. The cabin where his family had spent many seasons together, laughing and playing games, watching late-night movies, and making popcorn.

He dragged himself farther into the forest, away from the memories and the pain.

He dragged himself until he couldn't anymore.

The last thought his brain processed was how the elements of schizophrenia were similar to a winter storm.

Or was it the other way around?

His mother stood over him at the end.

She cried for him as his soul was ripped away and taken to a place where the pain was the price of entry.

John would never be cold again.

Vengeance

I HAD NO IDEA I would die that day, along with many other people. It's been ten years, and I still wonder how that day got so fucked up.

I had been looking forward to that holiday all summer long. Four of us had rented a cabin for Labor Day weekend, early September. It was our last party before university started for another year. We wanted to finish summer with a bang.

Boy, did we ever. I blamed many people during those ten years, but never myself. It's so hard to own something that tragic.

It's all my fault. Everyone's death, everyone's blood is on my hands.

I still kill to avenge their deaths.

***

Tabitha and I stopped at the last liquor store before the cabin to load up on alcohol. Scott and Allison pulled in behind us in their Jeep Cherokee. The sun was high, the air on fire, and we were sweating like crazy. My old Buick didn't have an air conditioner, so Tabby and I had driven for the past three hours with the windows down.

"Scott, how about this heat?" I asked.

He looked at me, raised his sunglasses to his forehead, and winked. "It's great. The inside of my Cherokee is like sitting in an igloo."

I jabbed at his arm. "And you'd know how it is to be in an igloo because you're a hard-boiled Canadian boy."

We laughed, wrestled around, and tried to get our girls to smirk. Tabby and Allison were both prepared for the heat. They looked great in their jean shorts and halter tops. I used to swear that these two girls called each other in the morning to coordinate their clothes for that day, making sure everything matched.

They hung back as Scott and I stepped into the small LCBO on the side of the highway. The Liquor Control Board of Ontario usually had larger stores, but this far north and in such a small tourist town, the store was small, and the selection smaller.

I looked at Scott. "Grab what you want, and I'll meet you outside."

He nodded, and we parted.

When I got to the till with my loot, I glanced outside at Tabitha. Three men, wearing a crazy-looking combination of leather jackets and green pants, were standing in a semi-circle around her and Allison. From where I was standing, it looked like they were blocking the girls' way.

"Forty-three, twenty," the clerk said.

I handed her a fifty-dollar bill, got my change, grabbed my bag, and headed for the door. It slid open, and I stepped into the hot sunshine.

"Everything cool here?" I asked, looking at Tabby. Her facial expression told me it wasn't.

Two of the men turned toward me, acting tough and showing off, no doubt, for the third member of their trio, who didn't look at me.

One of them had a goatee that dangled below his chin, the whiskers tied in a hair elastic. The other guy had no hair on his head, only a teardrop tattoo on each cheek. Under different circumstances, I would've laughed at how funny it looked. But today, the tension in the air gave me a good idea that laughing wouldn't be prudent.

"You know who we are?" the one with the stupid goatee asked.

I shook my head in the negative.

"I didn't think so," he said and turned around to show me the back of his leather jacket. I don't know much about biker logos, but it looked to me like a caricature of Satan with his hands out and the name Vago's with an M and a C on either side.

Goatee turned back around. "Recognize it?"

I shook my head and bent over to set my bag of alcohol on the concrete as it was getting heavy. A car pulled into the parking area. I looked over. An old man in a Chrysler parked and opened his door. If only it were a police officer.

"We're the Vago's Motorcycle Club. The symbol is Loki, the Norse God of mischief."

"Tabby, Allison, step over here," I said as I looked at the third member of their group. "We'll be leaving now."

Tabitha went to move off the wall, but the three men inched closer together, completely blocking her path.

"What is this?" I asked. "You're breaking the law. That's forcible confinement. Step away and let them go, or I'll call the cops."

Goatee and Tear Drop moved closer to me. The door to the liquor store opened, and Scott walked out. In my peripheral vision, I saw the old guy from the Chrysler slow his step.

"You'll do what?" Tear Drop asked, his voice sounding like sandpaper grating on steel wool.

"I'll call the police. You can't walk around acting like you own the world because you ride motorcycles. We have rights. Now, step back and leave us alone."

I didn't think my message was getting through to them. Their smiles, and the fact that they weren't stepping off, told me they didn't respect the same laws I had just mentioned.

"Do you know that the FBI and California's attorney general have all named us an outlaw motorcycle club? They say we're involved in drugs, assault, extortion, money laundering, murder, vehicle theft, witness intimidation, and weapons violations. Can you believe that?" He stepped closer to me, our noses almost touching. I could smell his last cigarette. "I'm trying to illustrate here that we've decided these two ladies will join us for the weekend, and then you can have them back unharmed. How does that sound to you?"

"What the fuck is this?" Scott asked. He set his bag down beside mine and reached for Allison's arm.

The gang member closest to her shot his hand in the air. A knife appeared out of nowhere.

"Touch her, and you lose your hand."

Scott hesitated. He looked at me. The old man to my right, who had nothing to do with this, moved away and ran for his car. I heard the lock click on the liquor store's door as they barricaded themselves inside. We were on our own in a small town where police response times would probably be too long to defuse our current problem.

In all my years of studying Shotokan karate, I never thought I'd have to use it for real.

Scott eased back farther, his face a mask of fear. Tabitha was trying to stay calm, but Allison cried quietly now.

Tear Drop was looking away from me. Only Goatee would see me move.

I dropped to my knees, grabbed the neck of a bottle of coconut rum, and drove my open palm into the chin of Goatee. I heard his teeth snap together, along with his cry of pain. I only hoped I caught his tongue.

The bottle was already in full swing by the time Tear Drop turned to address me. It hit him in the right cheek, breaking it upon contact, blood shooting from the split skin.

At the second he bent over and fell to the ground, I lunged past him and ran for the guy who was clearly the leader. He had turned toward me, his hands up, the knife shining in the sun.

I feigned left and spun to the right. He bought it, lunging with the knife. My left hand grabbed the wrist that held the knife and locked it down, while my right hand formed a fist. I drove everything I had into that punch, hitting him squarely on the jaw and spinning his head sideways. He brought his head back and smiled at me.

I knew it would take more to hurt this guy, and I didn't have the time, as Goatee would be attacking my rear any second.

I twisted his wrist as far as possible and drove my next punch into his throat. He tried to move out of the way but wasn't fast enough. His Adam's apple was my target, and I hit it hard enough to affect his trachea.

He dropped the knife, staggered back, and fell to his knees, his hands clinging to his throat, gasping for air.

I turned around just as Scott was kicking Goatee.

"Scott, that's enough."

I later learned that Goatee had stayed on his feet and was about to deal me a double-fisted sandwich when Scott surprised him with a kick to the stomach. I had no idea Scott was a fighter.

"Let's get out of here," I said, my stomach turning, my nerves feeling like I'd been tased.

Tabby ran for our Buick. After scooping up our alcohol, I followed, got in, started it up, and drove to the exit with Scott and Allison close behind. As I pulled out, I looked over my shoulder and saw Tear Drop pointing his arm at me. His hand was empty, but he was holding it in a mock interpretation of a gun. He dropped his thumb and lifted his finger as if his gun had gone off.

The message was clear: *you're dead.*

***

When we arrived at the cabin, I asked if we could avoid talking about it so as not to ruin our weekend. Everyone agreed, except Scott suggested we contact the local police and tell them what had happened.

We called North Bay Police, and they drove to the cabin on our second day. After we gave them our full statement, they said they'd be on the lookout. They also said that what we did was brave, but to be careful in the future. We could've gotten killed.

On Sunday, our moods were lighter. Everything was back to normal, and we were having a blast. The weather had been awesome, and the water in the lake was warm.

I stood on a large rock with Tabitha, and we both stared out at the view of Lake Nipissing. As the sun set, it cast stunning colors across the sky. A few boats raced over its surface on a journey to their docks before full dark. But it wasn't the beauty that stopped me. It was the tragedy. The real reason we had come to spend the four days here was because of my parents.

My insides twisted as I thought of them and how they had died one year ago today, on Lake Nipissing, in a boating accident. The autopsy confirmed death by drowning. I hadn't been on the lake since. I used to Jet Ski all the time. The lake had been a second home for my family. I'd talked about it at length with Tabitha, and I had decided that I would go out on a boat this weekend, but we hadn't yet. It'd be hard to look into the depths and know that this water took my family from me, but it was something I had to do.

"You okay?" she asked.

"I'm fine."

"Good, then you can help Scott and Allison with the rest of their bags. They're leaving early to get back to the city."

I headed over to their vehicle to lend a hand. When I was close to Scott's Jeep, he scrunched up a brown paper bag he'd taken from Allison's hand.

"You guys having an early evening snack?" I asked.

Scott looked at me. "We've finished it. Otherwise, I would have offered you some."

His manner seemed forced, somehow acting over-nice. *What the hell is that all about?*

I stepped up to him and grabbed his can of Pepsi. "The least you could do is give me a swig of your drink."

I only had the can on my lips long enough for one full swallow. Then Scott pushed me hard. I lost my balance, fell to the pine-needle-littered dirt, and dropped the Pepsi can.

"Don't swallow. Spit it out!" Scott shouted at me.

I leaned on my elbow and made to stand. "What's going on?"

"Allison doesn't know how severe your peanut allergy is. She had packed lunches for the road. Two peanut butter sandwiches. That's what you saw us eating as you walked up a moment ago. I didn't tell you because you didn't have to worry since they were gone now, and we were leaving anyway."

The symptoms for me can come on as quickly as the speed of sound.

"I had just taken a drink from that Pepsi," Scott explained. "When you grabbed it, I forgot, and I, oh man, this is not good."

I wiped the sides of my mouth and came away with a tiny brown smudge. I brought it up to my nose and smelled the distinctive aroma of peanut butter. When I tried to stand, my legs went out from under me.

"Get me to Tabitha. She knows how to use the Epi-Pen. I need a shot of epinephrine."

Scott leaned down and supported me until I got to my feet. With an arm wrapped around his shoulder, the two of us headed for the cabin. Halfway there, I heard rustling in the bushes. I thought, *Oh, great, a bear is coming, and we're all going to die.*

Fear enveloped me. That was the first symptom of my anaphylactic reaction: fear and abdominal pain. But now, it was mixed with what I saw watching us from the bushes.

Goatee's eyes. He was smiling.

My face felt flushed, and my lips were itchy. I heard Scott shouting Tabitha's name. My mouth grew tight. I couldn't warn anyone. Liquid began dripping from the corner of my lips. When I tried to speak, my voice sounded different. I suddenly felt tired, even though my heart was racing. The setting sun was on my back, but I had chills. My nose fought the air that struggled to enter it.

I was dying, and my friends would, too, if I couldn't warn them.

When I opened my eyes again, I was on the cabin floor, looking at the wood that formed the ceiling. Tabitha ran by me, shouting something about the medicine bag and that it was still in my Buick. The last thing I remember was Scott shouting into his cell phone for an ambulance.

Then a spurt of red shot out of his chest like a small fountain. Then another. I heard a cannon roar somewhere in the distance. I heard screaming. I couldn't keep my eyes open. I shut them as Scott fell beside me.

***

I walked to the front door. When I looked back, I saw myself on the cabin floor. Scott lay beside me.

The three Vago bikers from the liquor store stood over the two bodies. Tear Drop leaned down a white bandage on his cheek. He put his gun in my face and checked my neck for a pulse. He looked up at Goatee and shook his head. Then he checked Scott's pulse and shook his head again. I was dead, and so was my friend. I felt weightless, emotionless. It was an empty feeling, but at the same time, I felt like I had more life in me than at any other time.

All three men moved away from the bodies and disappeared into the rooms at the back of the cabin.

Tabitha ran back in, flipped the cap off the Epi-Pen, and prepared to inject me with it, but stopped and stared at Scott. She screamed and jumped back, her head spinning around to see if anyone else was in the cabin.

All three of Vago's MC members stepped out of the back rooms. They all had guns out and aimed. All three were smiling.

Then Tabitha did the smartest thing she could think of at the time. She dropped to her knees and rammed the Epi-Pen into my thigh. She needed me and knew that sometimes it could work fast.

I blinked, and the cabin disappeared. Tabitha and the bikers were gone.

I could feel pain in numerous places as I struggled to breathe and felt a gentle shaking. At first, I thought my headache had rhythm, but then I identified the drilling sound in my ears as a siren and the shaking as the movement of a vehicle. I was in an ambulance.

I fought the weight of my eyelids and struggled to open them. The paramedic told me everything would be fine, and we would be at the hospital soon.

By the time I got to North Bay's hospital, I had enough strength back to ask what happened. The paramedic said an officer would be by later.

As promised, the same cop who'd taken our statement about the bikers came to my hospital room.

I was dazed, reeling from what had happened. I hadn't talked to Tabby yet, either. I needed to know if she was okay.

I asked myself, *was it real, or did I dream it all?* Each time I asked myself that, I realized it wasn't a dream. It couldn't have been.

What happened to everyone else, then? What room were they in? Had Scott really died?

The cop removed his hat and looked down at his shoes.

"I'm sorry we didn't get there sooner." He lifted his head back up and stepped closer to the bed. "They had police scanners. They heard the call to come to your cabin to take your statement, and they followed us. That's how they knew where you were."

I motioned for him to continue. "Where. Are. My. Friends?"

"I'm sorry. Scott was shot."

"Tabitha?"

"She was found by the water."

I frowned, asking with my face as best as I could, *what does that mean?*

"They had done things to her that I can't talk about. She's dead. I'm sorry."

My eyes watered. Why did I deserve to live? How could I move on? I couldn't protect her when she needed me the most. I wasn't there for her. This all started because I was a hothead at the liquor store.

"The other girl is being hailed a hero," the cop continued. "She got behind the wheel of the Jeep, and instead of leaving, she turned the vehicle toward the water and drove over all three men. They were crushed and drowned under the Jeep's wheels. The problem was she had rolled up the windows and locked the doors to stay protected. As the Jeep sank, she couldn't get out. I'm sorry. Everyone died but you."

He paused and put his hat on again. "Maybe tomorrow, when you're feeling better, you can tell me your side of the story. Like, why did they leave you alive? I'll come by later."

He stepped out of the room, closing the door behind him. I was alone, truly alone. I had died that day and wanted nothing more than to die again. It was all my fault.

Since that day, I've quit school. I left my job and now travel state to state, hunting Vago's bikers. Their club's numbers are getting smaller, one by one. I've killed eighteen so far. Each one, I slice their throat. I violate each one inhumanely, as they did to Tabitha. And to each one, I whisper, "*For Tabitha*" in their ears as they struggle for their last breath.

I will continue hunting bikers until I die. If I'm ever caught and go to jail, I'll kill them in prison. My hands are weapons now; they're lethal. Nothing has stopped me yet. I've been stabbed, shot, and beaten to within an inch of my life, but you know what stops them from killing me? Fear, which is something I don't have anymore. That's their weakness.

I had no idea that dying would save my life but kill me in the process.

The Reaper

The day had finally come to kill. To remove a soul. What I do is a form of cleansing. I take great pleasure in easing the world of the souls that burden it. The only problem is each soul has to be worked, and—after eight years on this one—I need to move on. I'm old, tired, and ready to hand off some of my responsibilities to the younger generation. But first, I have to continue the ruse. What's one more hour in the life of someone as old as me?

"What bothers me," I started, "is our own child doesn't like us using the name we gave him." I turned around to look at my sleeping son, my little reaper, Jacob. Or *Mark*, as he would rather be called.

"I know, honey, but all we can do is continue to Novar and prove to him that what he's been saying can't be right. We'll take Jacob to where he thinks he was born and show him evidence to the contrary."

Grumpy and moody, I was angry this day had taken so long to come. I don't wait for people to die like my cousin, the Grim Reaper. We take people—think souls—early. It's justified. It's right. The problem is that I'm the only one powerful enough to know our purpose. My husband, John, has no idea who he is and won't for another hour. He actually thinks he's my husband and Jacob actually sees himself as my son.

If the world only knew how crazy I am, how much fun I have reveling in their misery, they wouldn't hunt me with pitchforks as they did hundreds of years ago—they'd send an army to decapitate me.

I sat in the front seat of our Nissan and stared at the passing trees, my arms crossed. The colors were vibrant green this time of year. Normally that would inspire me and cause me to snap a picture or two of the July sun if only to add another prop to my stage dressing. But I didn't because this play was coming to an end, and there would be no encore.

"I'm just tired of always hearing about his mother," I stated, fully encompassing my role in this incarnation. "How she washed clothes with her hands and how she made bread at home in an outside bread oven. His mother *this* and his mother *that*. Never memories of his first eight years with us." I raised my hands in frustration. "I know he remembers getting a PlayStation at Christmas and lots of other things since he was born, but I'm talking about what he says happened that isn't true. I mean, come on, we haven't let him watch that much television."

John put his hand on my leg to calm me. He knew all too well that I could really get fired up about this stuff. *I* am Jacob's mother. *I* wash clothes in a machine. *I* buy bread at a large grocery store, and we live in a city, not a village. We have electricity and only use candles for a romantic dinner. At least, that's how it all appears.

At first, I wondered if Jacob knew who he really was and what his mission had become for this incarnation. There were times when I was sure of it, but then I realized that he wasn't as old as I am, and only ones older than five-hundred years can do what I do with all the knowledge that goes with it. As I said earlier, I'm eight-thousand-two-hundred years old this June and ready to retire. My husband is a pawn, and my son is my successor.

I realized a few years ago, when Jacob began remembering a past life, that it was only a phase he was going through. But it didn't stop. Jacob continued talking about his past like he'd actually lived it. When he said he was born in the village of Novar, my husband and I decided to drive there to show him Novar so we could put his delusions to rest and I could complete my task for this incarnation.

"Everything will be fine," John said, attempting to reassure me but failing. I appreciated his efforts, but I had a nagging feeling that something was amiss. On this, the day of atoning, John still didn't indicate that he knew who he was. I worried that he wouldn't come around. If he didn't come around, I would have to kill him, too, which could become a problem.

My son had given details about a previous life that he couldn't have gleaned from watching TV. Barney a few years ago, then Blue's Clues, and now PlayStation. He could not know about churning butter, poverty, and a one-building schoolhouse. It didn't stop there, though.

Jacob had said just last week that if we drove to Novar, he would direct us to where he used to live. He would even show us the tree where he carved his name and the year he was born, 1931. He said that if we went this week, he had a surprise for us, one that I would be happy to learn. The mystery was enough for my husband and me to say we'd go. I should've known then that Jacob was well aware of my plans—our plans.

I wore a vibrant yellow, flowery dress, one of my favorites. I had wanted something bright yet calming and happy. I was prepared for a revelation of some kind, Jacob's mystery surprise, and a disgruntled husband. My human nerves were rattled.

"Ten kilometers left," John said.

I looked back and saw Jacob waking. He pushed himself up and glanced out the window as he rubbed his eyes.

"Hi baby, how're you feeling?" I asked.

"Okay, I guess."

"Are you worried about coming here?"

"No, I miss being here. We had great times when I was little."

We? What the hell does that mean?

"You still are little, Jacob. There are lots of great times to come," I said. *If he only knew.*

He looked at me. "Can you call me Mark for today? At least while we're in Novar?"

I stole a glance at John. He nodded, and I looked back at our son. I forced my teeth apart to say, "We can do that. But just for today."

John put the turn signal on to exit the highway, and I was immediately hit with déjà vu. I shook my head and came back to the present. John mumbled something beside me.

"What?" I asked him.

"Are you okay? You slumped down in your seat and paled like you were frightened."

"I'm fine," I stuttered. "I just thought for a second that I recognized this place."

What was it about Novar? Strange. An odd feeling.

"That's ridiculous," John said. "We've never set foot in this town."

He gave me a look that shouted, *Don't start talking like our son.*

Jacob directed his dad down several streets while I gawked at the familiar terrain. Why did I feel like I'd been here before? This was crazy. We were in Novar for Jacob—and our mission—and I was starting to feel like I'd been here before, too. If I had, I would've known about it. Odd.

"Where are you taking us, Mark?" I asked, feeling as awkward as always when using that name.

"To where I used to live. I think you'll recognize it, Mom."

What the hell? How could he say that? Better yet, why *would he say that?* He's not old enough to know who or what I am. Information like that can only be acquired at death.

I looked at my lap to avoid seeing the passing buildings. My right leg bounced up and down, my hands shaking even though I clamped them together on my lap.

"Why do you think I should recognize Novar?" I asked him. I heard my voice crack. Even John looked over at me. *And the play continues. Damn, am I good at this shit.*

"Because you were my mom in 1931. We lived here until our house burned down in the great fire."

I turned around and gaped at Jacob. What could I say? It was the first time he had said that his delusions of another life included me. In this incarnation, he wasn't supposed to know why he was here, yet he focused on this town and even said he used to live there. Something weird was happening. Something I didn't understand. I wanted no part of it. It fucked with my current reality. But should I react with how I was feeling about Novar? All I could do was turn back around and stare out the front windshield at the oddly familiar landscape. I was too close to the end to allow the ruse to be taken from me. No one could stop the killing now.

Jacob directed his dad to pull over. There wasn't much of a shoulder on the narrow road, but John did his best to keep the car from going down a small embankment. He put the hazards on, and we all got out.

The afternoon sun was warm and bright, but I took off my sunglasses. I wanted to enjoy every moment as the killing time approached, see everything, and feel everything.

I smiled to myself as John, and I silently followed Jacob through tall grass and weeds. We walked across a small clearing, and then my pulse raced as if I was in free fall. I felt faint. I grabbed my chest. John reached for my arm to steady me. What the hell was happening? This had never happened before in any of the thousands of incarnations I've lived in. Maybe my age was catching up with me. Perhaps it was *my* soul that was to be stolen?

"We lived right here," Jacob said, his arms wide.

I realized he was right. The earth under my feet was once my garden. I could see everything and understand nothing. I should remember it if I had lived here before. I looked around and noticed indentations in the foliage that resembled a pattern. When I pushed a few shrubs aside, I could see pieces of the foundation of a building that once stood there. When I looked up, Jacob was thirty meters away and moving fast.

"Jacob. I mean Mark! Where are you going?"

"I want to show you the tree," he yelled back over his shoulder. "And then you can have your surprise."

I'd had enough surprises for one day. I was having an involuntary epiphany. I didn't want to know what I was discovering. A part of my rational side rebelled. Anger rose in me—violence too. The killing was coming, along with it, the sweet rush of murder. So delicate and yet so satisfying.

Humans do it every day. They kill each other. They kill animals for sport. Everything down to a fly swatter kills, and they take great pleasure in it. I live on another scale, another plane greater than all others. My pleasure in death is immense. Watching it, causing it, feeling it, being killed myself. Everything to do with it is why I exist.

I am, therefore, I kill.

I followed Jacob another fifty yards, with John close behind. We came to a clump of trees, and there, scraped into the bark of the largest tree was the name *Mark* and the year *1931*.

I looked at John. If he didn't figure out who he was soon, he would wonder what all this meant. Was his son reincarnated or psychic? John would have questions. We were down to the end. I didn't want to have to kill him without the knowledge of who he is. It hurt when their last breath came out, their eyes darkened, and they had no idea why. Knowledge is power. I love death when we know why. It's a rich power. The only kind. That's why I do what I do and am so good at it. The power. The power of death and the power over death.

"Can I help you folks?"

Nothing pissed me off more than being startled.

My human body jumped a foot and let out a small squeal as all three of us turned around and stared death in the face. The man standing with the aid of a cane was twenty feet away. He must have been at least ninety years old. The side of his face looked melted like he'd kissed a fire and paid for it. He was simply gorgeous.

"I'm sorry, we were just looking around," John said.

Do you realize how dumb that sounds? Oh, we're just looking around in the middle of the tall grass and huge trees. We must've looked like complete idiots.

"I haven't seen anyone this far off the road in a long time," the old man said.

"Is this your property?" John asked.

"My papa owned it, and it fell into my hands when he died in the fifties. I've lived here since I was born in 1934."

I looked at Jacob. His head was down as he stared at something on the ground. I could tell he was thinking. Then my eight-year-old son spoke as he looked up at the old man.

"Your name is Kirk Sutton. I remember you because you always played with frogs. You actually had a few pet frogs that you wouldn't let anyone near. We used to tease you about it."

The old man looked at Jacob/Mark. He studied my son with a wry smile that turned into a scowl. A few seconds passed before he spoke. "How did you know my name? And how do you know about my frogs?"

"I know because I'm Mark. I used to live just over there in the thirties." Jacob lifted his arm and pointed. Then he looked back at Kirk Sutton. "I also know about your other obsession."

"Well, now, that couldn't be possible, little man, since you're only a boy. The family who lived in the house that burned down were the founders of our little village, Mr. and Mrs. Novar. They had a boy named Mark, but they all died in a fire in 1944."

I caught a breath in my throat. At that moment, I recognized Kirk Sutton. It came to me in a flood as the dam had surrendered. I remembered everything—the tree line, the landscape, even where the train tracks were. I saw men hammering spikes into the rails as they put the tracks in. My mind's eye showed me the details of their clothes and their tools. What surprised me more was why I hadn't known any of this before.

I used to watch my son Mark and his friend Kirk catch frogs as I sat on my porch and sipped lemonade. The yellow dress I'd worn today was the same one I had torn off on the day of the fire so I could protect my son from the smoke and flames that licked up the walls. Another incarnation, another time. What I found curious was why I had forgotten it.

Mark and I died in the fire. I knew that now. We'd failed in our joint mission in that incarnation because of Kirk, the man standing before us. And we came back together to live the life we never had the chance to. I stepped close to Mark/Jacob and reached for him.

That's why we're here now. Together.

Our eyes met, and we could see the secret between us that had lasted seventy-five years. Jacob knew. All those years, and he knew. Together we would kill today, and together we would be killed.

I simply couldn't wait to die. And what an honor to die with my son at my side again.

Jacob stepped away from me. He reached into his pocket and

moved farther into the foliage.

"Jacob, where are you going?" John asked.

Jacob ignored him as he moved deeper into the field. I would've ignored him, too. He was a straggler now, the only one who didn't know his part in all this.

"I know it was you," Jacob said loud enough for us to hear.

The old man looked from Jacob to me and then back to Jacob.

"You couldn't help yourself," Jacob continued. "But you got burned, too. I was told all about it, but I had to meet you for myself."

I had stepped into a new realm and left behind my old reality. The gig was up. No more playing human.

"Who told you about me?" the old man asked.

"Your brother. He's coming today."

John, that's you. Getting it yet? You're his brother.

"I don't have a brother, and I do not have to stand here and listen to this craziness."

John yelled for Jacob to come back. I turned and rebuked John.

"We'll handle this," I said.

The old man started away on his cane. I was ten meters from my son but still close enough to see the matches he pulled out of his pocket. He flipped the top, lit one, and touched the rest with it. The matchbook flared in his hand.

The old man glared at the flames in Jacob's hand.

"That's right. Watch the fire. That's what you did all those years ago. You watched the fire while your brother and I burned along with my mother. You listened to our screams and smiled. You stared so long that you got burned, too. It's mesmerizing, isn't it? Just watching the flames ..."

Jacob tossed the lit matches into the air. I expected John to scream in protest but heard nothing from behind me. The high grass was seriously dry for this time of year. The old man's house was too far away for him to escape.

Kirk Sutton used his cane like an expert as he tried to run from the flames. But it wasn't the fire he ran from. It was my husband. He'd finally gotten it. He knew who he was, or rather is.

"Get him, Daddy," Jacob shouted to his father.

My brain felt bent. Everything was good, as it should be.

I watched as John tackled the ninety-year-old man. They were lost to sight in the tall grass.

The fire rose above the waist-high foliage not one meter from Jacob, who was laughing as he watched the flames soaring higher and higher.

Something clicked in my head. I actually felt it. *Magical.*

John lifted the old man above the grass and carried him like a surfboard. Kirk shouted something about the police.

I walked closer to the flames to watch.

A loud crack resounded across the fields. I spun around to see a man running off the back steps of the old man's house. He had a gun in his hand.

"Stop what you're doing, or I'll shoot!"

Then I heard what Kirk Sutton was trying to say. His son was a cop.

The three of us circled the flames that had grown into a small brush fire. John stood the old man up and then, without preamble, shoved him into the center of the flames, where he fell on his back and writhed. He squealed and screamed as his flesh melted in areas spared in the fire of 1944.

The joy I felt as Kirk cooked in the flames was immense. My human body experienced a strong, vibrant orgasm as I listened to the wails and screams of pain. I almost fell to my knees.

The gun fired again somewhere behind us. John fell to his knees, blood spitting out of his mouth. I turned to see the cop aim his weapon at me.

The gun bucked in his hand. A bullet raced by me and shattered Jacob's face. What a sight, all the bone, and blood shooting into the air, caught by the grass, my son's soul free. The cop with the gun had no idea how happy he was making me at that moment.

I stayed low, grabbed John's hand, and reached for Jacob's to form a bond. All three of us lay on our backs and waited. I was the only one left unhurt, but my time was coming, and I looked forward to it.

Kirk Sutton had fallen silent in the fire. The new screams came from the cop. He stepped over and looked down at me.

"Who are you *fucking* people?" His face told me everything. The red cheeks, the wet eyes, the breathing. He was going into shock after hearing his father's screams. His mind was slipping into protective mode before he lost it entirely. Seeing someone crack in front of me was always a pleasure. Always a pleasure.

I smiled at him. It inspired him to raise his weapon and point it at me.

"Kirk, your father, murdered people," I said. "We came to make him pay. Shoot me, and we'll come back for you, too."

The gun went off, and I felt yanked away.

I've been at this for eight-thousand-two-hundred years. It's time to retire. My son is more powerful than I thought. I'm so proud of him.

Unlike my cousin, The Grim Reaper, we aren't lazy, waiting around hospitals for people to die. We take them, but we stick to the tormented souls. We're like the ultimate cleanser, ridding the world of scum.

Maybe one day I'll have to come for your soul. I could be your mother, brother, or school friend. You'll never know. But I'll lurk in the shadows, waiting for my chance to end a life.

Waiting for my reward.

The pleasure in murder is too great to stop.

I am, therefore, I kill.

I'm sure I'll see you soon.

The Ruse

WHAT'S LIFE BUT A river of tears? The chase for the almighty dollar. There are more billionaires in the world today than there have ever been in the history of man. I used to be like those people—money hungry. I didn't care who was in my way. If I could make a buck, I'd do it.

That was until I learned a lesson only life and death could teach. And now I am doing the right thing.

Be a stand-up guy? Or fall down?

Decisions, decisions.

But first, let me tell you how I got there.

***

My life changed forever with one text message.

I was a real estate agent. I played on the stock market. I watched the penny stocks, waiting for one to strike gold and be worth hundreds, or even thousands, overnight. I was the guy that handled the million-dollar homes in our little community on the Bay. The commissions were huge. I lived well, even if I only sold one house every three months.

Then I got a text message: "*John Turnbull.*"

At the time, that name meant nothing to me. I checked to see who'd sent it. The first red flag was planted as there was no return number. I'd never seen that before. There's always a number to reply to.

I'm usually a pretty organized guy. I use a day timer, a calendar, a notebook, an appointment book, and two computers at home to track everything about my clients. My cell phone is a mini computer detailing my day's routine, activities, and meetings. Each morning I sync it with my computer, and I go to do its bidding.

I'd never heard of a John Turnbull, though.

Two hours after I received the text, I was sitting at my desk in my office. Jessica, my company secretary, buzzed me to say I had a call waiting on line two. She said the caller wouldn't identify himself. That's Jessica, always fucking around. She's got issues, man. I mean, serious parent issues. They're dead. She's not. That's the issue.

I picked up line two to discover that I was talking to John Turnbull.

Of course, I asked him if he'd sent the text, and he denied it. Apparently, he doesn't even own a cell phone. John and his wife are in their late seventies. They'd won the lottery six months ago. After they'd won millions of dollars, every family member for hundreds of miles around began visiting and calling, looking for money. It drove them crazy. John said he wanted to buy a house on the lake, but he wanted to do it discreetly. That's why he didn't own a cell phone anymore, and he refused to say his name when he called the office.

I sold an expensive house to Mr. and Mrs. Turnbull a week later. They probably didn't need one that pricey, but a little charm, and smooth salesman talk, will do it every time. They overspent, but what did I care? The commission was worth it. Fuck 'em.

The mysterious text stayed unsolved, though. It started to piss me off. I wish I knew who warned me about the Turnbulls. But in the end, was it a warning? At the time, I didn't think so. I soon forgot about the stupid text. It was as if it hadn't happened.

Two months later, I received another mysterious text. A name again. I knew this one because it was my sister's name. I hadn't seen my sister in over ten years. After our parents died, their wills were *not* divided evenly. She got everything. I hated her for it. I refused to speak to her. Then she moved away.

I wondered if the text was another prophecy. I decided to block all my calls. I still didn't want to talk to her. I also realized at that moment that I was giving more credence to those ridiculous texts than I wanted to.

I decided that I could completely avoid incoming calls by leaving the office. I told Jessica I felt ill. She smiled at me in her usual stupid way. Like she knew what I was up to. At twenty-three, she thought she had the world figured out. She couldn't even figure out her own fucked-up head, let alone the world.

She was driving the car the night her parents died in the accident. To this day, she still thinks she is to blame. After three suicide attempts and two years of therapy, I took her on to be my secretary out of pity. She sometimes makes mistakes and screws up, but I get by at half the price of any other Coffee Maker.

On my way out the door, I asked her to take messages and wait until tomorrow to give them to me because I was turning off my cell phone.

There, problem solved. No more texts, no calls. The prophecy couldn't come true. I would not see, or hear from, my bitch of a sister.

On the way home, I decided I'd barbecue for dinner as I did on most Fridays. I pulled in and stopped at my favorite butcher shop. While selecting a T-bone, a woman walked up and stood beside me. I figured she was waiting to grab something from my side of the meat bin.

I was wrong.

I turned and looked into the eyes of my sister. I stumbled a little. Then I tried not to act surprised.

She'd lost weight. She was very thin. Sickly thin. She wanted to talk, but I didn't. I'd gone to great lengths to avoid her, yet here she was, in living color. She was so thin I assumed it was cancer eating her away from the inside.

What, all the money from Mom and Dad's estate run out? Can't afford all the drugs and chemo for the cancer treatment? Don't come crawling to me.

It wasn't my life anymore. These people I'd called "Family" had ostracized *me*. It's only DNA that connects us. I could be standing beside any other customer in the meat shop for all I cared.

I bought my T-bone and left the butcher shop. On the way out, she followed me and said she had something to tell me. Something important. I shouted over my shoulder that she could tell me in two weeks. Book an appointment with my secretary. Before getting into my car, her voice weak with whatever cancer does to people, I heard her call out, saying she'd be dead by then.

Deep down inside, I'm not a callous man. I think somewhere along the way I placed wealth at my core. People like me are money centered, and I'm okay with that. You will lose people you care about in the process. Maybe that was why I was single in those days. I didn't care about people much, so why would they care about me?

I looked at my cell phone a little differently after that. It seems my phone, or whoever sends those texts, knew something about my future. When a legitimate text came through, I always jumped. It was six months before I received my third prophecy. This one wasn't a name. It was a message.

To save a human life, be at the butcher shop at three p.m. This is your last chance.

That wasn't going to be possible. I had a house showing at three p.m., one of the huge mansions on Garrison Hill. This house was shaping up to be the biggest sale our little town had ever heard of. My client had toured other houses with me for over three months, with only a few he liked. It was just last week that this house went on the market. We drove by it four days ago. The owner's gardener was on the lawn, watering plants. My client, and his wife, toured the backyard and peeked in the windows. They said it looked perfect. The full walk-through was for today, at the same time as the prophecy.

I couldn't miss the appointment with my client. But how would I feel if someone actually died today and I could've stopped it?

I decided to do something completely uncharacteristic. I lifted my home phone and called the office. Before I changed my mind, I told Jessica, who was giggling for some reason, that I couldn't make my three o'clock. Get someone else to show my client the house, and if it sells, we'll divvy up the commissions accordingly. I told her to hold all calls and wait until the next day to give me my messages.

I couldn't believe it. What was I doing? I had two shots of scotch whiskey, looked at my watch, and started getting ready for my date with destiny.

I pulled into the parking lot of the butcher shop ten minutes early. Everything appeared normal. As I was supposed to be here to save a life, I'd thought of all kinds of scenarios. If there was a gun involved, I was toast. I didn't know CPR, so I hoped the intended victim didn't have a heart attack or something. I went through as many scenarios as possible on how I would save someone's life. I also thought about my client. I wondered who Jessica had gotten to show the house to.

At three p.m. exactly, I was standing in front of the butcher shop, right where I was supposed to be. Nothing happened at first. All my senses were on full alert. I watched anybody and everybody. I watched where they were walking in case a car was coming too fast. I especially watched older people. The area quieted down a little. I looked at my watch.

3:08 p.m.

Nothing happened. Anger seeped in. What if the sender of the text was a rival real estate agent, and at that moment, they were showing the Garrison house to my client? I decided to believe in the validity of the text. I had nothing else to go on, and they had come true twice. No one could've known my sister would show up at the butcher shop at the same time as me. I remembered it clearly. So the texts had to hold some greater purpose, something more than my ability to understand.

I decided to remain where I was and wait. At three-thirty p.m., my cell phone rang. Call display said it was the office. *Maybe my client wants to put an offer in*, I remembered thinking.

"Yeah."

"Hi." It was Jessica. She sounded broken up like she was trying to catch her breath. "How did you know?" she asked.

"Know what?"

"The house." She could barely get it out. "The house is gone."

"Gone? He bought it?" I asked, hoping that was the case.

"No, gone. As in destroyed."

What is she talking about?

"Destroyed? What's going on, Jessica?"

"They think it was a natural gas explosion. The house you were supposed to show at three p.m. has been leveled. It blew up like a bomb hit it."

I remember dropping to my knees so hard that little pebbles on the sidewalk left bruises. "Is anyone hurt? Who showed the house in my place?"

"When I called your client, he said they would view it when you were ready. They only wanted to deal with you. The owner of the house and his workers weren't there because they had expected the showing. I didn't call them because I was trying to get another agent in. At any other time, several people would have been there. Because you booked a showing for three p.m. and then didn't go yourself, you saved a lot of lives today. You saved yourself." I heard her stop, catch her breath, blow her nose, and then clear her throat. "But *I* killed someone. I'm so sorry."

What the fuck is she talking about now? I dodged a bullet. I'm alive, in one piece, and Jessica is talking her shit again.

"I killed someone," she repeated.

I heard her sobs and was disgusted with her.

"Is this about your parents, because if it is, you have really bad timing? I could've been killed today. I saved myself. It isn't always about you, Jessica. Get over it already, geez."

"I killed someone you know intimately."

"What? Are you mad? I didn't know your parents."

I was completely confused. Most of the phone call, I was in another reality, another field somewhere, stupefied at my good fortune that I was still alive.

"I killed … I killed your sister, and now I have to die."

"What the fuck are you talking about?" I was getting mad. I had no idea this woman was so fucked up.

She blew her nose into the phone. "Your sister called here looking for you this morning. When you told me to take messages and tell you them tomorrow, I didn't say anything about her. You canceled the three o'clock booking. I couldn't call her back anyway. She didn't leave a number."

"Where are you going with this? How could you have killed her? As far as I know, she has cancer. She's probably dead already."

"She asked where you'd be today, so I told her about the Garrison house. But you canceled. She was there. She was there."

Her twisted logic hit me.

"Were there any casualties at the Garrison house?" I asked.

"Yes. One. Your sister. I killed her by sending her there, and now I have to kill myself. Goodbye."

She hung up.

Shit. I couldn't have a dead secretary in my office. That kind of thing was bad for business.

I ran for my car while attempting to raise Jessica on my cell phone.

I was tired of the bitch. If she wanted to off herself, that would be one less person to eat the last apple turnover at my favorite bakery. One less person to take a seat on the bus from an old lady. One less person to nab the numbered ticket before me at the butcher shop.

I just couldn't allow her to do it at my office.

When I pulled into the parking lot, there was no indication a suicide had taken place, raising my hopes that she had gone home to do it or some ditch on the side of the highway.

I unlocked the front door and stepped into my office's foyer, acting as if nothing could bother the savvy real estate broker. It's not every day you have a dead sister and a secretary who wants to die.

"Jessica?"

The lights were all out. The blinds had been drawn.

"Jessica?"

I heard a police siren in the distance. After a few seconds, the siren drew closer outside. I realized they were stopping out front.

"Jessica, did you call the police?"

I stood in the main office, not venturing down the hall. If she did off herself, I didn't want to find the body. I wasn't willing to have bloody dreams for the next fifty fucking years.

The woman of the hour stepped out of my office. She had a gun in her hand. She raised it and aimed it at me.

"What are you doing?" I asked, trying to hide the fear I instantly felt.

"Do you want to die with me?" Jessica asked.

Oh, my shit. Every one of her marbles were on the floor because she had definitely lost them.

"I think I'll take a pass. Living is much more fun, and the possibilities are endless. Did you call the police?"

She nodded. "I can't kill myself. I've tried too many times and failed. I have to die like my parents did. Like your sister did. Indirectly. Death by cop is indirect suicide or whatever you want to call it."

"You don't have to do this," I said.

She turned her head sideways and looked at me with an expression that clearly showed her madness. In the little light of the room, I saw her eyes were completely bloodshot.

"Are you serious?" she asked. "I did not expect you, of all people, to try to save me."

Her condescending tone pissed me off. The world would be better without people like her, littering it with their demented sicknesses.

There was a loud knock on the front door.

"Police! Open up!"

"Umm, Jessica, we'll have to get that."

"Why? You worried they'll bust the door down? That could get expensive." She raised the gun, butt end extended to me. "Here, shoot me, and this ends now. Or get out of the way so I can open that door and have them shoot me. Either way, I die today, and the blood stain will be on your carpet. It was here that I directed your sister to her death. It'll be here where I direct my own."

"Can we talk about this?" I was getting seriously angry. "Go home. Do it there. Why do you have to ruin me in the process?"

Jessica moved forward. "You don't get it, do you? This is all your fault. If you felt love, even for one day, you would understand what was happening here. But you don't."

She walked past me and touched the door handle, the pistol in her other hand.

"Get what? You want to end it. That's easy. I get it. Just save me the name in the paper. Do it at home. And what does this have to do with love?"

Jessica hesitated. She held the doorknob and stared at the floor.

"If you loved your sister and didn't judge her for what your parents did, you would've taken her call. She would be alive today if you did that simple, humane task. If you could fathom what love is, *you* would be alive today. You're dead on the inside." She raised her head and stared into my eyes. "I lost my parents. I feel responsible. If I could go back, I wouldn't be driving that night. I'd had too much to drink. If I could go back, I wouldn't be working here for a soulless man who only cares about money. You're more dead than I will be in the next minute."

She turned the knob.

"Wait!" I shouted.

She stopped and looked at me.

"I'm sorry. You're right. Put the gun down and step away from the door."

"Why should I?"

"Because I can change."

She shook her head back and forth. "No one changes. This isn't about you. I die today, and ultimately, as much as it is my fault, it's yours, too."

I heard a noise in the back of the office. Maybe they were coming in through the rear entrance to surprise us. I hoped they hurried and disarmed Jessica before she did something I would regret.

"Please," I said, thinking I could disarm her first. "Give me the gun. We'll deal with this together. We'll get through it. I'm sorry I've been such an ass to you. Give me a chance. Show me what it means to love again. Teach me. I'll be your student. It's quite evident how much love you have to give. Your parents are gone, and it crushes you. My parents are gone, and I laugh about it. Bring me over to your side. Teach me how you are the way you are. Help me, and I'll help you."

Yeah, right. As soon as you go home, I'll fire your ass, and you can kill yourself there, in your own bathtub.

She let go of the doorknob and turned toward me. "Are you serious? No jokes?"

With a show of exaggeration, I shook my head back and forth. "No jokes. Realness here. Seriousness."

Someone was moving around in the back of the office.

Good. They're coming. I will have her gun in seconds.

I reached out. Jessica shivered as she started to cry. She handed me her weapon. Then she stepped over to her desk and sat down, resting her head in her arms on top of the desk.

I lifted the gun to look for the safety.

"Drop it!" a man yelled behind me.

A red laser pointer moved about on my chest when I turned around. Three men dressed in some kind of ski hats, with what looked like military fatigues, were battle-ready, guns aimed at me.

"I'm trying to flip the safety on," I said, my heart thumping in my chest. The last thing I wanted was for these guys to see weakness.

"Drop it!" the cop repeated.

I turned it around, my fingers shaking, found the safety, and used my other hand to flip the switch. I didn't realize that the barrel was aimed at the cop.

They fired at me.

A barrage of pops resounded in my small office. My heart felt like it had stopped. I lost all ability to stand. There was a pain in my chest. More popping sounds. I dropped the gun. Jessica screamed somewhere off to my left. My eyes closed.

***

When I look back, I realize the text messages were a chance for me to set things right to curb my personal evils. I could have done right by John Turnbull and sold a cheaper house to the lottery winners. I could have spent more time with my sister. I understand now why the text said that it was my last chance. It was my last chance at salvation.

I know I saved a life.

Mine.

There never was an explosion at the Garrison house. My sister approached Jessica six months before, and together they worked out an elaborate plan to bring me back to the land of the living. My sister acted like she was dying of cancer. The texts were a collaboration of work between Jessica and my sister. Jessica knew the Turnbulls were going to call in. She knew on most Fridays, I love to buy meat for a barbecue. She'd called my sister, told her to meet me there, and then sent me a text.

The suicide thing at my office was a setup. Would I save a life? Even after finding out, I'd just lost my only other family member?

The three officers had a key for the back door. Two were my sister's ex-boyfriends, and one was Jessica's brother. They fired blanks, and one of them tased me so I'd lose control of my body and assume that I'd been hit and dying. They took me to the edge of an insane reality and brought me back so maybe I could live again.

They did it because they love me.

Life is but a river of tears. At least now they flow from joy. I'm married, and I have two lovely children. I work from home to spend time with my family daily. For me, waking in the morning is a blessing. Every day I breathe is one more day I get what I wasn't supposed to have. Hearing my kids laugh, enjoying the smile on my wife's lips, eating ice cream, playing catch with my son, and watching a sunset are all life's little pleasures that amplify the beauty of my surroundings.

I know what's important in life. And it isn't money. It's hearing my wife whisper, '*I love you*,' while we have a family hug before bed each night.

I don't own a cell phone.

I don't send or receive texts.

The Witching Hour

DEAR VANESSA,

If you're reading this, then I have died.

You have no idea how much I wanted to watch you grow up, get married, and have your own children. I'm sorry that you have to go through this loss and pain. I tried to stop it from happening, but fate played a hand I couldn't beat.

If only I'd married another man. But then I wouldn't have had you, and having you made everything worth it. You're old enough now to move out and get away from your dad.

If you do anything for me, it will be to distance yourself from the monster you call a father. I don't know how he did it, but I assume he pulled it off to make it look like a suicide.

As I write this, I need you to know that I DID NOT kill myself. I would never do that. I love you too much to be that selfish. That's why I've been saving money for over six months and getting ready to run for it and take you with me.

Your father found out, and I got a phone call from your father's girlfriend today. He's on his way home right now. I'm scared. I have nowhere to go. I'd leave, but you're in school, and I don't have a car.

Remember that I love you and will get us out of this mess.

But if you're reading this letter, I failed you, and I'm sorry.

Please forgive me.

In the backyard, you'll find a small box with two thousand dollars wrapped in plastic. It's beside the oak tree on the left of the shed, buried about four inches deep. Get it and leave, but don't tell your dad or anyone else where you're going, or he will find you.

I love you. I'm watching over you.

I'll always be with you, my darling.

Love,

Your Mommy.

***

The bell signaled the end of another school day. Vanessa was outside and on her way to the town's small police station two minutes after the bell. The sun shone high and bright, doing its best to maintain a warm September.

Tomorrow it would be exactly two years since her mother had died. Vanessa found the note from her mother in her diary. Whoever left it there was playing a game, and who better to have access to her diary than her father?

Vanessa decided to discuss everything with James Redfield, the town's local sheriff. If there were anyone in the little town of Hover's Grove who could help, it would be him.

Then she would confront her father.

Her mother had drowned. That's what the police had said. Death by misadventure. Swimming in the lake at midnight by the light of the full moon.

They filed it as such, but it was rumored a suicide because who would go swimming at midnight when the temperature had dropped so low on that September evening? Her dad had said Mom was a good swimmer; at the time, Vanessa had just thought he was trying to put on a brave face and let her mother die with dignity.

Vanessa knew her mother would never have ventured out in the middle of the night for a swim unless she meant to kill herself. And it looked like she had good reason. Vanessa's parents were fighting near the end, screaming at each other at all hours of the night. Vanessa would lie in bed crying as her parents destroyed any kind of marriage they might have had left. Mom always wanted to leave Hover's Grove, and Dad said they had to stay.

Dad had a great alibi that night. He had to work the night shift at the private security firm where he was employed. He needed to check in every hour on the hour with an electronic device he swipes to pinpoint where he was at all times during his shift.

She had overheard her dad on the phone telling someone the police had cleared him of any wrongdoing. He said the police always looked at the husband first, but he was cleared.

In the days immediately following her mother's death, Vanessa had turned the world off. The funeral had been a blur. Feeling wayward and lost, Vanessa had wanted to join her mother in death. Now, armed with the purpose of unmasking the reasons for her mother's death, Vanessa was empowered. Something had to be done. She had a new note from her dead mother, who would not kill herself. And if her father was responsible, then he should pay for what he did, whatever that price may be.

Ten feet from the front door of the police station, a seagull squawked and flew low enough to catch her eye.

She watched as it lurched in the air, struggling to fly out toward the sea. It regained a semblance of flight but then chose to land on the grass in the park across the street.

Vanessa followed the bird's path, pulled in by its struggle, rapt by its faith in flight, and lost in its suffering. She stared until the seagull landed and waddled on what appeared to be a broken leg. Its white wings flapped while it tried to walk, but it finally gave up and slipped to the side, where it lay panting.

"Hey!" someone yelled behind her.

Vanessa jumped. She spun around and glared into the eyes of a woman in her sixties.

"Why did you just yell in my ear?" Vanessa asked, trying her best to keep the anger out of her voice.

"Missy, I'd advise you to catch the tone in your voice and monitor it for anger. Better to place anger in a jar, save it later, and release it on the most worthy opponent, yes?"

Vanessa stepped back. *What the hell is she talking about? And what the fuck is she wearing? A sari or something?*

"Didn't you see that bird?" Vanessa asked. "I stopped to watch it, and then you came up behind me and—"

"Shhh, just shhh," the old woman said. She stepped closer and lowered her voice. "I'm warning you. I think you might want to take the right-hand path. Do not take the left-hand path. You were spared last time. You may not be spared again. So take my advice and walk the right hand. Consider yourself warned."

Warned?

The woman lifted her arms and moved her hands back and forth like she was about to do a magic trick at a kids' birthday party. Her face contorted into a sneer, and then her hands dropped to her sides as she gazed past Vanessa.

It was like her eyes were riveted on a train wreck, horrified but unable to look away.

The woman met Vanessa's gaze. Then she gestured toward the grass on the other side of the road. Vanessa saw the seagull, still lying on its side, dead.

Two teenage kids from her high school walked by the bird and gave it a wide berth, commenting under their breath.

Sickened by death, angered for being startled, and pissed off for being talked to like a child by this weird stranger, Vanessa spun on her heels to tell the woman what she thought of her, but the woman was gone.

"That's fucked," she said out loud.

"What was?" James Redfield asked.

The town sheriff walked toward her. She collected herself and took a deep breath.

"The woman who was just here," Vanessa said.

"What woman? I didn't see any woman."

"She was right here beside me."

"I saw you walking up the street and then look into the park over there and curse out loud. I didn't see anyone talking to you."

Vanessa frowned. "You had to have seen her. She was wearing a long blue dress of some kind. Weird-looking thing. The crazy woman had huge rings on her fingers and nasty hair. You couldn't miss her. She acted all weird, waving her arms around and shit."

The sheriff shook his head. "Nope, I only saw you." He cocked his head sideways. "Are you feeling okay, Vanessa?"

Why would he lie? If he'd watched me walk up, he had to have seen the old woman.

"Did you see the bird over there?" she asked, pointing to where the seagull lay not twenty feet from where they stood.

The bird was gone.

What's going on?

"I don't see any seagulls, Vanessa. Are you sure you're feeling all right? Do you want me to call your father?"

"No! I mean, that's why I came to talk to you. Can we go

somewhere more private?"

"Of course, come into the office. No one is here, as usual. It's another slow day in the town of Hover's Grove, population 2644."

As they mounted the steps of the police station, Vanessa asked, "Why do you always announce the population number when you say Hover's Grove?"

"Force of habit, I guess. My daddy was the town sheriff before me, and his daddy before him. After the war, the population increased in the fifties, and my family remained proud of this little town." He paused to hold the door for her. "I remember growing up and hearing my father announcing the census numbers like he was proud. It's just something we do."

Vanessa wondered how much weirder her day would get. It was true, though. The town remained small even after the paper mill opened in the seventies. Her mom and dad moved them to Hover's Grove when the mill offered her father one of the top security jobs. Since then, they'd been stuck in this little town for almost five years.

Hover's Grove had one elementary school, one high school, and one small strip mall. They had to drive an hour to get to the closest Walmart, which her mother used to take her to years ago. Since her mother's death, Vanessa had only been there once with her father, just before last Christmas. Only geriatrics and people born in the Grove enjoyed the serenity of this seaside haven. Vanessa would be gone by next year. The only other option was insanity.

"Have a seat and tell me what's on your mind," the sheriff said, gesturing to a chair on the other side of his huge desk.

He sat with his hands clasped over his ample belly and leaned back, waiting for Vanessa to start.

"I've been thinking about my mother lately, and I was wondering, did she ever come to see you about anything before she died?"

James frowned and leaned forward, placing his hands together on his desk. "Your mother, rest her soul, was a good woman. All I remember is she was a good person. I'm sorry how everything turned out with her passing and all."

"Sheriff, I'm wondering if she ever came to see you about anything. Did she ever complain to you?"

"What's this all about, Vanessa? It's been two years this month since she passed. Is that why you're thinking about her again?"

Vanessa stood and looked down at the sheriff. "Is it something you can't tell me? Or has my father asked you not to tell me? Because, you know, I don't mean any disrespect, Sheriff, but I feel that you're purposely avoiding my question."

"Vanessa, Vanessa, Vanessa, come on now. It's so peaceful here in Hover's Grove. Whatever happened to your mother is history. I'm sorry for your loss, but you must let it go. Digging up the past won't help you find closure. Now have a seat and tell me what's really on your mind."

"I found a note." She said it before she could stop herself. "It was written by my mother. It said she didn't commit suicide, and my father abused her. What can you tell me about this? If it's true, I'd like to know. Otherwise, I'm going to talk to my dad, and then I'll call the state police to let them deal with his crimes."

Her throat tightened as the last words escaped before she could stop them.

"Now, now, I wouldn't advise getting them involved," the sheriff said as he stood, too. "The file on your mother's case has been closed for a long time. They aren't going to arrest anyone on an assault charge two years after the fact with the complainant dead. I'd recommend you let this go." He crossed his arms.

"So you acknowledge that you were aware of her problems before she died?" Vanessa stared at the sheriff's face, looking for any telltale signs of a lie.

"I've had just about enough of this line of questioning, young lady. Everything with your mother's case is closed and over. If you have further questions, you should forget them or ask your father. But I recommend you let this go. There's nothing to find in the answers but heartache and tears."

The sheriff walked around his desk and gestured for the door. Vanessa headed for the exit but stopped before crossing the threshold.

"I have one more question—"

"No, you don't," Sheriff Redfield said in his stern-cop voice. "We are done with this."

"It's regarding something else. Would you humor me?"

The sheriff waited a moment and then nodded. "One question, and then I've got a lot of work to do here."

That's bullshit.

"When I asked you about the bird, why did you lie to me?"

The sheriff blinked.

Got you, asshole.

"Vanessa, I didn't lie. What are you going on about now?"

"I distinctly said, *did you see that bird over there*, and you said, *I don't see any seagulls, Vanessa.* How did you know it was a seagull if you didn't see it?"

It was at that moment she knew for sure the sheriff hadn't spoken a single true word to her. He stumbled over his words. Then he became angry.

"Now you listen to me, Vanessa. How dare you march into my office, accuse me of neglect of duty regarding your mother's case, and then question my integrity. You had better let this go, or there will be a price to pay. Mark my words, *let it go.*"

Before she could respond, he grabbed her arm and pushed her through the door.

"Remember what I said. I'm warning you, *let it go.*"

The sheriff shut the door and locked it.

Vanessa shivered as she walked away. The look in James's eyes when he said those last three words scared her. And what is everyone *warning* her for? Warning her about what?

She had to talk to her father. She would find the answers, or she would take her questions to the state police and fuck Redfield.

Vanessa half walked, half ran home. Her father would be home from work soon.

She dropped her schoolbooks on her bedroom floor and grabbed her diary to read the letter one more time before her dad got home. When she opened her diary, it was empty. The note was gone.

"What the fuck?"

Someone had stolen the note. The only person who had that kind of access was her father.

A door slammed somewhere downstairs.

Her father was home.

Good. Now he can answer for what he's done.

With the empty diary in her hand, Vanessa entered the kitchen, where her father closed the fridge and opened a can of beer.

"Hi, Vanessa. How was your day?"

"Dad, I'd like to know what you did with the note I had in here." She held her diary out for him to see.

"What?" he asked as he pulled a kitchen chair out and sat down. "What note?"

"I'm the only one with a key to this diary. How did you get into it?"

"Whoa there, Missy. I didn't get *into* it. I've never even seen that diary before."

"Well, then someone broke into our house."

"Is that why you went to see the sheriff today? He said you riled him up a little. You want to talk about that?"

"He called you already? I was just there half an hour ago."

Her father gestured for her to sit. "Vanessa, have a seat. Listen, I know tomorrow's the anniversary of your mother's death. It's a hard day for all of us. But you need to let this go. You can't deal with the pain by asking questions and accusing people of lying to you."

Vanessa didn't sit. She stared at her dad as if he were a stranger. The beer in his hand, the tired look on his face, and the pain behind his eyes didn't match his words.

"You and the sheriff have no idea what you've done today, have you?"

Her father sipped his beer. "What are you talking about? I was at work all day. On my way home, the sheriff called, saying he was concerned about you. So here I am, hoping to help you through the next few days. I even requested time off work to be with you. So what else have I done today?"

"Since neither one of you are willing to give me straight answers, I will find someone who will."

His hand came down onto the table hard. She jumped.

"You watch your mouth. Don't you threaten me, ever. Do you hear me? Don't you *ever* threaten me. Now, these questions you have need to be forgotten. Everything is fine. The case is closed. Mourn however you want, but don't belabor this issue. Are we clear?"

This must be the side of my father my mother spoke of.

She needed to leave.

She nodded, hoping he would let it go. She knew it was over when he took another swig from his can of beer.

She went to her bedroom, grabbed a few personal things, and left the house. She walked up beside the shed in the backyard and stood by the oak tree. The ground below her feet looked untouched except for a small section by the wall. She dug down until her fingers touched something hard. After looking back at the house to ensure she wasn't being watched, Vanessa dug a small box out of the ground and unwrapped the plastic that sealed it. Inside, she found twenty-one-hundred-dollar bills, just like her mother's note had promised.

With the money stuffed safely in her pocket, she tossed the box onto the grass and hopped the backyard fence into the alley.

She screamed at the sight of the old woman standing in the alley, her arms waving like a lunatic.

Vanessa edged along the fence.

The old woman tossed something from her closed palm. A powder of some kind shot out and spread thickly in the air. Then it moved like a small fog with purpose, landing on Vanessa's face.

She coughed as the powder entered her lungs. She rubbed her eyes as some of it seeped past her lids. Whatever the old woman threw at her made her feel sick.

"What … did you do?" she managed to ask.

Vanessa dropped to one knee, coughing and hacking. Blood dripped from her mouth to the concrete.

She tried to look at the woman, but her vision blurred.

She hit the pavement with her left shoulder.

"I warned you to take the right path," the old woman whispered in her ear. "Now you will be my earth sacrifice. Your mother was my water, and you will be my earth. It is as it is and as it will be. Die sweetly, young thing, die sweetly."

Then darkness.

***

Vanessa floated between two worlds. One of sleep and darkness, the other, pain.

Her father's voice floated through her consciousness from a distance.

What's he doing here? Where am I?

Whack!

Something slapped her face. Vanessa tried to open her eyes, but an odd stinging prevented her from doing so.

Whack!

She tried to roll away from whatever was hitting her but couldn't.

Hit me again, and I will smack the fuck off your face.

She wrenched her eyes open. The ceiling above was old and stained. The smell of salt in the air told her the ocean was nearby. She was in one of the lighthouse rooms on the rocky shore of Hover's Grove.

On either side of her shoulders were small wooden walls, almost like railings in a hospital bed, so that she wouldn't roll off. She lay on her back, her legs secured to the wooden contraption.

"Why the hell am I at the lighthouse?" she asked and coughed as the earlier powder irritated her lungs. That must be what had bothered her eyes and was making them tear up.

She struggled with her bonds. "What ... is this thing?" The sound of her gravelly voice surprised her.

"Ahh, she's awake." A woman's voice. "Just in time for the witching hour."

"Witching hour? What's that? And why ..." She paused to swallow. "Why did you throw that powder shit in my face?"

She struggled against her bonds again.

"You persisted, little lady. No one can get away with meddling in my affairs without me knowing about it. I'm a solitaire. I work alone."

"You mean you play cards by yourself?"

The old woman drew closer and leaned over the wooden railing to look at Vanessa. "You can talk jokes and play your tricks, but I've got a trick or two of my own. For over two hundred and fifty years, my kind has reigned, and it is because of people like you that you must perish as my sacrifice to the four natural elements of the universe."

Vanessa suddenly remembered the woman saying something about her mother. This wasn't a joke. This was real.

She's fucking nuts.

The straps were too tight to entertain thoughts of escape.

"Back in the alley, what did you say about my mother?"

The old woman moved away. Vanessa heard something clang, like metal against metal.

"Your mother was my water, and you will be my earth. Each year I need four. The other two, fire and air, have already been extinguished. This is how I stay young. I harness my powers from the four elements."

Vanessa had to pee. She clenched and held it back. She shook all over, and her skin was clammy.

"Is that what you meant by the left and right road stuff?"

"The right-hand path of light is white magic, and the left-hand path is black magic. I might've spared you again if you had heeded my warning and not taken the left-hand path."

"Again?"

"Your mother took your place two years ago. Now, as my earth sacrifice, at midnight, by the light of the full moon, I will bury you alive in the coffin you lie in presently. My good friend and assistant, Sheriff James Redfield, is outside right now, digging a hole for you, one hundred yards from here."

Fear turned to rage as Vanessa thought of her mother. She had not killed herself, as reported by the sheriff, because the sheriff was in on it.

Her mother had been murdered.

Vanessa struggled as hard as she could despite knowing it was useless. The straps only dug deeper and cut off her circulation.

"An estimated 200,000 of my kind," the witch continued speaking from somewhere out of sight, "a few decent housewives were executed most brutally in the past. You've undoubtedly heard of the more famous event, the Salem Witch Trials? Well, we've been accused of sorcery, devil worship, and even baby-eating. None of that crazy stuff is what we do, and yet for years, we were killed. Now it is my turn. One by one, I take the souls of your kind to pay for what your ancestors did to my kind. In thirty minutes, it will be midnight, and it's a full moon. That's the witching hour."

Vanessa listened while locked in her coffin, immobile. The anger fled, and all that remained was a fear so intense she had difficulty breathing.

"I heard my father earlier," she said, her throat raw.

"He's here. He was brought in when I wanted your mother. She'd asked questions, too. I had him row the boat out and throw your mother into the water while I stood on the shore invoking the spirits. If I'd spared you back then, that was the deal. Your father had to do it." The witch's face appeared over the edge of the wooden box. "I wanted you for the water sacrifice that year, but your father proved to be a problem. He offered your mother instead. I took her. Now, to keep him in line, I'm taking you."

The old woman jerked her head back and laughed, eerie and guttural. It raised goosebumps on Vanessa's arms.

With the knowledge that her father not only helped kill her mother but was the one who threw her into the water, Vanessa really had nothing to live for anymore. These people had chosen for her.

A door banged open somewhere.

"James just received a call," her father shouted. "We have a problem."

"What kind of problem?" the witch asked.

"The state police are on their way. They will be here within five minutes. I just talked to him. He said they're coming with the FBI, too. Over forty cruisers are arriving in minutes. We can't do this now. We have to—"

"Slow down!" the witch screeched. "Who called the state police? How would they know where we are?"

"I have no idea. The state trooper called James. He said he was coming to the lighthouse before midnight. They said they'd be here in five minutes. We have to move now."

Someone else's feet pounded into the lighthouse.

"It's true." The sheriff's voice. "They received a complaint from a female. Apparently, this woman knew a lot about us. They're coming fast. We have to move now. There's no choice."

"A female?" the witch asked. "I need to know who this woman is. Redfield, find out. It wasn't Vanessa here. I followed her from school and stayed with her until now."

Vanessa could see the edge of the witch's head.

"You have won a reprieve for a second time," the witch said. "When this is over, I will hunt you down. I curse you to eternally look over your shoulder. From here on, you only exist to be my sacrifice." Her eyes were half closed, her face contorted and twisted as if she was experiencing a seizure.

After a moment, she looked away and addressed the men, who were out of Vanessa's view.

"You, take Vanessa to your car. You were out for an evening drive by the lighthouse. Redfield, get cleaned up and meet these officers. Talk to them and then get them out of our town. I will head down to the beach and walk home. Go!"

Hands reached in and started to undo Vanessa's straps. As soon as her arms were free, she punched and smacked her father, screaming at him.

"How could you do this?" she cried. "How could you hurt my mom?"

Her father's strong hands gripped her wrists and subdued her.

He gritted his teeth and said, "Don't fight this, or you will die. Obey me, and you may live a little longer. Are you listening?"

Her wrists ached in his grasp like they were broken. A moment later, he released her, and the sharp pain ebbed to a subtle throb.

He finished undoing her straps and lifted her from the coffin. Fireman style, he threw her over his shoulder and carried her to the car.

Everything she ever thought she knew was a lie. Her father was no longer her father. He was a monster.

He sat her down by the car, opened the back door, and eased her in. She contemplated running, but how far could she get? She no longer had the money her mother had left for her, and she was still groggy from the witch's powder.

Headlights shone through the window behind them, a long line of vehicles with red lights flashing. Her father stood outside, waving at the approaching vehicles.

What's he doing? How does he know that I won't tell the police what happened here?

"You can get out now, Vanessa. It's over. We're safe."

Vanessa stared through the windshield, not willing to do anything he asked.

"Come on. The police are here. Come on out."

"Never. When they ask me what happened, I'll tell them everything."

"I hope you do, sweetheart. I hope you do. I'm sorry it had to be like this. There was no other way. I hope you'll forgive me."

Sweetheart? Forgive me?

Vehicles stopped all around them. Car doors opened and closed. Men shouted orders.

A man in uniform, his hair in a military buzz cut, poked his head through the back door.

"Are you all right, ma'am?"

Vanessa nodded. She wiped her cheeks. Help had arrived. It was over.

"I've got someone here to see you," the man said. "Prepare yourself. This may come as a shock."

Vanessa nodded.

Her mother stepped into view and eased into the back seat to sit beside her.

A lightheadedness enveloped Vanessa, and for a brief moment, her vision wavered.

"Is it … really you?" she asked, shock settling over her nervous system.

"Yes, baby. Your mommy has come home. And we have your father to thank for saving both our lives."

***

Vanessa and her parents left Hover's Grove and flew to Europe, meandering through Italy, Greece, and Hungary before getting on another plane and flying to Australia.

During that year of travel, Vanessa learned the truth. Her father had heard about the mysterious disappearances around Hover's Grove when they first moved there. Then a family friend disappeared.

Vanessa's mother asked the sheriff too many questions. The witch warned her, saying her daughter would have an accident if she didn't stop asking questions.

When approached with the notion that Vanessa would be used in a sacrificial ceremony and given no other option, they hatched a plan. Her mother offered to take Vanessa's place, and her father would help kill her to show his allegiance to the witch and her cause. When he rowed out on the water that fateful night, he had given her mother a sealed package of money and a long straw to breathe through. Then she went into hiding.

Vanessa lay on the couch in their new home and asked why they didn't call the police then.

"Because the sheriff had videotaped your father throwing me into the water," her mother said. "With the report of death by suicide, the case was closed. If anything were to happen, the case would reopen, and the anonymous video recording would show up, blaming your father for my death."

"Why wait two years to deal with this? That was the worst two years of my life. The whole time I thought you had killed yourself. There had to be a way to involve the police sooner."

"The witch kept your father at a distance. He needed to be involved for the police to act. People still disappeared around town, but your father wasn't included in the planning. Not until they wanted you again. He had me write that note, hoping you would run from him, take the money and quietly leave town. But you did the worst thing you could, just like I did. You went to Sheriff Redfield and asked questions. Your dad told me to call the state police and bring them in just before midnight. And you know the rest."

"Twenty-eight killings and disappearances were attributed to that witch," Vanessa said, shaking her head and looking down at her hands. "After the sheriff's confession, only one thing remains unsolved. Where did the witch go?"

"I don't know. They're still looking for her. She apparently walked down to the beach that night and disappeared. No one has seen her since."

Vanessa felt a chill. She rubbed her arms and looked around the room. "Did you open one of the windows, Mom?"

"No, it must've been your dad. I'll check on dinner. It's getting late."

She left Vanessa alone on the couch in their remote shack in the suburbs of Port Denison, Western Australia.

Vanessa picked up a magazine from the coffee table and leafed through it while she waited for her mother to return.

Something banged the wall on the side of the house. Vanessa looked up in time to see a face move away from the window.

"Mom! Dad!"

She tossed the magazine aside and ran for the kitchen.

"Everything all right?" her mother asked. "You look startled."

"She's here. The witch is outside. I just saw her." She looked at the clock. "It's a full moon, and it'll be midnight in two hours. What're we going to do?"

"Now, Vanessa, you know she can't find us all the way across the world. Everything will be fine."

"To make you feel better"—her father lifted a large butcher knife in the air—"I'll go outside and walk around the house."

He stepped outside the kitchen door. Minutes later, he came in through the front door.

"No one's out there," he said. "Nothing to be worried about. Everything's fine."

Vanessa looked out the window where she'd seen the face. "It was this window. I heard a bang and looked up. The witch was watching me through it. I'm scared, Mom."

Vanessa leaned closer and stared out into the night. Something small and white waddled closer. It came into view, illuminated by the light from inside the house.

A seagull. It had a broken leg. It flapped its wings and then tucked them back in just before it fell over and died.

"Mom. Come and look at this. It's happening again." She pointed out the window. "There's a dead seagull outside our window, just like in front of the sheriff's office."

Her parents looked out the window.

The bird was gone.

Someone laughed outside.

It came across the wind and floated to them through the darkness.

Vanessa screamed as the front door burst open.

The witching hour had come again.

There would be no escape this time.

It's just the way things are …

Bound

Kramer Kay stood among shelves of glass figurines. Someone was dead. She could feel it, but she couldn't see them yet. As she walked around the display cases that held a variety of glass statues, the store clerk approached and asked if she needed any help. The store's lights were bright, the air stale and dry. She turned, moistened her lips, and judged the woman to be at least sixty years of age. Her nametag read "Beatrice."

"I'm just looking," Kramer responded. Beatrice probably heard that all day.

"Just holler if you need anything."

Kramer politely nodded and turned away.

Every sort of figure was done up in glass in front of her. Dolphins, wolves, deer, and even elephants. She went to pick up a glass rabbit and felt someone standing beside her.

A teenage girl held a glass figure of a deer with its head down in the grazing position. It appeared to Kramer that the girl, roughly eighteen years of age, worked here. Her name tag read, "Kelly."

"I've always liked this one," Kelly said. "It was my favorite."

Kramer caught the use of past tense. *Was my favorite.*

"Which one is your favorite now?" Kramer asked.

"It's still this one."

Odd.

"But I thought you said it *was* your favorite?"

"I did."

The girl placed the deer in Kramer's palm. Their eyes locked as the young girl spoke again.

"Help me. I lay where the deer play."

Her voice sent a shiver through Kramer's shoulders.

"What did you say?"

"I lay where the deer play. Help me, find me. Let me find peace."

Kramer blinked, and then she was standing alone. Kelly had been there one moment, gone the next.

Kramer turned and looked toward the counter.

"Are you all right, ma'am?" Beatrice asked.

"Yes, yes, of course." Kramer approached the counter, the figure of the deer still clutched in her palm. "I'll take this one," she said and handed the figurine to Beatrice.

"Oh my, nice choice. My former clerk, Kelly, just adored this one."

Kramer's head shot up at the mention of the girl she was just talking to. "Former clerk? What happened to her?"

"No one knows. She disappeared about a year ago. Not a word since. You must have heard about it. It was all over the news."

Kramer avoided the news for this particular reason. Too many people screamed for help once she knew about them. She reached into her purse, yanked out a twenty, and dropped it on the counter.

"Do you mean that eighteen-year-old girl with long blond hair?" she asked, now armed with what Kelly looked like.

"Yes. So you did hear about it. Tragic for the parents," Beatrice said as she handed back Kramer's change.

"I could only imagine. A tragedy."

Kramer gathered her things up and left in a hurry without saying another word.

I lay where the deer play.

What did that mean?

That's the main problem with earth-bound entities that are stuck. They have access to vast amounts of information, but they forget I don't.

She exited the mall and headed for her car, knowing she'd have to contact the investigating officer to see what she could find out about Kelly. Her contacts at the police department were pretty good, given that she'd helped them many times in the past on missing persons cases.

Bruce Wellington would help. Mostly because he kept asking her to dinner, but Kramer didn't date cops. She couldn't romance the very people she worked with.

From past experience, Kramer knew when someone from the other side, like Kelly, contacted her for something. They rarely left her alone until that something was dealt with.

***

She reached Bruce with her first call into the station after she got home. He promised to tell her everything he had on the case if she would agree to have dinner with him.

After ten minutes, she finally agreed to meet him at The Keg for nine that night. What would it hurt? She could use a good meal.

He had looked up Kelly's disappearance on the police computer and explained to Kramer that the case had gone cold eight months ago. Not a single lead had turned up as to the whereabouts of Kelly Walsh, eighteen. The parents had been interviewed extensively, even threatened with being charged in the hopes they'd break down and confess. They had been prime suspects in the case. But nothing came of it. The police had no one in custody and no idea where to look next.

Bruce asked Kramer why she was interested. Did she know something new? According to the file, Kramer's call had been the first about Kelly in over eight months. All Kramer said was that she would get back to him and hung up the phone after confirming the time for dinner again.

This venture to help Kelly seemed fruitless. Maybe she could talk to the parents? After that, if nothing led her to what *I lay where the deer play* meant, she would drop it. At least until Kelly came back with more for her to go on.

When Kramer looked into the local newspaper's archives via its website, she found excerpts about the missing girl and interviews with the parents. Wendy Walsh and Mark Walsh still lived on Somerset Boulevard.

Two hours later, at three p.m., she parked down the street and walked up to knock on the Walsh's door. The sun was hidden behind dark clouds that threatened rain. It reflected Kramer's mood and caused her to question why she was wasting time at the Walsh house. After losing their daughter and going through however many sleepless nights and grueling interviews with the police and media, the last thing they needed was Kramer asking the same questions, re-opening old wounds. She had turned to step off their porch when the door opened a crack. A single eye peeked through the gap.

"Yes?"

"Hello, Mrs. Walsh?"

"Who wants to know?"

"My name is Kramer." Now, what was she supposed to say? She didn't want to make up a lie or scare Mrs. Walsh by saying the wrong thing, yet she had to get her talking about Kelly. She decided to try the truth. "I came here today because I saw your daughter, Kelly."

There was a moment of silence. The awkwardness made Kramer fidgety. She adjusted her coat and stepped back on the porch. The door opened far enough for the woman's face to be exposed.

"That's impossible. No one has seen Kelly for over a year."

"I know, but I'm different. Let me explain. People who have unfinished business come to me after they pass away. Earlier today, I was shopping in the mall and met Kelly, where she used to work."

Mrs. Walsh audibly gasped, raising a hand to her chest. "Are you playing games with me? Is this about money? What kind of person are you?"

Kramer was surprised by Mrs. Walsh's response. Usually, when she told people that she was a psychic, they either asked questions of a psychic nature or stated that they didn't believe in the other side. It was rare that she would be accused of trying to cheat someone out of money.

Kramer described Kelly to Mrs. Walsh. "I read her name tag at the figurine store. I called the police and found out the case had been cold for eight months. After meeting Kelly, I thought maybe we could talk. Maybe something will click for me."

"You talked to the police?" Mrs. Walsh opened her front door all the way. "They give out information on a case so easily?"

"Ma'am, I've worked with the police for years on missing persons cases. My reputation is sound. I respect confidentiality. They wouldn't work with me if I didn't."

Kramer wondered if it would start to rain before Kelly's mother decided to either let her into the house or send her on her way.

"Did the police send you?"

"No," Kramer said.

"How about the media? Were you sent here to dig for more clues, or did you come on your own?"

"I came on my own."

Mrs. Walsh made an exaggerated attempt to step out on the porch and look up and down the street.

"Am I able to trust you? You're saying no one sent you? You're here to talk about Kelly, and no one knows you're here?"

Why are we still going over that point?

"It appears you've been hounded to the point of paranoia," Kramer said. She raised her hands in an *I surrender* gesture and said, "I just want to talk. That's it. No one and nothing is behind my motives."

Mrs. Walsh stepped back into her foyer and nodded at Kramer, but she didn't step aside to allow Kramer entry.

"Maybe we could continue this conversation inside," Kramer said. "If possible, I want to see Kelly's bedroom."

"Okay," Mrs. Walsh said and moved to the side.

Kramer stepped into a modest home. It was clean and tidy, but she felt something was wrong again.

"Please understand. I'm usually pretty cautious when answering the door. We used to get reporters wanting interviews, and all sorts of weirdos, knocking at all hours."

Oh, so now you only allow crazy psychics into your home.

"Kelly's bedroom is up there," Mrs. Walsh said as she gestured at the stairs and started for them, slamming the front door hard. Kramer followed close behind.

When they entered Kelly's bedroom, she saw they'd turned it into a library. She also saw Kelly sitting in a rocking chair in the corner.

"Are you okay?" Mrs. Walsh asked.

It must've shown on her face. "Yes, yes, I'll be fine. What happened to Kelly's things? Aren't you expecting her to come home?"

"Sadly, no. She wasn't the type to run away. My husband and I decided to move on. If and when she comes home, we will turn her old room back to how it was."

That's odd. Mrs. Walsh knows more about Kelly's disappearance than she's letting on. Something is very wrong here. And how come she didn't respond when I told her I saw Kelly's ghost—which is confirmation her daughter is dead and not just missing?

Kramer heard a whisper. She looked over as Kelly was mouthing the words *where the deer play.*

"Was there a certain area where Kelly set up her glass deer?"

"Oh, my, you really are psychic." Mrs. Walsh walked to the closet and stood beside it, pointing into the corner of the room. "Before this bookcase was here, we had set up a circular rug in the corner. When she was little, Kelly would play for hours on that rug so none of her glass figures would break on the hard floor. She always played with her deer right here."

Kramer walked over, being careful now to keep a little distance from Mrs. Walsh. Everything in her soul screamed at her to *RUN*. She had to leave, come back with Bruce, or never return again.

Kramer used her hands to inspect the bookcase to look like she was onto something. She ran her hand down the side of the wall and felt a slight depression in the drywall.

Someone else was coming as footsteps resounded along the outside corridor. She turned to see who it was. Mrs. Walsh's facial expression had changed. She now looked angry.

The footsteps stopped outside Kelly's bedroom door.

"Everything okay, Mrs. Walsh?" Kramer asked. "Have I offended you in some way?"

She hadn't seen the rubber mallet in Mrs. Walsh's hand before.

"You big city bitch." Her voice had taken on a high-pitched squeal as if this was her real voice, and she had deliberately deepened it earlier to converse at the door. "You come here and want to start shit. Who do you think you are?"

Kramer had felt it. She should have run. She regretted getting this involved in the first place.

She turned to look at the chair where Kelly sat. Kelly was crying, her face red, tears streaming down her cheeks. She was shaking her head back and forth and mouthing the word, *No*.

Kramer's stomach dropped even further. She stepped back and bumped into the bookcase.

A man entered the room behind Mrs. Walsh. His physical features led Kramer to believe that she was now standing in the presence of Kelly's parents.

"I'll leave," Kramer said. "I'm sorry to have bothered you."

"Oh no. You won't be leaving." Mrs. Walsh lunged at her.

Kramer ducked out of reflex. The mallet hit the bookcase above her head, stopping its descent. Kramer looked for an escape. She felt trapped, locked in the corner of the bedroom, both Kelly's parents blocking her.

Before Mrs. Walsh could raise the mallet again, Kramer dove past her legs and tried to crawl through the door.

A large hand grabbed her from behind. As much as she writhed and protested, Mr. Walsh held firm and lifted her as if she were weightless.

"We got us a pretty one here," he said, his breath smelling of onions and garlic.

"No one knows she's here," Mrs. Walsh added. "Take her to the basement and do what you do best. Treat her to a little Kelly treatment."

Kramer grabbed hold of the doorframe and tried to arch herself in a quick twist to dislodge his grip, but he was too strong. The man had to be at least six and a half feet tall.

Mrs. Walsh dropped the mallet again, connecting with Kramer's wrist where she held the doorframe, audibly breaking it.

Kramer screamed. The pain was more intense than anything she had ever felt.

"That'll teach you to go nosing around in other people's business," Mrs. Walsh shouted in Kramer's face. "Who do you think you are? Now you're gonna pay, you little bitch."

Mr. Walsh dragged Kramer out of Kelly's bedroom, but not before Kramer caught a glimpse of Kelly, still sitting on the chair in the corner, her head in her hands, crying, her body wracked with sobs.

Kramer's pain became too much. Blackness covered her peripheral vision and then moved inward until Kramer slumped, completely out.

***

Kramer woke in a basement. It was dark and smelled of oil. A tiny light shone out of a single bulb that dangled from the ceiling.

She looked over at the source of her pain. A rope tied her swollen wrist to a long nail protruding from the wall. The injury looked horrid. It was already a dark purple, her hand sitting at a bad angle. She looked at her other arm and then down her body. Nothing else was damaged yet.

She examined the basement as best as possible in the little light. It was a mess. Tools scattered around different makeshift tables told her the guy wasn't organized. Something hung from the ceiling to her right. It had chains and a small black strip that looked like a seat.

Then it occurred to her what she was looking at. The tools on the tables weren't just any tools. They were items used in some kind of fetish. The thing hanging from the ceiling was a sex swing of some kind. Behind a beam, barely visible in the light from the bulb, she saw a medieval stockade with a hole for a head and two smaller holes for the hands. Black ropes dangled around the side of it.

What the hell is this place?

Footsteps started down the stairs. Mr. Walsh came into view. He was wearing shorts and a white wife-beater shirt.

They couldn't hold her for long. Bruce would miss her at dinner and wonder what happened. He knew she wouldn't stand him up. They'd had a deal. But would he come to the Walsh house and expect to find her tied up in the basement?

"I see you're finally awake."

He stepped up close and sniffed her. It was repulsive, like a dog sniffing its food.

"Good," he said. "I smell fear."

He lifted the edge of his shirt and wiped his nose, snorting as he did it.

In all her experiences with the dead and working with the police, she had never been in such a bad place.

"What are you going to do?" she asked. "Whatever it is, there will be no going back. You won't be able to undo it." Kramer hated that her voice sounded so weak.

He stared at her for a long moment before responding. "I never *want* to undo nothing."

"What about Kelly? Wouldn't you want to change that?" She had nothing to go on. She had to try to keep him talking.

"Never. Kelly was good. One of the best. I left her locked in that stockade over there for almost a week once, and she still begged for me to do it to her. The more they beg, the faster I release them. You'll learn this rule because you're a bitch, too. You'll learn. All women are fucking whores and should be treated as such. When you get in touch with your own understanding of this, you'll be allowed certain freedoms. But until then, I treat you as my personal slave, my personal whore. Over time you'll learn to love me. Or you'll fight with the truth, a truth polite society has implanted in your head, and die for that truth."

Kramer's insides twisted. She almost lost the contents of her bowels as her urine, warm and sudden, rushed down her leg.

Mr. Walsh looked over at her feet.

"Good," he smiled. "That's a start. I love when a whore is self-lubed."

He moved closer and placed his hand, open-palmed in the small puddle that formed at her feet. She leaned into the wall as hard as she could to escape him, but it was no use.

He lifted his hand and sniffed it. Then he opened his mouth and licked her urine off his fingers.

His smile was evil. His eyes, Lucifer's.

"You taste good."

For a large man, he stood up with ease and speed. One second he was on his knees, and the next, he was standing, his chin coming to her forehead.

"You'll do fine. After one or two months of being my pet, I'll bury you in the wall like all the others. Unless, of course, you're a good pet. One who enjoys pleasing me."

Kramer couldn't help herself. She spat in his face, the phlegm landing beside his mouth in a glob.

He licked around his lips, caught a piece of her saliva, and dragged it into his mouth.

"Damn, do you ever taste good."

Then with an athlete's quickness and deft speed, he lunged forward, grabbed her jeans on both sides, and yanked with his vise-grip hands. They snapped and dropped, leaving her exposed to him, her panties the only thing separating her privacy from his insanity. Kramer screamed as long and as loud as she could.

"Oh, you are going to be fun. Maybe later, my wife could join us. I usually leave her out in the beginning. I love all the bodily fluids except blood." He turned and tossed her jeans away and then looked back at her. "My wife only likes blood. You end up minus a finger or a toe when she joins us. After a few weeks, you'll never walk again, and then, eventually, she takes too many pieces, and I'm left with a dead trunk, and that's no fun. Well, maybe for a few days, but that doesn't concern you because you're already gone by then."

He laughed. Then he slapped his knee. The laugh grated on her already raw nerves. Kramer cried. Was this it? Could it be that easy?

A loud bang from upstairs made her jump. Pain rushed through her broken wrist.

Mr. Walsh looked up at the ceiling.

"Wait here," he said.

Where am I going to go, asshole?

As Mr. Walsh reached the bottom of the stairs, Kramer heard a gunshot somewhere above. He heard it, too, and stopped. She thought she could see the doubt on his face in the dim light.

He ran from the bottom of the stairs to a table littered with gadgets, lifted one, and walked over to stand beside her.

The door opened above. Light shone down the stairs. It looked like someone was holding a flashlight.

"Kramer? You down there?"

"Help!" she yelled, but only half the word escaped her lips before Mr. Walsh clamped a hand over her mouth. Breathing became a chore she couldn't accomplish.

The tool in his hand was a metal OBGYN-type speculum with the ends shaved down to points like knife tips. Mr. Walsh turned the sharpened ends toward Kramer's chest and pushed it forward with all his strength.

She had little wiggle room between his grip and the ropes on her wrists, but it was enough to arch her back and spin her chest away. One of the pointed ends of the speculum entered between two rib bones and punctured her right lung, which caused immediate stress on her breathing ability.

A gun went off somewhere in the basement.

Mr. Walsh's hand came away from her mouth and nose. Breathing was even more difficult than before. It seemed like the one bulb in the basement went out for Kramer.

***

Kramer regained consciousness as she was being loaded onto a stretcher. An officer was standing over her.

Bruce.

"What happened?" she managed to ask.

"We got 'em, thanks to you. You're going to make it. You'll be okay."

"Got who?" she asked, her own voice sounding miles away. "You mean, Mr. Walsh?"

Bruce nodded. "You didn't show up for dinner. The great Kramer would never stand me up. I figured you'd come to the Walsh house, so I thought I'd do a drive-by tonight. I found your car parked a block down. The engine was cold when I touched the hood. It set off my internal radar. When I came to the door, Mrs. Walsh was acting weird. Then I heard someone screaming from the basement. I asked to check it out, but Mrs. Walsh said no. I called for backup, explained that I had probable cause, and entered the house anyway. I cuffed Mrs. Walsh and then got startled and fired my weapon by mistake. I found you in the basement."

A paramedic stepped forward and tried to push Bruce away. "Sir, we have to get her to the hospital."

Kramer lifted her good hand and touched Bruce's arm. He turned back.

She tried to speak, but nothing came out.

"What? What are you trying to tell me?" Bruce asked.

"The …" She waited, breathed in, cringing with the pain, and said, "Wall."

"The wall? Is that what you're saying?"

Kramer nodded.

"What about the wall? Is there something in the wall?"

Kramer nodded.

Bruce went to ask something and then stopped. He stared down the street, then looked back at her.

"Is Kelly in the wall?"

Kramer nodded.

"Okay." He looked at the paramedic. "Take her away and bring her back in one piece. Nothing happens to this one, you hear?"

Kramer was lifted into the back of the waiting ambulance, where Kelly sat beside her all the way to the hospital, smiling and mouthing the words, *Thank you.*

The Painting

MATT KEPT HIS HANDS below the table so his wife wouldn't see how much they shook. In order to eat, he brought them up, sliced another piece of meat, dipped it in the steak sauce, and then dropped them out of sight again.

It would be too uncomfortable to be questioned about the source of his anxiety.

After empty conversation, Matt left his salad on the plate, stood, and placed his dishes on the counter—to his relief, without dropping or breaking anything. He told Fran that he'd do the dishes while she was out on her evening run. Then he retired to his office.

After twenty minutes, he heard Fran getting ready to take her evening jog along the nature trails in the woods behind their house. It had never occurred to him why she would run right after dinner each night.

Maybe she's not running. Perhaps it's just a fast walk.

A buzz of energy passed through him when he entered his den. He looked up at the picture hanging on the wall.

That damned picture.

He willed the painting to move like it did yesterday. He was sure he'd seen it actually move. The water in the creek had been running, the trees billowing softly in the imaginary breeze that traveled through the painted landscape. He tried to convince himself that what he'd seen the previous night had to be an illusion. Pictures that hung on the walls of people's homes didn't have moving parts or double as a TV screen. At least *this* one didn't … until last night.

He had bought it for five dollars at a garage sale two years ago. What impressed him about it was the deer sipping the creek's water and the trail behind the deer. It looked like the trail behind his house. It was so close to a replica, in fact, that guests had commented on it over the years, wondering if it was a landscape painting of out back. Many times Matt had wanted to tell them it was, just to mess with them.

He turned away from it and crossed the small room where he sat in his leather armchair, which was still close enough to be able to watch the painting for any sign of movement.

The previous evening while sipping his scotch, he'd felt the same buzz of energy in the air. The painting was moving when he looked around to see what had changed. The creek ran through the center of the canvas, flowing into the frame. Upon closer inspection, the leaves lolled slowly, and after a few moments of staring, Matt felt himself being physically pulled into the landscape.

He'd rubbed his eyes, checked how much scotch he'd had, and looked again. The painting was a still image once more.

The telephone had rung, forcefully yanking him back to the here and now. The call went unanswered as he'd needed a few moments to collect himself. For reasons unknown, the painting that hung in his den for years had transfixed him hypnotically.

Now, sitting before the canvas with his wife out jogging, Matt stared at the picture from his reading chair just as last night. A part of him wasn't just nervous. He felt fear, too. Would it repeat itself? What was its purpose? Was the house haunted, or just the picture? Could a picture actually be haunted?

After ten minutes of intense scrutiny, Matt looked away, assuring himself that nothing as ridiculous as a moving picture would happen tonight. A feeling of foolishness made him frown.

What the hell am I doing? Sitting in my chair, waiting for a painting to move?

He looked around for something to read. The new Koontz novel sat on his desk. He grabbed it, flipped to the bookmark's location, and stared at the words.

A noise startled him. It sounded like someone was yelling his wife's name. Goosebumps covered his arms as he sat still, trying to hear the voice again.

He edged forward and then stood from his chair.

The silence around him was absolute, the house empty. The proverbial pin could drop in another room, and he'd hear it.

Then the picture moved.

The deer that had sat idle for years lifted its head and looked to the right. Startled by something, it turned the other way and bounded out of the picture.

Matt felt his heart rate spike as his eyes widened.

Am I going crazy?

A man shouted Fran's name again. This time Matt could tell it came from the picture. It was like he was watching a widescreen TV hooked up to the wall. Only it wasn't a TV. It was a five-dollar picture from a garage sale.

A man stepped into the scene and walked to the creek's edge. The man stopped about a dozen feet from where the deer had been.

Matt recognized him. It was Charlie Houghton, his ex-business partner. Their small pizza business had gone under in the last year as a large corporate pizza company moved into the neighborhood. Two months ago, they'd severed ties. Matt hadn't seen Charlie in at least six weeks, but he easily recognized the walk, the way he swaggered like a 70s car salesman with too much jewelry around his neck.

What the hell am I watching? Better yet, why am I seeing this?

Charlie called out Fran's name again.

His wife slowly entered the picture by the right side of the frame. She walked up to Charlie, and they embraced and kissed a long, deep, sensual kiss.

She wore her normal jogging suit.

Without realizing what he was doing, Matt shouted her name. He watched as they yanked away from each other.

"What was that?" Fran asked.

Charlie shook his head and scanned the area. "I have no idea. It sounded like Matt." He turned to look Fran in the eye. "Could he have followed you?"

"No way. I jogged here. He can't run, the fat fuck."

They shared a laugh. Then they kissed again.

Matt watched, stunned into silence now. After a long moment, they pulled away from each other.

The creek water entered the painting on the right and oozed through the landscape, exiting on the left.

Matt was past disbelieving. He had lost all doubt. Whatever he was witnessing had some psychic quality to it.

"Are you going to be able to do it this time?" Charlie asked.

Fran pulled away and looked down at the ground. She kicked at a pebble and then glanced back at Charlie.

"Yes," she said. "I told you I would."

"But this is your sixth time. You've told me six different times that you *would* do it. You must understand that this erodes my trust and commitment."

Fran nodded. "I understand. But you can count on me. I love you. I will not let you down." She stepped back to Charlie and grabbed his lapel. Staring him in the eyes, she said, "I will do it tomorrow night. When we meet out here again, Matt will be already dying and, soon after, dead."

Matt gasped and covered his open mouth.

"Good, because getting my hands on ricin is seriously hard. We had to find something that the body metabolizes, so no toxicology reports would ever detect what killed him. Also, it's so uncommon that when he gets to the hospital, the doctors will identify it too late and won't know how to treat him."

"I promise," Fran said and then kissed Charlie again. "Tomorrow night. I'll make lasagna, his favorite dish. He can't resist eating extra when it's lasagna."

Charlie stepped away from her and crossed his arms like a scorned little boy. Matt watched as he dipped his head and raised his right eyebrow.

"Are you serious this time? This is it? No more excuses?"

Fran nodded.

"I need to hear it."

"I will murder my husband tomorrow night. You have my word." She held up her hand as if swearing on a Bible.

Matt clenched his hands into fists and rested them firmly on the filing cabinet under the painting.

"Until then," Charlie said.

They embraced and kissed long and sensuously. After separating, Fran and Charlie walked backward, staring at each other as if they were about to duel.

Then Charlie said something that caused Fran to pause and Matt to punch the metal cabinet his fists rested on.

"Do this, Fran. Do it right for us. After tomorrow, there will be no going back. You prove to me your love in this action. *Don't* do it, and

I'll know who you really are. Understand?"

Fran lingered near the edge of the frame. She nodded at Charlie.

Charlie turned and walked away. Fran stood a moment longer and then disappeared past the frame of the painting.

Exhausted, angry, and scared, Matt turned away from the picture and sat back in his chair. He blew out a long breath and tried to think.

He dropped his face into his hands and wept as his emotions overcame him. His partner had deceived him. His wife had cheated on him. Everything he knew was a lie. And now she planned on killing him—tomorrow night.

He rubbed his eyes and tried to stop crying. When Fran came home, he couldn't have bloodshot eyes. He wiped harder to clear the wet, salty proof. When he looked up, the deer was back in the picture. The creek had stopped moving. It was as if nothing had ever happened.

He poured himself a double scotch, sat in his armchair, and stared at the ceiling to think. He needed to do something.

Slowly a plan came together.

Matt smiled to himself.

He would show them.

***

"Dinner's ready."

For the last hour, Fran had been in the kitchen making their dinner. She had told him that she was making lasagna and adding a new Italian cheese called ricotta instead of cottage cheese. Because it was a new recipe, he had been banned from the kitchen for the last hour.

But now it was ready.

Dead man walking, he said to himself as he started for the kitchen.

The smell was incredible. He was going to miss this. When

everything was said and done, he would probably have to learn how to cook lasagna for himself.

He entered the kitchen and took a long, deep breath.

"Wow, that smells amazing."

Fran turned to him and smiled. "It is. I think you're really going to love the ricotta."

He was elated to see she had used the glass casserole dish. Without it, his plan would be more difficult to execute.

"Bring your plate over so I can serve you," Fran said.

"Nope. Not tonight."

Matt stepped over and grabbed a hot plate. He tossed it on the table without looking at Fran's reaction.

How dare you try to kill me? You're nothing now. I don't care if you stare. I don't care if you wonder what I'm doing. Fuck you if you think you have the upper hand.

He grabbed the oven mitts and picked up the lasagna pan.

"We'll put this baby on the table so I can easily grab seconds and thirds without leaving my chair."

Fran nodded and moved out of his way, undoubtedly happy that he would be a willing victim.

Matt stepped toward the table, fumbled the dish, and tripped, tossing the lasagna in the air. Fran shouted behind him. He hit the ground and rolled away from the flying glass as the lasagna pan erupted on impact with the marble kitchen floor. Meat and pasta were pierced with chunks of Pyrex.

Food ruined. Mission accomplished.

Matt got to his feet and feigned regret. He hugged Fran and thanked her for the effort involved in making such a dish, even though it repulsed him greatly to touch her, knowing what her plan had been.

"We'll order Chinese or pizza. I'm so sorry."

An hour later, the pizza finished, and Fran said she was heading out for her evening run.

Matt only nodded. He didn't want to talk to her anymore.

She changed, put on her running shoes, and slammed the door when she left.

He got up and ran to his den. He poured a scotch and sat in his armchair to steady his hands and calm his nerves. The picture was as it should be. Everything remained intact. Nothing moved.

He waited. He drank more scotch and stared. Still nothing.

Matt finished his beverage and got out of the chair. With each step forward, he waited to see the picture animate, but it didn't. He stood one foot from the landscape and waited, both hands placed open palmed on the top of the metal filing cabinet.

The river started first. Then the deer got spooked and bolted off. Charlie entered the painting from the left and Fran from the right.

"You didn't do it, did you?" Charlie asked.

Even from his vantage point in the den, Matt saw the look of failure on Fran's face.

"It wasn't my fault," she pleaded. "He was carrying the lasagna to the table and tripped. The Pyrex shattered on the floor, ruining the dish." She looked down at her shoes. "I'm sorry. I tried."

"You're lying."

Her head snapped up. "What did you say?"

"You're lying. This was your seventh attempt. If you really wanted to kill your husband to be with me, you'd have done it by now. I've waited too long for this charade to play out. Goodbye."

Charlie turned away from her and started to walk off the landscape.

Fran ran after him. She grabbed the shoulder of his jacket and spun him around.

"How dare you!" Fran screamed.

It sounded as if she was in the same room.

"You said you loved me," Fran said. "I was willing to kill my husband for you, and you dare to just walk away. How dare you?"

"You weren't killing your husband for me. Let's be clear on that."

"What are you talking about?" Fran asked, her voice rising to a shriek, one Matt had heard numerous times. "What was I doing it for then?" She stepped back and crossed her arms.

"You were doing it because you are a stupid bitch. I have manipulated you from day one."

Fran shook her head and frowned. "What are you talking about?"

"With your husband dead, not only do I get to fuck his wife for a while, but I also get his half of our little business venture as agreed upon when we started up, in the advent of death. After a month, I would explain to the authorities what you had done and that you'd just told me all about it out of guilt. You'd be arrested, and I wouldn't have to deal with you anymore. See what I mean? You're a stupid bitch."

Matt didn't see it coming. He could tell Charlie didn't either.

Fran dove forward, hands outstretched, lunging for Charlie's throat. Before he could respond, she was on him, and both fell to the ground.

Matt shouted at the painting and slammed his hands on the top of the cabinet.

Charlie and Fran rolled off the path.

Matt shouted again for them to stop. He had no idea where they were on the path as he had only walked it a few times throughout the years. He never jogged it routinely as Fran did.

He heard grunts and groans as his ex-partner and his soon-to-be ex-wife fought in the bushes.

Then Charlie rose up on his knees. Matt gasped. Charlie lifted his right arm and drove a fist down below the line of sight.

"Noooo!" Matt screamed as he banged his fists on the top of the cabinet. He grabbed the phone and dialed emergency services without looking.

"Do you require an ambulance, police, or fire?" he heard through the phone.

"Police. My wife is being attacked in the bushes behind my house."

The phone clicked. A man said, "Police, what is your emergency?"

Charlie raised his arm again and again, dropping his fist into Fran's face. The only difference was his fist was covered with blood now.

"My wife is being attacked on the path behind my house. Please help. Come fast. He's killing her!"

Matt tossed the phone and ran for the front door without looking back at the painting.

He hit the sidewalk running, the pizza jostling in his stomach, trying to slow him down.

The access to the trail was two blocks away. Matt ran, knowing it was too late to avoid serious damage. He was hoping to at least stop Charlie before he killed Fran.

A police siren wailed in the distance.

Good, they're coming.

He hit the opening to the path as a police cruiser rounded the corner twelve houses back.

Matt tried to maintain his speed but was slowed by a lack of routine exercise. Sure his wife had wanted to kill him, but he couldn't sit by and watch her be murdered.

After a hundred yards, he entered an area familiar to him from the picture in his office. He heard the authorities not far behind.

He recognized the creek. The tree to the right. The spot where Fran had stood was five feet away. He stepped up, afraid to see what had become of Fran. There was no sign of Charlie.

He saw the blood first.

Blood had pooled in little puddles over two feet from her broken body. Her nose sat askew on the top of a ruined face that looked like a farmer's plow had gone over it. Matt couldn't tell where the cuts started and stopped. Above her sightless eyes, a sizable dent in her skull dipped inward at least an inch, like a golf ball had impaled her.

He dropped to his knees beside her, overcome by sadness.

He tried to lower her eyelids, but they were missing.

What the fuck did Charlie do to her?

The cops caught up to him. Matt leaned down and wept.

What had Charlie's fists been made of, bricks?

Then he saw the culprit. Two feet from Fran's ruined face sat a jagged stone the size of an average running shoe. It had edges covered in blood, and part of Fran's hair was matted to the surface of it.

Matt grabbed the stone and turned to the cops.

"His name is Charlie. He did this to my wife, and he used this rock. I saw the whole thing."

Matt set the stone down as it seemed to be unsettling the cops. One was calling for backup, and the other had stepped back, his hand resting on the butt of his gun.

"How do you know it was Charlie?" the one cop asked.

"Because I saw the whole thing."

"Could you explain how you saw the whole thing?"

Even in his heightened state of emotions at the loss of his wife, he realized no one would understand what had happened. No one would believe him when he told them about moving pictures on the wall.

"What I mean is, I heard the scuffle and knew Charlie's voice from over there. I just couldn't get here fast enough. Charlie is my ex-business partner, so I know his voice. He has been fucking my wife, and when she rejected him, he did this to her."

More officers approached. Backup had arrived.

The cop who had asked him the questions turned to the new

officers. "We wanted to wait for you. He claimed to see someone else doing this, but when we pulled up, he ran into the bushes with us on his ass. He knew exactly where she would be. He said it was an old business partner. Something about the guy fucking his wife." The cop stopped talking and pointed at Matt. "And look at his hands. They're all red like he's been slapping and punching something."

Yeah, a metal filing cabinet in my den, asshole. The one beside the painting where I watched all this happen.

Two more officers walked up, making it six in total now.

"This is my wife," Matt said. "I did nothing wrong. I did not touch her."

"Then explain to us what we're looking at," one of the new cops said. "Help us understand."

"It all started when I overheard Charlie and my wife planning to kill me …"

Two officers turned to the others and smiled like they'd all heard this story a thousand times.

"Look, asshole. I didn't do anything. Stop making out like I'm guilty."

"Mister, stand up and place your hands on your head. Do it now."

"I will not. I did nothing wrong."

"That's not for us to decide. Stand up and place your hands on your head. I will not tell you again."

Matt let go of Fran, gently set her broken head down on the grass, and started to stand. Five of the six officers held their hands over their holsters. The one talking to Matt had handcuffs in his hands.

Matt looked down at his wife. "Is this what you wanted? Was this how I get killed?"

"What's that?" the cop asked.

Matt looked back at him. "You're in the picture now."

"I'm not following."

"If I were back in my den, I would be able to watch you. You're in the picture now."

"Hands on your head. Now. Last chance to do it peacefully."

"There's nothing you can do to me that would hurt me more than what has already happened. I'm innocent here, and fuck you if you think otherwise."

Matt made it three steps before he was tased. With no muscle control, Matt fell and rolled away, down the small embankment, and into the creek. He slipped below the water's surface and moved from the edge with the strong current.

The officers ran to the edge and looked over. Matt was already four feet from them and moving away fast.

Nothing in his body seemed to work properly. He could only breathe. He took in a large breath. His mouth filled with water, his lungs enlarging with it.

He detected a splash nearby. But it didn't matter anymore. Nothing else mattered.

Maybe he didn't see the picture in his office move. Perhaps he knew about Charlie all along. But could he kill his own wife? *Did* he kill her?

Or was it the painting that showed him the truth?

He drifted down the creek and in and out of consciousness.

His chest hurt. His heart hurt. His head ached.

And then nothing hurt.

No Trespassing

I DIDN'T KNOW I'D find death as I searched for the rarest leaves I could find.

I'm a leaf collector. For me, the leaves glisten in their hammock of twigs. At times, they call to me with disdain. I hear my name whispered among them as a soft breeze caresses their undersides. They don't yell, only whisper.

I love leaves.

I fear trees.

The trees watch me. I feel them watching. When they see me coming, I hear my name. That's their way of telling the other trees I'm close. I often hear a branch move, a twig snap. In the past, I would jump and look around. No one would be there. I soon realized the trees were stalking me. They don't like me because I take their leaves and the art they created and put them on display. I steal their protection. I steal from their crown.

But I respect them. I steer clear when walking through the forest and don't respond to their small noises. But I listen. Oh yeah, I listen because they call my name.

I carry numerous pieces of magazine paper in my satchel to keep the leaves safe and dry. I also have bear spray. I keep it clipped to the rope I use for a belt. Alongside that is my trusty umbrella. I couldn't be out collecting leaves only to have it rain and soak my work.

I slow to pick up a leaf, then stop myself. I can't. I have enough regular leaves. Today I only want Honey Locust leaves.

"Seve ..."

I hear my name, Seve Johnson, whispered, drawn out. The trees whisper it. They always take their time saying my name. I feel it as much as I hear it. I feel pleasure like I belong here, but it's fleeting. A stronger breeze has touched the leaves, and they use this chance to sing to one another.

I forge ahead. Somewhere in this area, I will find a Honey Locust tree. I know it because it was documented in the Botanical Journal last week.

I ease a branch out of my face and look upon a clearing. The only movement I see is the various trees passing messages back and forth amongst themselves. I ease away from the clearing and slip down a small embankment, where I open my satchel. The banana and jelly sandwich I prepared for lunch is soggy and mushy. I fish it out, take a bite, and listen.

Whenever I break to eat, I can almost hear the trees hatching their plan. A root stuck out nonchalantly, left exposed to trip me. A branch swinging back to swat my face. A dead tree knocked over to block my path. Whatever they devise, I can usually avoid it as long as I hear them. As long as I listen. I've realized they fear me just as much as I fear them.

After finishing my sandwich, I close my satchel, move the umbrella to my left side, hook the handle into my rope, and start back up the embankment. Within ten paces, I'm in the clearing I saw earlier.

There's a shadow a hundred yards up on the right. The area I'm looking at is an extension of an old forest. I suspect it's the section of forest the Botanical Journal spoke of. Convinced the Honey Locust I'm searching for will be in that copse of trees, I start walking.

Halfway there, I encounter a barbed-wire fence. Every twenty yards or so, there are small metal signs adorning the length of the old fence. The signs face the other way, so I can't read them. I approach an area where it's been trampled down. It's no more than two feet off the ground where I step over the barbed-wire barrier.

On the other side of the fence, I turn and see the Honey Locust tree.

I've found it.

Elation sweeps over me. I need to touch it to make sure it's real. I smell it, feel it, and set a leaf on my tongue. I realize with the addition of the leaves of this tree to my collection, I have almost completed my legacy. My display of rare leaves will sit in botanical museums for years to come.

It takes no more than fifteen minutes to collect the leaf samples I want, gently placing them in the magazine papers I'd brought. I ensure insects, diseases, or the environment doesn't damage the leaves I'm collecting. I also want ones attached to a small part of the twig with a lateral or terminal bud.

It isn't even midafternoon, and I've found the tree I was looking for. Overjoyed, I turn to the sky and shout with glee, more like a baying. I'm not much into yelling. I try to do a fist pump, but it just shakes my arm too much.

Before I step back over the barbed-wire fence, I read one of the posted metal signs.

NO TRESPASSING. VIOLATORS WILL BE SHOT.

I didn't see a house. There isn't a farm nearby, so I can't cross this fence and walk back the way I'd already come. I realize the signs are facing me, which means I've trespassed the whole time.

I shrug and make my way back across the clearing. I walk past the embankment where I'd had lunch and am halfway to my car when I hear the trees again. Of course, the trees want to say something. I didn't think I was going to get away that easy.

I hop behind a dead trunk. I'm being smart. Dead trees don't talk. This one will provide shelter while the others talk, trying to figure out a way to get me to give back what I have stolen from their forest.

They never get their leaves back, though. Seve always triumphs. I pull out my bear spray. I want to be ready for anything they throw at me.

A twig snaps. I press my back against the dead tree. I am less than an hour's walk to my car. This is their last chance. I swipe at the sweat collecting on my forehead. The hand still holding the bear spray—safety off—pauses mid-swipe.

Cold steel touches my neck. I panic and freeze at the same moment, my eyes wide. My heart slips and stutters.

"You was supposed to read the signs," a man beside me says.

Someone's talking to me. This clear voice could never come from leaves. I look to the left as far as my eyes can go without moving my head. To look farther, I'd have to turn my head, but I don't want to startle the voice's owner. The cold steel is pressing hard near my lower jaw, so hard I think my skin might break.

I begin to understand. I get it. Everything comes to me in a rush of knowledge. I'm going to be shot for collecting leaves. The trees will finally win. The cold steel is a gun held by a man gone insane. A man who lives out here. A man who hears the trees talk, night and day. They drove him crazy. It's not his fault.

With speed I didn't know I possessed, I jolt forward, away from the gun's tip, and spin to the left. I aim the bear spray and depress the trigger. The liquid shoots out and covers the face of the man.

The long-barreled weapon falls to the ground as the man wails inhuman cries. He drops to his knees, his face already turning a patchy red. His eyes lock shut. He bellows a symphony of agony.

I don't know what to do. I've never hurt anyone before. I'm shy and reserved. I don't like violence. I resist confrontation. I hate yelling. Yet here is a man kneeling before me, screaming a tune I have authored.

I have to help him. He was a victim of the trees. It wasn't his fault. After I help him, I will get out of here. I have to get home and press my new-found leaves.

Besides, how many people actually get shot for trespassing nowadays, anyway? He was just protecting his land, his house.

I holster the bear spray and pick up the long gun.

"Which way?" I ask. My voice sounds foreign to me. It's been a long time since I talked. But this isn't a time to be passing notes. The man's eyes are locked shut. He wouldn't be able to read anyway.

"Whaaaatttt!" he bellows.

"Home! Which way?" I have to shout to be heard over his screams. It gives me chills. I almost run at the sound of my own voice.

He's still on his knees. He's using his hands to claw at his eyes in a wasted effort to remove the pain. One of his arms comes undone, and he points down a path.

I get him to his feet. It's maddening how we stumble through the foliage, the elbows of roots sticking up here and there. I thought the man would be tough to guide, but the gun was a real nuisance. With every step, it seems to gain weight, getting heavier and heavier.

After about twenty minutes, my stranger stops screaming. He moans a lot, though. His eyes run with tears. Another clearing is coming up, and I can see a house. We cover the distance fast because my stranger can walk better now and there aren't all those trees purposely sticking things in our way, trying to trip us up.

The house is small for a farmhouse. I wouldn't live in it. There aren't any trees close to it.

In a window on the second floor, something moves. Something flashes by so quickly that I can't grasp what it is. We are almost at the back porch, and my stranger is still whining. I look at the window again, which gives me goosebumps this time. A woman is peeking out. She's wearing glasses. She has a telephone at her ear. I can tell she's quite animated by the way she's waving her arm and gesturing with her head. Whoever she's talking to is getting an earful.

This woman scares me more than the trees do.

The stranger mumbles something about a bathroom, and I understand him. He wants the bathroom sink to wash his eyes out. The bear spray gives off a wicked stench. I wish he hadn't pointed the gun at me. I don't like hurting people. Why can't they understand? When the trees are stalking me, I need to be left alone. I do bad things when I'm in the woods with people.

It's not my fault.

Jimmy shouldn't have touched me like he did.

It wasn't my fault he died all those years ago when we were ten years old.

We reach the back door, and my stranger opens it. Entering the house is tricky because I can't stand beside him supporting his arm anymore, so he takes the lead by feel.

I wonder why I don't feel remorse for what I did. Maybe because I'm harmless. He shouldn't have put a gun in my neck when all I wanted were leaves. Maybe this is a lesson he needs to learn.

I follow him out of a room where shoes and coats go, past a washer and dryer, and into a narrow hallway. There aren't any lights on, but I don't think the half-blind stranger minds.

I stop by the bathroom door and wait. Why didn't I put the long gun down? I'm still holding it in the hallway of this stranger's house. I could've put it on the dryer or the washer. I step back into the laundry room and try to lift the long gun up onto the washing machine. It snags on something. I pull hard, but it's still snagged. I look down and see my umbrella's wooden handle caught in the trigger guard.

What are the odds?

I twist the gun and give it one last pull, but this time a roar belts out as the gun fires and jerks in my hands. The recoil bites into my unprepared shoulder, tearing at it like a noose yanking on a neck.

A serious fire shoots through my arm. My eyes and mouth widen at how much pain my shoulder is experiencing.

A hole has formed in the drywall. Through the hole, I can see into the hallway.

The woman from the upper window appears before me. The pain must be intense because I hadn't noticed her standing there. She has a large rolling pin in her hand.

Before I can get out of the way, she's on me. I try to protect my head, but my left arm isn't working well, and my right arm is pinned to my chest. It had been holding my aching shoulder.

The rolling pin smacks me on the head. I'm not sure what I'm feeling now. There's a pounding, but I can't breathe too well. My shoulder still doesn't feel like it belongs to me. I try to move my head, but it aches. I move it anyway. I'm screaming now.

The woman is convulsing on top of me. Her weight makes it difficult to breathe. I roll, and she falls off. My nose inhales deep, my lungs fill, and the pounding in my head drops from a ten to a seven.

Something moves in the doorway. My stranger is there, his face still red. No doubt called by the roar of the long gun and the shriek of the strange woman.

"Asthma," he says before he bolts from the doorway.

A moment later, he's back with an inhaler, puffer, or whatever they call it.

I lean against the wall, the gun beside me. The woman is sitting up. She appears to be breathing better. My stranger can see and talk, although his eyes are quite red. He's explaining to the odd woman what happened and how stupid he must have been. He should never have entered the house with pepper spray on his face and a lingering scent on me. He should've known she'd react to it.

The woman says the word, *police*.

I use the wall to stand. Halfway up, I grab the long gun. Might need something to defend me if the police are coming.

The strange man looks at me with a question on his face. I shrug and gasp. Man, does my shoulder hurt. Funny how I took for granted a shrugging motion, and now it tosses coal on the flames of a fire I can't ignore.

"What are you gonna do, Mister?" the stranger asks.

I don't talk much to people. They're okay, but years ago, I decided I wouldn't talk to people anymore. Only when I really had to. I even pretend at times that I can't talk. I use a pen and paper to communicate with tellers, waitresses, and cab drivers. I point at my mouth and show them with my hands that I can't use it.

All my life, people had laughed at me when I talked. It wasn't always this way. Only after those teenagers nearly killed me. The doctor said I was beaten to within an inch of my life. Brain damage. They had jumped up and down on my head. But it never took away my love of leaves, so it's okay.

At least I remember why I was beaten. It was because of the death of Jimmy Urdith. No one believed me when I said it wasn't my fault. They laughed at me then, and they laugh at me now.

So I try hard not to talk to people.

I step away from the man and the odd woman on the floor and lock the bolt on the laundry room door. I use the long gun's barrel to point them up and out of the room. I push and prod them into the living room.

The redness in the man's face is diminishing quickly. It looks like everyone's going to be fine. I'm happy about that.

Except if the police come. Then I will have to explain things. And I don't want to talk. I just want to pick leaves and go home. I only want my leaves.

Why can't everyone just let me be?

When I saw the woman in the window on the phone, she must have been calling the police. Especially when she saw her man being guided to the house, his face a mask of tears. With me holding the strange man's gun, it might have made her think I was hostile. Why didn't I realize this earlier? I shake my head back and forth and smack my temple.

The living room has a long couch where I get them to sit. I use shoelaces to tie up their feet. I don't want hostages. I only want them out of the way while I do a field press on my new-found leaves. Then I will exit this strange house in a strange land owned by strange people by way of the back door and disappear.

They will never see me again.

I figure the cops will take at least fifteen minutes to get to this remote setting. I had spent ten here already. I need to hurry.

I am happy with all my clear thinking. This is becoming fun in a way. I haven't been in control of a crisis for a long time. Neat how it all comes back to you, dealing with unpleasant issues.

Once they're secure, I run to the kitchen. I set the long gun on the counter, locate the wax paper and rip off a strip. I flatten it out on the kitchen table. I carefully take the leaves out of the magazine pages I'd placed them in and set them gently on the wax paper. I make sure they are flat and ready.

Now I need newspaper. After a frantic minute of running around the house, I can't find any. I walk into the garage and locate a recycle bin. There's enough in it for my purpose.

When I get back to the kitchen, something's different. I place the newspaper on top of my leaves and look around. For some reason, I can't figure out what's different about the kitchen.

It's time to leave. But first, I want to check on the strangers in the living room. I go to the counter to pick up the gun, but it's gone.

That's what was different.

The gun's missing.

My stomach clenches like I chewed on rocks, and now they weigh it down. My shoulder throbs. My head feels like it's an egg that got cracked. I need to do what I don't want to do. I need to check on the strangers in the living room.

When I get there, the living room is empty.

Why are they doing this? I just want my leaves. I just want to go home. I wish everyone would leave me alone. I didn't ask for this.

It was the same when Jimmy followed me into the woods that day. We walked and looked at all the trees and their wonderful leaves. We marveled at the colors, shapes, and sizes. After about three hours on our own, Jimmy wanted to return to the teacher and the rest of the students. I didn't.

We argued. I remember walking away from him. He grabbed my arm and spun me around. I was shocked. He yelled at me. He said we had to return to the group. We had to go back to school. We were supposed to go home.

He had touched me and yelled at me. Those two actions made me run. I always run when people touch me too much or when people yell at me.

Jimmy was found dead a week later. He got lost on his way back to the school bus.

It wasn't my fault.

I ran from my dad. He always yelled. He died from yelling when I was twelve. Yelled and yelled and yelled. Then his heart blew up.

I come back to the room in my head. The strangers are not where I put them. Maybe they left the house. I'll get my leaves and go.

I turn and discover the strange man has the long gun. It's pointed at my midsection.

"Get down," he says.

Now, what do I do? I don't want to get shot. For my leaves, for my Honey Locust leaves, I get to my knees.

"All the way. To your stomach."

I refuse to talk, so I shake my head back and forth.

The strange man raises the gun to his eye and points it at my face. We're in a long hallway, the living room opening to my right, and I think he might shoot me.

"I said all the way down."

I shake my head again.

There are footsteps behind me. For fear of being shot, I don't move. I want to turn around, but I don't want a bullet for it.

"I thought I told you to get outside and stay outside," the strange man says to the owner of the footsteps behind me.

"I know, but I can't leave you alone." It's the woman's voice. "What if you needed my help?"

"I don't need no help. I was just getting him to the ground to tie him up until the police get here."

"He don't look like he's on the ground. He's only on his knees."

"I was working on it. Now let me do this."

The long gun takes up its position, aimed at me again. I push off the wall on my left and dive for the dirty rug on the living room floor.

A loud boom echoes throughout the house. My hearing disappears and is replaced by a loud whine. I race my hands over my body. No blood. No wounds.

I scramble to my feet as my hearing ebbs back. But all I hear is screaming. A woman screaming.

She was directly behind me in the hallway. The gun went off. I wasn't there to get hit. She got hit.

The strange man is a blur as he runs by the living room alcove. I peek around the corner. He's on the floor, holding the woman's foot. Blood on the carpet, some on the wall. It looks like an ankle wound. She'll live.

I bolt for the kitchen. My field press is waiting. I carefully wrap a string around the newspaper like a present and pick it up. When I peek into the hallway, the man has a cloth of some kind. I can see he's applying pressure to the woman's wound.

I hate her screams. I have to leave. In three steps, I'm in the laundry room. I unlock the deadbolt and move out into the early evening air.

A voice comes at me from all sides.

"We heard a gunshot. Is everyone okay in there?"

It sounds like one of those handheld metal things cops use to make their voices louder.

"We've got the place surrounded."

I look left and right. I don't see anybody. I drop my shoulders and start for the trees. Maybe they won't see me.

I've done nothing wrong. I helped a man back to his house. This is all a bad case of mistakes.

I'm running hard now. I'm thirty yards from the trees. I'm going to make it. I feel great.

"Hey! You there! Freeze!"

I hate it when people yell at me. I always run when people yell.

"STOP! POLICE!"

I run harder. I didn't run hard enough when the boys came to put boots to my head all those years ago. The trees are steps away now. Shelter, security, and comfort await me.

I already hear the trees calling my name.

Serenity can be found in the strangest of places and the oddest times. I thought of the many journeys I've had in forests just like the one I'm entering. How many times I've sat and stared at the sky while having lunch. How many times I've fallen asleep in a bed of grass and soft leaves.

Ohhh, the leaves. How I love leaves.

My arm doesn't hurt anymore. I feel whole. When I sit up, I'm surprised at how fast I'm standing. It was like I stood with the effort of thought.

I see my satchel on the ground. I see the umbrella, too. It's still attached to the side of a man the police officers are surrounding.

One of the cops is using both hands to push on my chest. They've holstered their weapons.

They must have shot me.

The field press sits by itself a few feet from my body. I'm standing by it now. My fingers try to touch the Honey Locust leaves before they're blown away in the breeze.

They tumble from me. My soul aches. My spirit cries. I can feel it.

I'm a leaf collector.

I love leaves, and they love me. We have an understanding. They whisper my name. They never yell.

I look around. The trees have won. All I ever wanted was to leave a legacy. All I ever wanted was to be loved and adored.

I had trespassed one too many times in a forest where the trees didn't want me taking from their crowns.

But in the end, I don't blame the trees. I know in their own way, they love me because I love them.

After the light allows me passage to a new home, I have all the lovely trees I can handle. I play with the leaves, set up displays, and rummage through forests for hours and hours.

I love leaves, and they love me.

I'm home now. No one yells here.
I'm a leaf collector.

Blood Money

I CAN'T BELIEVE THAT I'm doing this. People might see me. What if it's someone I know? My neighbors wouldn't laugh, but my friends would, and isn't that an injustice?

I'm not a thief.

There, I said it. Everyone seems to think so after cops found me in a stolen car. The car was removed from its rightful owner by a friend of mine. At least, I thought he was my friend. He picked me up to cruise in his *new* car. I actually thought he'd just bought it. Guy bailed on me at first sight of cops.

I'm picking up garbage on the side of the highway because I was ordered to do this community service for ten hours by a judge who didn't want to listen to reason. I know everyone says it, but in this case, I am innocent.

A car races by me as I reach for another piece of garbage. I looked too fast. The cut on my forehead made me wince. I touched the bandage with my palm. My supervisor sat on the other side of the road, having coffee and chatting with one of the other community service guys.

Here's my chance to hide from public view.

I drop below the edge of the highway and make my way into the ditch. It's quite wide, opening to a flat area about twenty feet long before another small drop into a line of trees. This is the perfect area to pick up garbage without being seen by anyone driving by.

It's not just me I'm protecting here. It's my brother. He's second in charge at the police station in our little town of 15,000 people. Everyone talks about everything in this shitty hole of a town, and I wouldn't want him embarrassed more than he already is.

Thinking of him reminded me about tonight. He's supposed to be coming over for pizza and beer.

I notice a small tree bent in half to my right. If a storm caused this deformation, how come none of the other trees around it seem to have any damage? I realize that I'm probably too far from the shoulder of the highway, but I have to get a closer look. I drop down a six-foot embankment and step up to the little tree. There's a large gouge in the earth about three feet behind it.

Something huge came through here. I part the branches of the small pines and see a car upside down, items from the interior spread out on the grass. Where it sits, this vehicle would never be noticed from the highway. When I was five feet away, I couldn't see it because the tree line was so thick.

I want to search the car but wonder if I will find dead people. I hope not. The last thing I need is to be in the newspapers for discovering a dead body.

Much to my relief, there are no humans here, dead or alive. I notice a garbage bag perched on the sill of the broken back window. There's a rip in the bag.

I gasp when I see a wad of hundred-dollar bills sticking out of the rip.

I tear the bag open and discover it's full of bundles of hundred-dollar bills. They're wrapped fifty to a pack, which would be five-thousand-dollar bundles. I deduce that I'm looking at half a million dollars or more.

Questions race through my mind while my heart rate triples. Do I report it? Or do I take the money home and let someone else find the car one day? The court's already convicted me of theft that I didn't do. I might as well just take it. This can't be called theft because I found it.

I have to decide and decide now. No one can see me from the highway. If my supervisor happens along, I'm toast. Since it appears no one was hurt here, and whoever was in this car accident left the bag of money behind, then I guess it's mine.

Finders, keepers, and shit ...

I quickly take out one of the bags the court provided me to collect garbage and pile the bundles of cash inside. Then I take off my sweater and toss it on top of the money in the bag. No way is my supervisor going to let me take a garbage bag home. If I show him the sweater and tell him it was too hot out, that I had to pack a few things in this bag, I might get away with it. I get up and start back for the highway, my nerves jingling against the beat of my rapid pulse.

***

It's around seven in the evening. I've got all the lights in my house turned off except the one in the kitchen. The money is spread out before me on the table. I keep trying to count it, but there's just too much. There's got to be over a hundred bundles here.

My gut keeps twirling. What if it's drug money? What if someone very powerful comes looking for it?

I think it's time to call my brother. I grab the hands-free on the wall and dial.

"Hello?"

"Heh, bro," I said, trying to keep my voice calm. "How's it going? You sound like you're driving."

"I am. What's up?"

"I was doing my community service thing this morning and was surprised to see the constant flow of traffic racing by me."

"You called to talk about highway traffic?"

I heard the laughter in his voice. I wonder what he hears in mine. "I just thought, since you're a cop and all, I could ask you about accidents around here. I mean, some of those drivers were acting crazy, passing each other without much room, and so on. I don't read a lot of newspapers, but everyone hears about the highway carnage. Do you have to attend to accident scenes?"

"Sometimes. Why the interest?"

"No interest, really. Just curiosity. What about people or cars that go missing? Does that come up often?" I was going too far. Why would I be asking these questions? My brother would think it out of character. I suddenly felt the urge to terminate the call.

"Why? Do you know something about a missing car? We are looking for a Chrysler."

"You are?" My voice cracked. I couldn't believe it. If my brother were a psychologist, he would know I was hiding something. Stupid, very stupid. This money suddenly became scary.

"You remember what happened three days ago. The Brink's truck robbery downtown. Some guy rammed the money truck so hard that the guards got knocked out when the truck flipped over a curb. By the time we responded to the call, they had garbage bags of money filling the bed of a pickup."

"So why aren't you looking for a pickup?"

"Because we got that already. One of the guys jumped out during the pursuit and carjacked a woman in her Chrysler. The woman and her car are still missing. Did you see a black Chrysler 300C somewhere?"

"No, not me." Again, he'd know I was lying if he was a psyche major.

"It's okay. All the money has been accounted for except one bag. Hey, listen, we can talk about it in a minute. I'm pulling into your driveway."

"You're here?" He must have heard my surprise as I almost shouted those two words.

"Yeah, remember, we talked last night about how the chief said I should take a night off because I've been working so hard lately. You and I are supposed to have pizza and beer tonight."

I heard his car pulling up out front. The money was still all over the kitchen table. I realize now that I'm done. I mumble something into the phone and hang up. I grab a new garbage bag from under the sink and start shoving all the money into it. I'm halfway through when the doorbell rings.

"Coming!" I yell. "Gimme a sec."

The last batch of bundles won't fit. I stuff the bag under the kitchen sink and get a little shopping bag for the rest.

My front door opens. "Hey, I let myself in. How come it's so dark?"

A light flicks on from down the hall. My heart almost stops. I don't have time to pack the last fifteen bundles or so. Scrambling on my feet, I head down the hallway to prevent my brother from entering the kitchen.

"Have a seat in the living room. I'll bring you a beer." I'm trying so hard to keep my voice in check, really focusing on it.

"That's okay. I'll go in the kitchen and get one myself while you order the pizza."

I step in front of him. "Not this time." I say it like a command.

My brother stops and looks me in the eye.

"No," I said. "You order the pizza. I'll get the beer. Every time we do this, you complain about the toppings. I want you to order whatever you want. No complaints."

I turned away from him and headed to the kitchen without waiting for a reply. In thirty seconds, I have the rest of the money hidden in my kitchen cupboards except for the one bundle I had opened. That one I shove in my pocket for safekeeping. With beers in my hand, I head out to the living room to try to have a calm evening without knowing how much trouble I could be in.

A half-hour later, the doorbell makes me jump almost out of my skin. My brother looked over at me. I know that face. Ever since we were kids, that was his, you're-weird expression. Wanting to extract myself from the living room, I tell him the pizza's on me.

I open the door, grab the pizza box and reach for my wallet. It's not in my pocket. Then I remember leaving it on my dresser when I got home from my community service highway cleaning. Since no one will notice a one-hundred-dollar bill missing amongst all the others I found, I reach into my pocket and use one from the open bundle I'd stashed there.

The evening with my brother went over rather well, all things considered. I had one scare when he helped himself to another beer. He stood right beside the cabinet that held the money, but there wasn't any reason to start opening drawers, so everything worked out.

***

The phone rang. It's 8:15 a.m. My second day at the highway doesn't start until noon, and I barely slept all night. Whoever's calling can get the machine.

"Hey, man, pick up." My brother. "Something weird happened. Remember that robbery we talked about last night? All the money taken was serial numbered, and the local retailers were informed which series to watch out for. Apparently, the pizza joint we ordered from last night had a hundred-dollar bill turn up. They're trying to locate the delivery guy to find out if he remembers which house he got it from. It was a slow night. He'd only done six deliveries, so there's a good chance he'll remember. I'll call you later."

I was up now. Even if I wanted to sleep, I couldn't. This just went from bad to worse. I grabbed the phone and called my highway supervisor to tell him I was sick and wouldn't join them today. I really was sick. I'm not a criminal or a thief. The money just happened to fall into my hands. At least, that's what I keep telling myself. I'm sure no one else will see it that way.

In ten minutes, I'm dressed, car keys in one hand and a garbage bag of money in the other. I decide to look outside first. No one in sight. When I opened the front door, the phone rang.

I hesitated to hear if the caller would leave a message. I heard my brother's voice again and the sound of an engine revving in the background.

"Hey, pick up. I need to know what's going on. Pick up the phone. We just talked to the delivery guy. He said he remembered the house because the guy had a wad of hundreds in his pocket. I was told to visit the address. It's your *house*, man. What's going on? Pick up the phone!"

I bolted. I jumped in my car, threw the bag in the back seat, and peeled out of my driveway. It took me less than fifteen minutes to get to where I was cleaning garbage yesterday.

Out of the car, down the little embankment, and through the line of trees. Everything looked just like it did yesterday. I set the bag half in and half out of the back window like I'd found it. I turned away and started for the road. When I stepped out of the line of small trees, there was a cop car parked behind my vehicle. I stopped in my tracks and watched my brother scan the area. He called my name.

I reached into my pocket and pulled my wallet out. Overhanded, I tossed it as far as I could up the tree line. I saw where it landed and marked it mentally by a large rock sitting about ten feet to the right of the highway.

Then I stepped out and waved. My brother was watching me now. I wonder if he saw me throw my wallet.

"You won't believe what I just found," I yelled.

My brother cupped his hands around his mouth and shouted. "What are you doing down there? I called the community service guys. They said you called in sick. Then I spotted you racing out of town, so I followed you. When you parked here, I saw you get out, but I was too far back to see which direction you ran."

"I lost my wallet when we were working yesterday. I felt sick, but I still needed to get my wallet."

The branches rustled behind me, and then I heard the distinctive sound a bag makes.

When I turned around and peeked through the line of small trees, I saw a man holding the garbage bag in one hand and a tall blond woman in the other. He looked injured, leaning to the side. I stepped through the trees toward them. I could hear my brother yelling for me to stop.

After pushing branches aside, I entered the clearing. The man and the woman were gone. Not ducked down behind the car or hiding by a tree, gone as in completely gone.

I decided the only way to save myself was to find them. My story would be completely clean if I were a hero. I could even explain using the hundred-dollar bill for the pizza guy. I could say that I'd found a small bundle out here by the highway yesterday. Not thinking anything of it and subsequently losing my wallet, I used some of the money. It may still look bad, but who doesn't spend the money they find?

I bolted down the line of trees away from where my brother would come after me. I knew running from a cop probably wasn't a good idea, but he was my brother. He wouldn't shoot me. And the guy with the woman was close by. I had to be the one to find them first.

Roughly ten yards down, I turned into the line of small trees and jumped through. Cars whizzed by on the highway. My car still sat on the shoulder, the cruiser behind it. My brother was nowhere in sight.

I bent over to look for my wallet. It had to be around here somewhere. I was within two yards of the rock I'd used as a marker. A loud rig raced by, blocking out sound momentarily.

My left arm was wrenched behind me in a flash, and I was thrust forward. I hit the ground hard. A knee jammed into my back while my right arm was wrenched farther back. Handcuffs hurt when they're slapped on. After he secured me, he flipped me over, and I lay on the hard ground, looking up at him.

"You really did it this time," my brother said.

"I didn't do anything," I protested. A piece of grass had been sitting on the edge of my mouth from being pushed into the ground, and I hadn't felt it until I talked. "I just saw the guy who robbed the Brink's truck and the girl he kidnapped. They took off with a garbage bag full of money."

I have to admit there was a sense of loss thinking about how close all that money came to be mine.

My brother said police stuff into a lapel microphone. Then he turned back to face me. "There was no woman kidnapped. I only told you that to gauge your reaction. We had witnesses to the Brink's holdup. They described a man of your hair color and weight. When I came over to your house last night, it was to see how you were doing. I told the chief that your case of severe split personality had been handled years ago with therapy and medication. I told him there was no way you were mixed up in this, and he let me do an unofficial investigation. But we matched the blood on the windshield of the vehicle that rammed the Brink's truck. It's type O negative, the same as yours, and it's on the windshield in exactly the same spot where your bandage is."

I shook my head back and forth slowly. "How could I have done it and not known about it? No way, it wasn't me." I said this but didn't completely believe it.

"Remember when you were going for therapy years ago in Toronto? We learned that in one personality, an individual could be allergic to cigarette smoke, but in another personality, the same individual is a smoker with no allergic reactions. Each personality is isolated from the other. I think they call it Dissociative Identity Disorder now or DID. I specifically remember yours was accompanied by memory loss, or what your doctor called, *losing time*. I never forgot the actual term was Dissociative Amnesia."

"But that couldn't be …" I stopped talking because my brother stepped away from me. He mumbled into his lapel microphone again. A moment later, my stomach in knots, he turned back toward me, a grave look on his face.

"I'm gonna have to read you your rights."

"Are you serious? You can't arrest me. Where's the proof?"

"When I followed you to the highway earlier, a judge signed a search warrant for your address based on the passing of that hundred-dollar bill last night. I was just notified of what they found there."

"They couldn't have found anything." I said this with a clean conscience. I know for a fact that I didn't ram a Brink's truck and steal money. My only possible involvement is if this DID stuff was real.

"They found half the money in your basement along with a journal. The first few pages they've examined detail all your plans for the robbery. Now come on, tell me where the rest of the money is?"

"I thought you said you guys got all the money on the phone last night?"

"I planted that in your head to watch your response."

"But I saw a woman and a man back by the car with the garbage bag," I said.

"Has to be your imagination, your DID. You saw them because I told you they were real."

I recalled the therapy years ago. I thought I was cured. This couldn't be. I banged my head two days ago on the concrete when I tripped, that's why I have a bandage.

My brother was talking. "You have the right to remain silent …"

We made our way to his cruiser. We stopped at the back door. Another cop car was pulling up behind my brother's. I felt lost. Could I really have this other personality?

"I just hope they don't try too hard to match the handwriting in that journal," my brother whispered.

"What are you talking about?" I asked. "Handwriting?"

"I would hate for them to realize that the evidence was planted. No one will believe you over me, especially with your history of psychological disorders. This was the best thing for both of us. I get a lot of money quickly, and I get to keep it because everyone thinks someone else took it. Don't you think I deserve it after all I've done for this little shit town? No one would believe in a million years that I, a recognized police officer, would frame my own brother. This helps you, too. My plan was genius. You can continue to get help for your problems and have a place to stay and eat for free."

He shoved me by my head into the cruiser's back seat and slammed the door on my life, my fate.

Don't Shoot

THE KNOCKING IN THE wall came again.

Jim Bower sat in his basement apartment and listened to the knocking in the walls. No one could be behind the wall. The knocking, the noises, and the talking at all hours of the night permeated the wall of his apartment. The noises drove Jim to obsess over who tormented him. He wanted to learn their methods. Maybe whatever was alive in the walls was evil. Or perhaps they were nice and only wanted a companion. He just needed to figure out how to get to where they were.

Jim removed the oversized headphones from his ears. No sound emitted from them. He wore the headphones to keep sounds out. But the knocking always got in.

"Go away," he shouted at the wall. "Go away, or I'll come in after you."

The wall knocked again. He replaced the headphones on his ears to remove the noise, but they weren't soundproof. The knocking always got in.

"Stop it. Don't come back. Don't stay here. Don't shoot."

A sense of peace and comfort always pervaded him when he said, *don't shoot*. It'd been his axiom since he was a child. Those words had kept him alive.

Someone whispered something.

"No, no whispering." He grabbed the headphones, then chanted, "La, la, la, la, la, la," in a quest to silence the voices.

He closed his mouth and listened. When he heard nothing, he picked up the hammer that sat on the floor by his foot. The table beside him had magazines and books scattered on its surface. With a sweep of his arm, they all fell to the floor, but he barely heard them land as his headphones were doing their job.

Jim dropped the head of the hammer onto the table, tapping it in rhythm. He maintained a tempo that soothed him.

The clock on the wall said it was 4:44 a.m. They always came in the middle of the night.

When was the last time I ate?

He couldn't remember.

"Don't shoot," he whispered to the empty basement.

The wall always looked so innocent. He walked over to the wall that had turned his life into a living hell. The hammer swung in his hand like he was practicing with a baton.

Thumb tacks held up a poster of Rita Hayworth. Out of respect for a book Jim had read many years ago, he'd chosen it to conceal his digging. At the bottom of the poster, he'd affixed a small clip so that when it was lifted out of the way, the clip would hook onto a nail at the top.

His phone rang. He frowned.

"But I don't have a phone."

The ringing stopped.

Jim lifted Rita and clipped her into place. The hole he had made was magnificent. He loved the hole he had bored into the ground. Screw what the landlord thought. He needed the hole. Whoever knocked on the walls in the middle of the night was somewhere. He'd dig until he found them. He needed to get back to work. Being a member of society was fun. It felt good to buy things. They wouldn't put him back in the Amy Greg Asylum if he performed well in the community.

If only he could get rid of the whispering and the knocking, he would be okay.

His favorite World War II RAF aviator goggles sat dangling around his neck. He eased them up to cover his eyes. The hammer smacking into bits of concrete and rock maintained a muffled existence to his headphone-covered ears. He shuffled the excess dirt to the apartment floor, where he'd sweep it into a pile and remove it on garbage day.

Two weeks into digging, the hole was big enough for him to crawl completely in and be covered when the poster of Rita Hayworth dropped back into place. He knew buried power lines and gas lines were close by, but since he was digging slowly and with the claw of a hammer, he felt he'd have ample warning before puncturing one.

An hour passed in a daze. Another pile of dirt. Another few feet gained.

The knocking started up.

Someone was at his door. He lifted the headphones off and listened.

"I know you're in there," someone yelled. "Open up!"

The landlord.

If he stayed quiet long enough, the landlord would go away.

Another knock. "Come on. I need the rent money. You're a week late." He knocked again. "Come on, Jim, I know you lost your job. Let's talk about it, or I will call your brother. You know how he likes to keep tabs on you."

Yeah, and makes me do stupid things like eat and shower, Jim thought. *No way. If you come through that door, I won't let you leave. I've got a hammer.*

"I heard you in there banging something. I know you're home."

"Go away," Jim whispered.

Waiting was hard, but he did it. Eventually, Owen, the landlord, stopped knocking. Owen wasn't his real name, but Jim couldn't remember names very well, so Owen it was. People called Jim names all his life, so it was only fair if he called people by names he liked. Others seemed to like the names they chose for him because they laughed and had fun with it.

Jim chuckled to himself a little to see how it felt after calling the landlord, Owen, but he couldn't see the humor.

He felt the urge to pee and allowed it freedom. The wetness coursed through his ragged, torn jeans. It didn't matter. Anytime now, he would find peace. He would do it as soon as he figured out how the people living in the walls did it. People made themselves invisible all the time. The books called them entities or ghosts, and the only way to become invisible and move with just a thought was to die first, but Jim had an idea that he could do it without dying. The answers were buried in the wall.

The people in the wall would tell him how to do it. The people who visited him in the night and whispered horrible things. The things they told him to do were scary, but he'd do it if they would explain how to be invisible. They were alive. They made noise. They traveled around. So Jim concluded they weren't dead.

He tossed the hammer onto the fresh pile of dirt and dug with his hands. The process was slower but a lot quieter.

The hole smelled bad. He knew it had to be him because he hadn't changed his clothes in a few days, and he hadn't used a toilet or the shower in that time, yet his body still voided. Nothing else mattered, though. He'd deal with the smell as it was mixed with the richness of the moist soil.

The ground softened. His energy waned. The earth moved around him.

Jim slowed until he stopped and looked back into his basement apartment. Dim light entered through the closed blinds in the small window near the ceiling. It seemed to brighten a little, beckoning him. He refused its call by unhooking Rita Hayworth and letting the poster fall into place, covering him where he lay on the bed of dirt.

He rested his head back, closed his eyes from behind the goggles, and whispered, "Don't shoot," before falling into a deep sleep, riddled with nightmares of death.

***

The knocking woke him.

He wondered why it was so dark. The headphones were snug around his ears. Whoever was knocking had to be excessively loud to have awakened him.

He squinted his eyes, held his hands over the headphones, and whispered, "Go away, go away, go away …"

His bladder released, the warmth comforting him. Today had to be the day. He would find the people in the wall. He had to. The landlord would use his key soon. Or he'd call Jim's brother. Someone would enter his apartment, and he would not be able to explain the mess.

There was shouting, but the headphones muffled it enough that he couldn't discern what they said.

He rocked his head back and forth, trying to free himself of the noises. Then he paused and listened. The noises were gone. He exposed his right ear but heard nothing.

He flipped his body around without lifting the poster for light and continued digging. With each handful of dirt he tossed behind him, it was one closer to being able to transcend this place. Maybe he could be the *haunter* instead of the *haunted.*

His mother's voice told him everything was okay. When he looked up, all he saw was the brown dirt.

"No, Mom, it's not okay," he said, removing dirt bit by bit. Then his father's voice beckoned him to stop digging. Jim continued anyway until he hit a wall.

The houses on his block were built in the early 1900s. They were tall and statuesque, covered in faded brick and weathered roofs. On his street in downtown Toronto, each house had a small front yard and a tiny backyard that led onto an alleyway. The houses, built side by side, had only a walkway between them. Jim always wondered how the bricklayers got up so high in between the houses to lay their bricks when the houses were so close.

He looked at the poster that hung over the opening and mentally measured how deep the hole went. He guessed it to be eight feet long. He laid his whole six-foot-three-inch frame out and still couldn't touch the poster with his toes.

He wondered about the dirt above him. Why hadn't it caved in? He hadn't rigged anything for support to keep it from falling down.

Voices whispered again. He clenched his teeth and grabbed the headphones, pushing them onto his ears. The voices wouldn't stop. Most were indecipherable. A scrambling of people telling him to do unspeakable things.

He edged toward the poster, moved it out of the way, and then hopped down to the floor of his apartment.

"Hello?" he asked.

He pushed his eye goggles down around his neck and lifted the headphones off his ears.

Wisps of air moved by the kitchen in the shape of people. He thought he saw the apartment door sitting open, but when he looked directly at it, it was closed.

He had a sparsely furnished apartment with a small kitchen table that lay broken on the floor. There was one chair, a single cushioned television seat, and a bed mattress. His brother had wanted to help, but Jim had insisted on doing it alone. The job at the warehouse would pay enough. Doing it on his own was part of the terms for being released from the asylum.

The voices and knocking were always just there, and he had come to accept them. He wouldn't do their bidding even though he wanted to at times. They always came from the wall. But now that he had dug an eight-foot hole into the wall, the voices were in his apartment. Maybe he had opened a portal of some kind.

Whatever he'd done, it was worse now.

"Get out!" he shouted. "Don't shoot!"

The air moved two feet in front of him. He swung an arm at it. He moved back fast until he hit the wall beside his television. A framed picture of him, his brother, and his father connected with his right shoulder and fell to the floor, smashing the glass frame. He looked down at it. That was one of his favorite pictures because it was the first one of the three of them after their mother was shot and killed.

Anger welled up so deep he felt it bristle with his sanity. He turned back to the beings in his apartment and growled, his breath seething in and out of his clenched teeth. In rising tones, he yelled, "Get out. Get *out*. GET OUT!"

But they didn't listen. He heard one of them clearly ask who was shouting. They pretended he wasn't there, but they knew he was.

He felt his chances of being one of them slip away as he gripped onto a tenuous sanity that had ebbed years before.

They all disappeared at once as if to discount him, to show he meant nothing.

Someone knocked on the door.

"I know you're in there. It's Owen. You know, your landlord. You're over a week late on the rent. Your apartment smells horrible. I am calling your brother if you don't open this door, Jim. Let me in."

Owen knocked again.

Jim walked over to the hole, lifted the poster, and retrieved the hammer. He unlocked the apartment door with it firmly in his right hand.

"Come in," he said.

Jim held the hammer slightly behind his right leg. One last look confirmed the entities had retreated to wherever they resided.

Owen stepped in.

"Oh, man. What have you been doing?" he asked and raised the neckline of his sweater over his nose to breathe through it. "Oh, Jim, what has happened to you? What have you done? Where did all that dirt come from, and what happened to your pants?"

So many questions, Jim thought. *Only one answer.*

"Don't shoot," Jim said.

"What are you talking about, *don't shoot*? I'm not shooting anything—"

The hammer's claw end embedded in Owen's skull directly above the right eye, cutting off his words. Owen tried to push him away as Jim attempted to remove the hammer for another blow, but the tool was stuck in the bone. He shoved the landlord hard and then yanked with both hands on the wooden handle of the hammer, pulling it free with a gush of blood.

Owen stumbled until his back hit the wall. Jim was on him in seconds with another hammer blow to the top of Owen's skull. This time, without knowing it, he had turned the hammer around. The business end connected above the center hairline, crushing the skull bone and permanently denting the landlord's head.

As he slid down the wall to the dirty carpet on the floor, Owen did an epileptic seizure dance that made Jim smile because the noises were silent at that moment. He lifted the hammer again and waited. Did he need to strike anymore, or was the landlord gone?

He waited.

Owen's body slowed, then stopped. Jim looked at Owen's chest and saw it wasn't moving. He lowered the hammer. The movements in the air had stopped. All whispering had ceased. He couldn't see or hear a thing.

Jim dropped the hammer and walked into the small kitchen, where he grabbed a large chopping knife. He closed and locked the apartment door and undressed the corpse. When he was finished, he placed all the clothes in a garbage bag and tossed the bag over by the wall under the gaping hole he'd created.

With the knife in hand, he began the grueling task of cutting his landlord up. It took him a full hour to dismember the man into manageable pieces that would fit into a recess of the wall.

Was this really happening? he asked himself. *Did I really kill someone? Am I supposed to feel bad?*

Questions. Always questions. There was only one answer.

"Don't shoot," he whispered.

He put his aviator goggles back on to avoid sweating in his eyes.

"Okay, things are bad, but I can handle this. At least now he can't call my brother, and there will be no more knocking."

It took three trips to the hole in the wall with every piece of the landlord now lining the tunnel. The garbage bag had been pushed in first, and now it rested at the deepest part. The only evidence in the apartment was the blood on the dirty carpet. Jim figured it would turn a darker color over the next couple of days, and no one would ever know what it was.

He climbed into the hole and dropped the poster behind him. Alone again, with no knocking and no noises of any kind, he rocked back and forth in place, trying to think about what would come next. The future wasn't something he'd considered. Tomorrow showed up, and he lived it. Then the next day. Then the next. But he had done things. Bad things. He was sure of it.

The asylum might take him back. He hated being there. They said he had delusions and hallucinations. They said he was having schizophrenic episodes. He suffered from a schizoaffective disorder where he would have a bunch of episodes. He was told they were depressive and manic episodes, but they were wrong. He wasn't depressive or manic. He just heard people talking. He saw things that weren't there. Not a big deal.

Bits of dirt crumbled down beside him as he rocked harder. He felt dizzy as the intensity increased. He rocked so fast that his back and shoulder smacked each side of the little cavern. There was a shift in the dirt. For a moment, he felt disoriented. He tried to shake the dirt loose from his goggles, but it remained. He tasted dirt in his mouth.

He struggled to get loose but couldn't. He closed his eyes and surrendered.

***

When he opened his eyes, the noises were back. A violence formed inside him. The landlord was easy. Whoever knocked at his apartment door was going to pay as Owen did.

He edged toward the poster, flipped it out of his way, and dropped to the floor.

Jim watched as his brother, a man in a suit, and two uniformed cops milled around the apartment. None of them seemed to notice him. There were no wisps of air, no subtle hints of a presence. These people were actually standing in his basement apartment like the landlord had. He removed his headphones and let them fall to the floor.

"Can you tell us what would have caused this?" the man in a suit asked Jim's brother.

"Maybe an episode of some kind? I don't know. I didn't expect it. I would've come more often if I had. He seemed to be getting along quite well."

His brother used a Kleenex to blow his nose.

"Do you think something set him off? What did he sound like when you last talked to him?"

"That was about two weeks ago. I came over for a beer. He said, *don't shoot* a few times. That was usually an indicator he was about to experience an episode, but he had done so well over the last few months that I thought we were past those things."

The suit looked up from his pad, a frown on his face. *"Don't shoot?* What does that mean?"

"When I was ten years old, and little Jimmy was eight, our house got robbed. My dad and I were out at a ball game. Jimmy had the flu, so he stayed home with our mom. When we got home, the front door was wide open. My dad told me to wait in the car. He found my mother shot to death. He couldn't find little Jimmy. My brother was missing for five full days. You'd never guess where we found him."

"No, I probably wouldn't," the cop said. "Tell me."

"We found him in the basement, under the stairs. He'd removed a panel to hide in. It probably saved his life. For those five days, he'd only used his hands to dig …" Jim's brother stopped and grabbed another Kleenex to wipe his nose.

"Dig?"

Jim stood there watching this exchange as rapt as hearing his brother tell it as the officer did.

"Yeah, he was digging into the wall, trying to get out of the house. He kept saying, *"Don't shoot, don't shoot,"* repeatedly. We found out later that the guy who robbed the house had given my eight-year-old brother a pistol and told him it wasn't loaded. He had him aim it at Mom and pull the trigger for pretend. The guy whispered something into mom's ear, and then Mom said to go ahead and play the game. According to Jimmy, the gun went off, and half of mom's face went with it. Little Jimmy was never the same after that. When things were overwhelming for him, he'd chant, *don't shoot*."

The suit lowered his notepad and stared at Jim's brother.

"That's some story. I'm sorry."

"It's okay. That was over thirty years ago."

Jim's brother walked over to the TV and bent down. He came up with the broken frame and the picture of the three of them after their mother's death.

Someone knocked on the apartment door and stepped inside.

"Are you the landlord?" the suit asked.

"Yeah, my name's Mike. What a fucking mess. This will take me weeks to clean, and how will I fix that wall? Shit!"

The landlord's alive? His name's Mike? What the hell's happening?

"Where's your sensitivity?" his brother asked.

Mike looked over. "Ah, shit. Didn't see you there. Sorry."

One of the uniformed cops yanked on Rita and pulled the poster down.

In a second, Jim was standing beside the cop. He recognized his own socks. They were buried in the hole on a pair of feet.

He suddenly felt joy that he'd done it. He could now be like the entities that floated around. He had dug far enough. They allowed him into their world.

He raced over to his brother and tried to take the picture, but he couldn't grasp it. He tried again and again, each time with growing vexation.

"Did you feel that?" his brother said out loud.

"Feel what?" the suit asked.

"A breeze of some kind. Like something ran by me."

"Nope. Didn't feel a thing. Look, we can do the positive ID thing back at the morgue."

His brother walked over to the door and leaned on the wall beside it. "I'll stay here. I'm going home to make funeral arrangements when I leave this apartment. I don't want to drag this out."

"Suit yourself. Removing the body properly will take a while, but it's your choice."

Jim watched everything with growing disdain. He wanted them to leave. This was his apartment. He headed for the kitchen to grab a knife as a warning.

His mother approached from the side.

"Mom?" He couldn't believe it.

"Yes …"

It was her voice, but still, he refused to believe it. Where had she come from? *Why* had she come? She looked as radiant and beautiful as the day he shot her.

"It's time to come home," she said.

"But I am home. This is my home."

She shook her head. "No, this was your earthly home. You need to realize that and move on."

"No, you don't understand. I finally made it. I'm invisible, like the entities that have always haunted me. I'm very much alive. You can't convince me otherwise."

"Jim, it's okay. Come with me."

"No!" he shouted. "I don't need food, and I don't need to breathe. I'm able to move at a thought. I'm free. I finally did it. So don't come around here telling me I'm dead. I'm more alive than ever before."

He reached for the knife on the counter but missed. He went for it again. The knife remained on the counter.

When he turned back around, his mother was gone. He looked over his shoulder and saw everyone staring in his general direction.

Jim screamed as loud as he could.

The men visibly jumped. The landlord slipped out the door. The suit started for the door, and Jim's brother edged along the wall closer to it.

Jim had made it. He could stay and make noises for others like they did to him.

It was Jim's turn.

He rallied all his energy and shouted his favorite two words, "Don't Shoot!"

The men ran from the apartment, leaving Jim alone in his darkness, waiting for others to enter his domain.

He climbed into the hole in the wall and lay down, where he knocked incessantly and whispered hateful things for a very long time.

The Burning

Monday, October 18, 2011 ...

Jared Tavallo stood in the clearing as his gun's echo reverberated off the valley's mountainous walls. The sun shone brightly on the bushes into which the doe had scurried, making it impossible to see blood on them from where he stood.

He pumped his legs through the thick snow, breathing rapidly through his mouth as he ran after his kill. He was certain the doe had taken the bullet about the neck area. There was no way he could've missed.

The bushes thickened in the area where the deer had entered. Jared hit them hard and fast in the hopes of finding and securing his kill before anyone could see how close he'd gotten to the city of Banff, Alberta.

The Banff National Park strictly prohibited hunting, which left him in a dilemma. He was close to the park's border or already inside, but the deer was too tempting to let go.

Determined to see this through, he would locate his doe, cover it in the recently received snow, and that evening, his hunting partners would come and help him haul the carcass out.

No one in the National Park had to know.

The kill was his and his alone. He'd worked too hard for it—fought the cold temperatures and stumbled a long way from home—to let the deer go simply because it didn't follow man's rules on geography.

He pushed harder through the brush and stumbled, dropping to one knee in the thick snow.

"Damn it!"

Back on his feet, he slung his rifle over his shoulder and trudged on through the white powder. The deer tracks led deep into the thicker foliage. A line of lodgepole pines were on his right. The doe's tracks turned toward them.

A light snow began to descend from the dark gray clouds above. Jared stopped and examined his surroundings. A tall tree to his left sat beside a boulder the size of an SUV. He would use that as a marker to find his way back. He had no way of telling how much snow would fall in the next hour, and getting lost would only move him one step closer to hypothermia. All he needed to do was return to the clearing where he had taken the shot. Then he could find his way back to his cabin.

But first, he had to locate the wounded deer. The cold had worked on Jared all day, but he was just now starting to shiver. He collected himself, took a deep breath, and started toward the line of pines.

The deer's tracks disappeared beyond the scatter of bark and needles, leading into the darkness beyond. Jared struggled with his left sleeve, lifting it far enough to see his watch. Thirty-five minutes to sundown.

"Shit."

A slight breeze brought with it the smell of something burning. Jared let his sleeve fall back into place as he looked around to see if he could tell what was on fire. He stopped breathing and listened to the silence of the area around him.

Maybe it's a nearby cabin's wood stove or fireplace.

He released his pent-up breath and inhaled heavily, taking in the acrid smell of something burning that wasn't just wood.

"What the hell is that?" he asked out loud.

He sniffed again. His stomach rolled. It smelled like burning hair or flesh.

"What a putrid smell," he whispered.

He'd leave the area within minutes whether he found the stupid deer or not. He would never call the fire department even if he saw a house on fire unless he could block his number and make an anonymous tip. He couldn't allow any officials to see him on park property with a rifle. The fines would be too much, and the uproar ridiculous. Whether he shot the deer a kilometer away or where he stood made no difference to Jared, but the powers that be always had an ear of corn up their asses for someone just like him.

He stepped into the relative darkness of the tall pines and tried to follow the tracks again. Ten minutes later, he entered another small clearing.

The smell of something burning intensified.

He decided it was time to turn back. If he'd hit the deer, it would've dropped long before now.

Then it occurred to him that there had been no blood in the pure white snow where the deer took the shot. Maybe he had missed it.

"What a fucking waste of time."

If he'd hit the animal, there would've been blood. All he had followed were white tracks in undisturbed snow.

"Amateur fucking hunter," he said out loud again.

Something banged against a tree. Jared jolted and looked to the right, where the noise had come from. He could just make out the edge of a shack or cabin. The animal's tracks had turned that way.

Maybe that was the deer falling over.

He stepped around a tree and took a closer look at the cabin wall. The chimney appeared dormant. No smoke billowed from it.

That's weird. Then what's burning?

He stepped forward, intrigued. He covered his mouth with his glove and breathed through the cloth, the burning smell intensifying as he drew closer to the cabin.

Fifteen meters from the building, he saw that it had been a large house once. The wall he had walked up to was a small part of the garage area left over after a recent fire. He moved around the side of the building and stepped toward the front, where he took in the immaculate features of a beautiful two-story wooden chalet. It had the traditional look of many of the resort homes in the area. Someone had taken great care to keep this one in top shape. Many hours of labor had gone into the intricate detail surrounding the windows and doors. Cherubs and angels acted as trim. Gargoyles framed the edge of the roof along with a crazy-looking weather vane in the shape of a beast he couldn't identify.

He had never seen such a contrast. A modern wooden chalet half turned into a historical, gothic building.

"Fuckin' weird."

There were no other tracks in the snow except for the deer. If no one had come or gone in the last twenty-four hours, and there was no vehicle in the driveway, then who started the fire? Had there even been a fire?

The deer's tracks led to the front porch of the chalet. Jared held the glove over his nose as he walked toward the front door. The smell of burned flesh and hair was as powerful as a fine pepper spray. He wondered if he would vomit from the pungent odor.

The deer's tracks stopped at the edge of the closed door.

What the fuck? Where did it go? Inside the cabin?

The white button on the doorbell was quite small. He held his breath, pulled the glove away from his face, and yanked it off his hand to use his bare finger for the bell.

"Holy shit," he shouted.

He jerked back as soon as he touched the white button. The tip of his finger reddened and began to blister.

"I just got burned by a doorbell button," he said to himself.

He leaned in and examined the doorbell closely. It was plastic. But that was impossible. To burn his finger as badly as it did, the plastic should have melted.

Maybe it was an electrical burn. A short in the wiring. Making sure to protect his finger, Jared closed his hand into a fist and knocked on the door. He wanted to ascertain whether a fire raged inside the cabin's walls or not. If anyone was home, were they in need of any help?

And where was the deer he'd shot?

His knuckles rapped the door again and began stinging the second he pulled them away.

What the fuck!

He examined his burned knuckles.

How could that happen?

The wooden door didn't have electrical wires attached to it like the doorbell button did. There had to be a very hot fire raging just beyond the door with an enormous amount of heat radiating through it.

He waited for a response from within and reexamined his hand. He slid his glove back on and walked along the porch until he could see inside the front bay window.

The furniture inside appeared normal. A couch and a loveseat completed the living room ensemble. A gorgeous marble coffee table sat in the middle. Near the rear of the house, beautiful high-backed chairs surrounded a long wooden table in the dining area.

Everything appeared intact, and he could detect no sign of a fire.

As he stepped from the window, something moved on the floor by the base of the three-seater couch. Charred and still smoking, the edge of someone's hand dragged away from his sight.

He covered his face with the glove again to keep down the sandwiches he'd had for lunch.

Someone was in trouble and needed his help. He now had no choice but to make an anonymous call to the police.

But first, he wanted to see what the problem was.

Jared pulled his weapon off his shoulder and leaned it against the wooden railing that framed the front veranda. Then he stepped back to the front door and knocked on it with the tip of his boot. Little puffs of smoke rose from where his boot touched the door.

With no answer, he lifted his boot higher and kicked at the door. It gave way and opened wide. The horrid odor was instant and overwhelming, hitting him like burned cow manure permeating the air.

He would take a quick look inside, then leave. Under a minute was all he needed. Then back the way he came and home for a drink. But he feared it would take days to eliminate the smell in his nostrils.

Jared stepped into the cabin with his glove firmly in place over his nose. From where he stood, the back of the couch sat exposed.

There was no one behind it, burned or otherwise.

The hand had been attached to something, but that something was gone now.

Outside, heavy clouds darkened the sky and brought early dusk. He had followed the deer too far and waited too long to head back. He stood in the foyer of someone else's house as it grew dark outside. He figured he had ten minutes left with any source of light.

"Hello?" he called out. "Anybody here?"

A light smoke filled the air, like fog floating throughout the main floor. He tried to detect the source, but since there wasn't a breeze inside, it only floated, not moving left or right.

"Hello?" Jared called again, louder.

He moved farther into the house. Could the person behind the couch be able to drag themselves into the kitchen? There were no pictures on any of the walls. Nothing adorned the cabinet to his right. It was like no one lived here and cared for the home, yet it seemed to be in top shape.

Could be a vacation home for skiers, he thought.

At the archway to the kitchen, he stopped and waited for his eyes to adjust to the darkness. A red light glowed from inside the stove. He leaned closer to get a look, but from the doorway, with little to no light coming in from the outside, he couldn't see much.

Evidently, someone was home and cooking something in the oven. No lights were on, and it got harder to see with each passing second, but Jared didn't want to touch anything. He didn't want to get burned again.

Heat rose under his feet. He stepped away from the kitchen door and looked down. The rubber soles of his hunting boots appeared to be melting. Bits of smoke rose off his feet to add to the already dense foggy air surrounding him.

It's definitely time to leave. Fuck the deer.

He pivoted on the spot, but his boots stuck as if glued to the floor. He'd left part of his rubber sole behind.

"That is fucked up."

A loud bang was accompanied by the loss of light. The front door had slammed shut. He searched in the dimness for who had closed the door, but nothing moved. No one was around. Jared stood stock still, his stomach revolting at the smell, his nerves on edge. He felt goose bumps rise on his arms inside his thick jacket.

A game? Someone is playing a game with me?

"Okay, Mr. And Mrs. Fuck Off. You know what you can do with this stupid game."

He stepped toward the door and left the rest of the sole of his right boot on the wooden floor behind him. Jared yelled out when the thick winter sock on the underside of his foot touched down. The cloth couldn't hold back the searing heat from the floor. He pitched to the side and landed on the back of the living room sofa.

"Son of a bitch!" he yelled.

He twisted up to examine the wound but, in the dimming light, could barely make out the shape of his foot.

"What the hell is this?" he asked, scanning the room wide-eyed. "Where are you guys? What the fuck did you do to the floor? You fucked up my boots, man."

He hauled himself upright on the couch. At least the couch wasn't hot.

How could the house not be burning up and falling apart with this much heat?

He tapped the pockets of his jacket and found a purple Bic lighter. A fast flick of the ignitor and a flame shot out. He held down the tiny black tongue and turned the lighter in all directions to see who was setting him up. He couldn't make out much past the limits of the small flame and the smoke floating by.

"Where the hell are you?" he called out.

The fog he'd seen when first entering the house began to collect around the flame of his lighter. At first, it moved slowly and then increased in speed. He watched, fascinated by the intense movement of air, or whatever was in the air, dance around his small lighter. The flow intensified, rushing toward the flame. One moment the fog was simply moving toward the light, and the next, it overwhelmed it.

The Bic went out.

"Shit."

He tried to restart it but couldn't. Every flick with his thumb brought nothing but pain to his skin.

Outside the window lay only relative darkness.

Inside the rank house that smelled of burned hair, Jared now sat in almost absolute darkness. There was a very tiny amount of light coming from the kitchen.

The stove.

He had to get out of the house.

But how?

Everything he touched was too hot. It felt like everything was on fire but without flames. He couldn't walk on the floor. His boot had all but melted off his foot, and he couldn't touch anything.

But maybe he could walk on the cushions of the sofa.

He grabbed each cushion on either side of him and tossed them to the floor. Then he slid sideways and pulled the one out from under his butt. He held on to that one to use when needed.

On his feet now, favoring the burned foot, he stood on the arm of the couch and got ready. His eyes had adjusted to the darkness enough to make out the faint outline of the square cushions.

Then he leaped off the couch and landed solidly on the first cushion, where he waited and balanced himself for the next jump toward the front door.

Something moved underfoot. He looked down but, in the darkness, couldn't make out what he was seeing. It appeared the cushion was also melting, becoming one with the floor of the chalet.

What the fuck?

He couldn't believe it. Wood couldn't be that hot. Decayed wood ignited at 150 degrees. It was a stupid fact he'd looked up because of the burns he'd received at a campfire cookout years ago. There was no way the wood on the floor was below 150 degrees, which meant he should see flames. To melt his boots, it had to be higher. He was sure of it.

Something very wrong is happening in this house. I need to get the fuck out. Now!

He jumped from the first cushion to the second one and realized his mistake. The first cushion and the second one had been melting into the floor the whole time, just as his boots had.

The second cushion had shrunk to less than half its size and was almost no comfort when he landed on it. Standing on his good foot, he was down to seconds before his other boot would start to melt, and he'd be left standing on two sock feet.

Jared tossed the cushion in his hands and jumped on it when his boot began merging with the floor. He was still four feet from the closed door. The same door that someone had slammed shut just minutes ago.

Fucking assholes.

He'd make them pay.

He reached for the knob but couldn't touch it from where he stood. He would have to take one step on the burning wooden floor. Why hadn't he stayed on the couch and used his body weight to shift it along the floor? On second thought, why wasn't the couch burning? How were the couch's legs withstanding the heat?

Before leaping at the door, he turned around one more time to look at the couch, but in the darkness, he couldn't see it anymore.

Jared squinted toward the living room right in front of him. As far as he could tell, it was completely empty.

"Now that's messed up, man."

All the furniture was gone. The cushion was also not there if the couch wasn't there and had never been there.

He jerked his head to look down at his feet. The square cushion he thought he stood on had disappeared. The wood below his socks turned a deep shade of red. The heat coming through his skin registered, and for every sense, his mind had understood since he was born, he couldn't understand this one. He rejected it. Denied it. There was just no possible way to explain what was happening.

Then the pain was too much.

Jared screamed and ran for the door like one of those guys who, at the last moment, turned into a non-believer at a Tony Robbins motivational seminar walking on hot coals.

The door wouldn't budge. He yanked and pulled on it with renewed fervor, but to no avail, the whole time bouncing from foot to foot.

Finally, before he completely collapsed onto the floor, Jared turned from the door in a panic and ran for the kitchen, his feet barely touching the floor in his haste.

The oven still glowed red with its prize, but now the door was open, the remains of an animal inside. He moved closer for a better look.

Then he threw up. All the nerves and all the fear gave way to a clenching of the stomach, dislodging his lunch and tossing the half-dissolved contents onto the kitchen floor, where it sizzled and began to fry. He considered his sanity and how it was slipping away.

The heat overwhelmed him. Jared lost his balance and fell. He rolled on the floor as the intense heat rushed through his jacket. His hair caught on fire, lighting the dark kitchen with the flames.

Jared screamed and rolled until he hit the wall, batting at his head.

Something lifted him. The pain decreased for a passing second. His mind surrendered to the chaos of uncertainty as he levitated.

One rational thought seeped through. *Who's carrying me?*

Then he was utterly and absolutely consumed by flames.

***

Friday, May 18, 2012 ...

Tessa saw the police car approaching before she heard it.

"Eric," she shouted down the stairs. "Looks like we have company."

She set down the paintbrush she had been using on the plastic floor cover and took the turpentine with her to the bathroom to wash the paint off her hands. She hated using oil-based paint because of the lingering smell, but until they got the chalet aired out after a long winter closed up tight, she would rather breathe in paint fumes than the charred smells from last season's woodstove fires.

She dried her hands on her painter's apron and headed downstairs just as the doorbell rang.

Eric stood next to the front door. Before opening it, he looked up at Tessa as she walked down the wide staircase. He frowned and shrugged, nodding at the door. She shrugged back in a, *don't ask me* gesture. Neither one knew why the RCMP would be visiting them.

Once Tessa was beside him, Eric twisted the knob and opened the door.

"Good afternoon, Officer."

The Royal Canadian Mounted Police Officer came dressed in full uniform. He wore the Stetson hat, the pressed shirt, and even the red stripes down his pants leg. But he had no horse.

As Tessa extended her hand, the officer took off his hat and nodded at them, leaving her hand where it was. She waited for a heartbeat, then let it fall to her side.

"Afternoon, folks. Just wanted to do a routine drive-by to see how things were going."

Eric shot a look at Tessa, then back to the cop. "Everything's fine here, Officer. It's beautiful here, warm, and we're in our brand-new house in the mountains. Nothing could be more right."

The cop looked from Eric to Tessa and back to Eric. The expression on his face made Tessa wonder if there was more to the visit he wasn't telling them.

"Good to hear. I'll be on my way then, but first, here's my card." He handed a white business card to Eric. "Call me if you need anything."

"If there were an emergency, wouldn't 911 work just as well?" Eric asked. "Or is there something we should be worried about?"

Tessa could tell that Eric wanted to know what precipitated the unannounced visit, but he was too shy to ask the cop directly.

"Nine-one-one would work well, but I live two kilometers away," the cop gestured behind him. "I could respond faster than any cruiser on duty in Banff." His eyes turned downward. "I can see you're wearing a Medic-Alert bracelet. I'll let the local paramedics know." He met Eric's eyes. "Just in case." The cop stepped back and examined the front of the house. "See, we all stick together around here and get to know one another."

Eric stole a glance at Tessa again. In his eyes, she saw him working up the courage to be more forthright.

"Thanks again, Folks," the officer said. "Sorry to bother you." The cop turned and walked toward his car.

"Wait," Eric said. "Is there something we should know about? This unannounced visit got me thinking—"

The cop turned around so abruptly that Eric didn't finish his sentence. Then he scanned the length of the porch and the front of the house. After a moment, he stomped his feet in the dirt, leaned on the hood of his cruiser, and examined the underside of each boot, one by one.

Weird, Tessa thought.

"There's nothing to *know* about," the cop said. His tone bordered on sarcasm. "Consider this a personal housewarming gift from a neighbor who happens to be a cop."

"I need to be honest," Eric pressed. "As kind as this seems on the surface, it feels like there's more purpose than a neighborly gesture. Has someone escaped from a local prison? Are you here investigating something?" Eric snapped his fingers and snuck another look at Tessa. "Or did something happen here? In our house? Is that why we got it so cheap?"

"Nothing happened that we know of."

His voice changed an octave. Tessa was sure he had just lied to them.

"What does that mean? Did something happen that you *don't* know of?"

"Look, just call me if you need me. Really, everything's fine. I only wanted to welcome you to the area."

The RCMP officer placed his Stetson in the passenger seat and turned to get in his car. Anxiety rose in Tessa, starting with a nervous stomach. Could there have been a crime committed on their property? Or something worse? She had never been welcomed into any new home by a local cop offering his personal phone number before.

She watched the cop as he got into his car. When she looked at Eric, he was staring back at her. She knew he'd seen her expression of concern.

Eric leaned down and addressed the officer. "Sir, please …"

Tessa was too far away to hear what the cop was saying from inside his cruiser. She stepped down front the steps and moved closer to get within earshot.

"A man, Jared Tavallo, went missing last October after hunting in this area. We had found his footprints in the snow, but they were quite faded when we located them. At this point, he's still missing, and now that most of the snow is gone, his family has been roaming the area looking for his body.”

“What’s that got to do with us?” Eric asked.

“His tracks were found around here.”

“But there’s nothing wrong with the house, right? I mean, we did get it pretty cheap.”

“Jared’s hunting rifle was found on your front porch. But when we searched the house, we found nothing.”

Tessa could tell the cop was lying again. During the entire conversation, he had looked at neither one of them directly when he talked. He seemed sure of himself. But when he said they’d found nothing in the house, he looked away and fiddled with his car keys.

Eric would’ve caught it, too. He was a writer and a people watcher. He studied them to grab the nuances and character traits he could offer his characters.

“Okay, thanks, Officer. We’ll keep our eyes open, and at least now we’ll know what they’re doing if we see people wandering around the property.”

The cop nodded and put the cruiser in gear. He backed the car up, spun the wheel, and drove down their narrow driveway too fast for the curves.

“What was that all about?” Tessa asked. “I’m seriously creeped out now.”

“I don’t know, but I intend to find out.”

***

Tessa remained on the porch as Eric walked back into the house, no doubt on his way to the computer to see what he could learn about Jared Tavallo.

I know him too well.

She inhaled deeply, detecting the faint smell of something burning.

It had been permanently stuck in her nose since they'd moved in. So far, they hadn't found its source.

Eric shouted something. She jumped on the spot, a startled yip escaping her lips.

"What?" she yelled back, almost too harshly.

"Get in here."

Tessa ran through the front door. Their furniture lay piled in the center of the living room, covered in a white sheet until the room could be painted. The cathedral ceiling was sixteen feet high, with a wooden railing along the top that led from one bedroom to the other. He wasn't upstairs by the railing where she'd last seen his computer.

"Where are you?" she asked.

"In the kitchen," he said.

At the archway to the kitchen, Tessa stopped and gasped, covering her mouth with her hand.

"Why did you do that?" Eric asked.

"You know I didn't do *that*," she said, pointing at the oven. "I'm not capable of doing *that*."

"Then who did?"

"I have no idea," she said.

Eric looked away. "You don't have to be sarcastic. There's only the two of us, and since I didn't do it, I naturally assumed it had to be you."

The smell intensified as the oven's door sat open. Tessa wanted to cover her nose but instead crossed her arms and stared at Eric.

"That's funny," she said. "I was just thinking the same thing. Is this some kind of prank?"

"You're kidding, right? You set this up, and now you're pretending it was me."

"Okay, Eric, I trust you." She unfolded her arms. "But if I didn't do this and you didn't, then who did?"

He glanced at the stove and then back at her. "I have no idea. Could someone have come in while we were talking to the cop?"

"How? The back door is blocked with furniture. They would've had to walk right by us as they entered through the front door." The smell slowly became overwhelming. "Can you grab that thing and toss it in the bush, and then we'll talk about this outside? I can't breathe in here anymore."

Eric opened the cutlery drawer and pulled out the barbecue tongs. Carefully, he leaned into the stove and applied the tongs to either side of the rat's burned carcass. With the blackened rodent's body held firm in the tong's grip, Eric walked across the kitchen toward the door. Once outside, he continued away from the house and tossed the body into the trees.

"There, it's gone," he shouted as she stepped outside.

Tessa took a deep breath and shuddered the length of her body. "We've been here since yesterday. Do you think that charred smell was the rat all this time, and we just found it?"

Eric shook his head in the negative. "No. The oven light was on when I returned to the house after the cop left. This is new." Eric rubbed his chin and looked sideways, lost in thought. "Funny how it coincides with the cop showing up, though."

"Yeah, funny," Tessa said, using the sarcasm in her voice on purpose.

Dark clouds moved in and formed overhead. Only bits of blue sky were left, and the sun shone down on them in the late afternoon position.

"It looks like we might get a sun shower," Tessa said, hoping to alleviate the tension between them.

"Tessa, I'm going to run into town to see if I can find our real estate agent. After that, I'm going to see if the library's open. Maybe they have newspapers or records on the Jared Tavallo missing person report. I'd like to know more about it. I couldn't find anything online. Will you be okay here?"

"Yeah, but maybe you could walk through the house to make sure whoever stuck the rat in our oven isn't still here?"

"Of course," Eric said and moved past her.

He entered the front door and skipped up the steps two at a time. Tessa stood alone, staring up at the gorgeous chalet they had just bought for a steal. They paid less than half the going rate without wondering or asking why. Full disclosure didn't reveal that any murders or suicides had taken place in the home. As far as they could tell, the mysteriously anonymous previous owners just wanted to unload the property as fast as they could.

Tessa wasn't religious in the organized religion sense or into believing about the Other Side, but the weird trim on all the windows scared her when they first visited the house. The gargoyles lining the roof had a certain beauty to them, but the exterior would need to be renovated. It was the interior that had won them over. They'd always wanted a quiet year-round home in the mountains where Eric could write his historical thrillers, and she could dabble in gardening and cook extravagant meals. Now the oven would need a serious cleaning before she'd put any food in it.

A moment later, Eric ran out the front door, car keys dangling in his hand. "The house is clean," he said. "No one's in there." He slowed as he reached her. "I'm starting to believe the rat was in the oven since yesterday, and that's what we've been smelling."

"Yeah, that has to be it," Tessa agreed.

He kissed her and ran for the car. "Gotta hurry. It's getting late, and the library may close. See you in an hour or so. Call my cell if you need me."

Tessa waved to him as a light rain began to fall. A soft sheet of drizzle dropped from the gray clouds above. The sun still warmed her as water collected on her face.

Eric's car fired up, and he was off down the driveway, driving almost as fast as the cop did fifteen minutes before.

Tessa turned toward the house and started for the porch but stopped so suddenly that her arms pinwheeled to keep her balance.

Steam rose off the roof as the rain made contact with it. She stepped closer and examined the porch railing. It was happening there, too.

It reminded her of what water did when it hit the burner on the stove after overflowing a pot's lip, sizzling and bubbling up, and finally disappearing. She touched the railing to see if it was hot. Her fingers came away cool but not wet.

As fast as the rain started, it slowed and then stopped with only the occasional drip here and there.

Tessa walked into her house and discounted what she'd just witnessed. It had an explanation. She just didn't know what. Probably the home had heated up with the direct sun all day, and the warm rain only dissipated faster than expected.

Who knows, she thought. *I'm going to paint and not worry about dead rats and sizzling rain.*

***

Friday, June 1, 2012 ...

It had been almost two weeks since Officer Clayton had visited the new couple who had bought the cabin. He stared up at the façade of the house. The house that the area's people had started calling, *The Burning Chalet*. It looked like any other summer home in the Banff area, but he'd been on the police force long enough to know that strange things had happened here.

"Strange things indeed," he mumbled as vehicles pulled up behind him. He removed his sunglasses and watched the line of seven cars crawl up the drive, with Arthur McKay bringing up the rear. Good old Arthur—the longest-standing resident still alive in the National Park. Clayton was certain Arthur would hit ninety-five years of age this year, but people had stopped asking how old he was a dozen years ago. He was still spry, eating bacon and eggs for breakfast and still driving his own car, but Clayton suspected this would be the last year Arthur drove anymore.

The vehicles broke left and right and parked where they could find room.

"Gather around," he shouted as everyone filed out of their cars. "I want to talk to all of you before we start."

The search team assembled in a loose circle around Clayton. He counted ten people, including himself.

"Okay, here's what we know. According to the real estate agent, a young couple bought this house and were supposed to arrive for the long weekend in May a few weeks back. They never showed up. The problem is their family in Calgary said they left for Banff and came here on the seventeenth of May. I've asked you to help search the area in a grid formation. Once we've covered every square meter of the property and found nothing, we will leave as a group and go home. I will report to the family personally with what we find, which I'm figuring won't be anything. Got it?"

Heads bobbed up and down.

"Okay, we'll start in that corner in a single line and walk the property. We've all done this before. Let's go, let's go."

Arthur stood at the back, leaning on his cane. Clayton headed over to Arthur as the searchers started for the property line corner.

"You sure you're up to this?" Clayton asked.

Arthur's old eyes watered constantly. Arthur said in a high-pitched, grandfatherly voice, "You're damned right I am. No house will spook me." He turned and started after the group, leaning into his cane more today than on other days.

The ensemble of volunteers started by ten in the morning and finished the left side of the property by the lunch hour. Everyone returned to their cars for food and sat on hoods and trunks to eat.

Mike Lewis gestured toward Clayton, the remnants of a tuna sandwich in his mouth. "You really think that couple came here?"

Clayton shrugged. "I have no idea. Everything points to the negative."

"I heard that whoever comes around here goes missing eventually," Barbara added from a few feet away.

"We don't want to encourage fairy tales," Clayton said.

"What happened to that hunter last year?" Mike asked.

"Who knows?" Clayton bit into a gala apple. "People go missing all the time in the mountains."

"Yeah, but I heard his rifle was found on the porch of this house."

"Ghost stories," Clayton said. "That's all it is."

"I don't think so," Arthur chimed in. "There's something wrong with this house. I can feel it in my bones. Can smell it in the air."

Clayton swallowed the chunk of apple and took a deep breath. "That's just somebody nearby with a campfire. Probably roasting marshmallows or hotdogs."

"I smell something burning," Arthur said. "And it ain't marshmallows."

"Okay, Folks. Let's finish this up and get the rest of the search done. I want to be home in time for dinner."

They gathered their garbage, tossed it into a bag Clayton had brought, and assembled at the opposite corner of the property.

After two more search lines were covered, they came upon the old well near the back of the property line. In order to walk around the raised stones that marked the well, Clayton would have to move away from one of the volunteers on either side of him.

"Everyone, slow up. I want to scan the base of the well, so we don't have to revisit this spot."

The line stopped. Clayton got down and circled the well, seeing nothing but overgrown grass and stone. He rose to his full height and looked down into the open hole of the well. Darkness covered the bottom. As far as he remembered, the old wells in these parts had dried up years ago.

He grabbed the flashlight off his belt, flicked it on, and shined the beam down the hole. Something reflected off it near the bottom.

"What was that?" he asked out loud.

A moment later, Mike stood beside him, leaned down, and scanned the bottom of the well.

"I can't make it out, but from here, it looks like a woman's purse."

"What would a purse be doing at the bottom of a well?" Clayton asked no one in particular.

"No idea," Mike answered.

"Okay, everyone, continue the search without me. I'm going to get my fishing rod out of my trunk to see if I can hook that purse and bring it up."

As Clayton walked out to his car, the volunteers formed their line and moved away.

Minutes later, he stood at the lip of the old well, a large lure with a double hook at its base affixed to the ten-pound line.

He let the line go until the lure touched the bottom and began the monotonous work of trying to hook the purse in the little to no light at the bottom of the well.

The volunteers finished scanning the property and came up empty. There was no indication anyone had spent time at the house in the last few years.

Just as it was beginning to seem a fruitless effort, the hook caught in the front flap of the purse.

Gently, he pulled the fishing line up and began to reel it in. Mike grabbed the fishing rod's tip to stabilize it and reduce sway.

"You're getting it. Slowly, slowly."

Clayton paid attention to the line, ensuring he didn't jerk it.

"Five feet left. Someone reach down and grab it when it gets close."

Clayton didn't look up to see who volunteered. He kept his attention on the rod. Getting this close and accidentally dropping the purse back into the well would piss him off.

"Got it!" Barbara shouted.

Clayton let out a pent-up breath. He set the rod down and reached for the purse. It didn't look old, but the strap was broken and the outside leather worn. However long the purse was in the well, it had weathered beyond repair.

"Everyone, thanks for coming out. Time to go. I'll have this, and its contents analyzed and let you all know what I find, if anything. Thanks again. See you all in town."

Clayton walked away, but not before Arthur grabbed his arm.

"I don't think you'll find anything in that purse. The house doesn't want you to know."

Clayton stopped walking. "What makes you say that?"

"Up there," Arthur pointed at the second-story windows with his cane. "When you got that purse into your hands, something was in the window, watching you."

"What are you talking about?" Clayton asked. "You think someone is in the house right now?"

"No, not someone. Something."

"Arthur, I hope you're not seeing things," Clayton said as he turned to go.

Arthur grabbed his elbow with surprising strength and spun him back to face him. "Whatever it was I saw, I can tell you it was real and angry. I didn't see eyes, but I felt it watching us. Then it glowed a fire-red, orange color. When you touched the purse, for a brief moment, the whole second story of the house looked like it was on fire. Flames licked up the window panes. They turned a deep shade of red, and by the time I was ready to point and tell you to look, it all went away."

"Arthur," Clayton lowered his voice and leaned in. "You didn't see anything of the sort. Go home and get some sleep. Thanks for your help today."

Officer Clayton walked away with the purse, wondering what he'd find in it. He also wondered if Arthur had started brewing his moonshine again or if he was finally losing his mind to age.

When he reached his car, he stopped to look back at the house and saw Arthur in the open door.

"What are you doing now?" he asked. "That's breaking and entering."

"I'm going inside to *investigate* what I saw. And the front door was unlocked. I was invited."

Arthur had snarled the word, *investigate*. Clayton knew what that meant. He'd had heard that some people in the area didn't think he did his job well enough.

"Hold up, just one second."

He placed the purse on the passenger seat and walked to the front door. Arthur stepped inside the house. Clayton followed.

It was dark, and the air smelled like burned flesh. Sitting on the floor by the door was a small pile of luggage. On top of two suitcases sat a VHS video camera.

Clayton examined the recorder as Arthur stepped farther into the house.

"Hey, Arthur, hold up. Don't go too far. We shouldn't even be in here."

"I'll do what I want," Arthur said.

Clayton hit the eject button and popped the cassette tape out.

More evidence.

"Hey Arthur, look at your shoes." Smoke had started to come off Arthur's feet.

The old man leaned on the wall to lift his foot. Half of the sole of his loafer was missing.

"What the hell—"

Clayton felt heat in his boots, too. Smoke also came out from under his feet now.

"Arthur, we need to leave. Now!"

Even at his age, Arthur could still move fast. He skipped across the living room, and together, they walked out the front door and down the steps to the gravel drive.

"What was in the floor?" Arthur asked.

"I have no idea," Clayton said. "But I've got a VHS tape to watch. Maybe there'll be something on it that'll help us understand."

Both men walked away with less than half their footwear still intact, but Clayton's confidence wavered.

***

Friday, May 18, 2012 ...

Tessa finished the first coat of paint in their bedroom. While washing her hands, she heard Eric pulling up to the front of the house.

Eager to hear what Eric had found out in the town, she ran down the stairs, gave the kitchen—the oven—a wide berth, and opened the front door.

The anger on his face was quite evident.

"What happened in town?" she asked.

"Nothing," he said, his voice confirming her suspicions of ire.

He had gotten out of the car and fiddled with something in the trunk.

"What do you mean, *nothing*?" she called to him. "Wasn't the real estate agent in? Did you get to the library?"

He popped his head out from behind the open lid of the trunk. "No, and no."

He doesn't have to be so bitchy to me.

"What happened then? Tell me. You sound pissed."

"I am pissed."

He slammed the trunk, and she jumped at what he held in his hands.

A silver handgun.

"What are you doing with that?" she asked, her voice weak and feminine, which she hated at that moment. "We don't believe in guns. We've talked about this."

"Yeah, and look how many kilometers we are from town." He walked around the car. "Someone came into our house and burned a rat in our oven. We're so far out of town that the local sheriff offers us his personal services if and when we might need a cop. Tell me that doesn't spook you just a little."

"There are two things that have me spooked. One was the rat in the oven. The other is you right now."

He walked up beside her and slid back the top of the gun until it clicked. "Well, Tessa, I'm sorry, but you'll have to get used to it. I will protect you and this house, and I won't allow you or anyone else to dictate *how* I choose to do that protection."

He walked past her and disappeared inside.

What the hell has happened to my Eric?

She found him in the kitchen, checking to see if the window over the sink was secure.

"Where did you get the gun?" she asked.

"Officer Clayton had an extra in his trunk."

"What?" She slapped her forehead. "Are you serious? That was smart, real smart."

He stopped sliding his hands along the frame and turned to her. "What does that mean?"

"Tell me what happened in town." She crossed her arms. "Everything."

"Okay. The real estate agency was closed by the time I got downtown. With all the tourists in town for the long weekend, it took forever to get to the library. It, too, was closed. I missed it by five minutes."

"Then what?"

"Officer Clayton pulled up in his cruiser and asked me to get in. I did."

"Why? We just saw him."

Eric raised his hands and said, "I have no idea. He said I looked scared, so I told him about the rat. He offered the weapon, and I took it. Coming from a cop, I thought it was a safe move."

"This is insane. You didn't consider my feelings —"

Something snapped upstairs, and the house shuddered with the bang.

Her eyes wide, Tessa whispered, "What was that?"

"I don't know, but I'm going to find out."

Eric ran past her, the gun held high. Tessa was scared about the cop's gift of a gun. If Eric shot someone and ended up in court, there was no way a member of the RCMP would take the fall by admitting he offered a weapon to someone as untrained as Eric. Something was wrong with Clayton.

She ran into the back storage room and opened three different boxes until she found her old video recorder.

She could hear Eric calling for her to come upstairs.

"In a minute," she shouted.

"*Now*," he yelled back down.

What the fuck?

She opened the tape drawer and saw it held a VHS tape.

Whatever's on this tape is about to be erased.

She grabbed the cord and plugged it into the back of the recorder as she ran for the stairs. When she got to the top of the stairs, she saw why Eric had called her.

She gasped and almost dropped the recorder.

"Who did this?" Eric asked. "Did you?"

She shook her head in an exaggerated twist back and forth, her chin almost touching each shoulder. "Never," she whispered.

"How did it happen, then?" Eric asked, his words coming out in tight, short beats.

"What? You don't think I had anything to do with this, do you?"

"Look, Tessa, I drove into town, and when I returned, the room you were painting in was ruined. Unless we have company, you did this. And don't suggest otherwise. Unless you really want to get crazy and say this house is haunted, we both know that's not the case. *We* don't believe in that shit."

She was stunned at what she saw in the room and at Eric's words. His tone hurt her. Eric had never talked like that before, and now he stood in their new home with a gun in his hand. For the first time in a long time, Tessa felt fear. She was afraid of what was happening to them.

"Eric, we should leave. Maybe this was a mistake."

He threw his head back and laughed. "You know, you're a real fucking joke. How could you say *that*?" Spittle flew from his mouth at the last word. His face reddened, and the sclera of his eyes lost their white to a red hue. "Someone is fucking with us, and you want to leave. Give me a fucking break!"

"I'm sorry." She raised her hands in defense. "Please stop shouting at me."

"Don't tell me what to do," he screamed, storming past her.

What's happening to us? This morning when we arrived with the paint, he was so happy. We were so happy. What has changed?

Tessa stepped into the master bedroom and looked at the first coat she had spent several hours applying. It had bubbled up and flaked off like she'd tried to paint the side of a barbecue. Flakes of charred paint lay around the room at the bottom of every wall where the paint had been applied.

The original wooden wall showed through in all its ugly brown and black surface. The room had lost the smell of paint, too.

Only the faint odor of burned hair remained.

***

Friday, June 1, 2012 ...

Officer Clayton poured himself a glass of wine and sat on his couch. The purse had come up empty. He'd kept it sealed at the house so the volunteers would think it would be opened in a lab. Everyone watches CSI nowadays and is an amateur scientist. When he got to the station, he'd walked into his office and opened the purse to find it empty.

He had fast-forwarded and rewound the VHS tape to loosen it up. It took him more time to locate his old player in the garage than it took to get the tape ready.

With it hooked up and the tape ready to play, Officer Clayton sat back and sipped his wine. He wasn't sure if he wanted to see the tape or not. Should he just let it go? How many more people would go missing before someone else noticed and raked him over the coals for not doing more about it?

Maybe it was time to deal with *The Burning Chalet*. Ever since that fire in 1978, no one had ever done a thing about that house. Why did it have to fall on Clayton's shoulders?

He pushed play on the remote and drank more wine.

The tape started with the man and woman who had bought the house, Eric, and Tessa, playing at a beach somewhere. He leaned forward to speed the tape up. The scene changed.

As far as he could tell, Tessa held the camera. A man's voice in the background was too far away to be holding the camera. The image on the screen was of one of the bedrooms. The room was quite sizable.

"This is the master bedroom," Tessa's voice said. "I finished painting the first coat fifteen minutes ago, and this happened after cleaning up and going downstairs."

The camera moved closer to the wall. The paint had chipped off the wood, leaving behind a mess on the floor. What didn't surprise him was the way the paint had come off. It had burned off wherever it had been applied.

The camera slowly panned down the wall to the floor. Littered around the baseboards were blackened chips of paint, their charred edges sending a chill down Clayton's back. He shivered, jolting the wine glass in his hand.

The picture on his TV broke, and went back to another time at the beach. Then it broke again, and he was back in the house. He could tell Tessa was filming over an old trip to the beach.

To protect his sanity, Officer Clayton almost turned off the tape. But he couldn't. If he did, he would spend the rest of his life wondering what came next. Halfway through the scene, his stomach gave way. Officer Clayton vomited into his wine glass and across his coffee table.

"I'm damned to hell," he said as he watched Tessa do the unthinkable.

***

Friday, May 18, 2012 ...

Tessa finished filming the bedroom and headed downstairs to see what Eric was doing. She didn't want to be too far from her man if someone was in their house.

Eric was in the kitchen with his head stuck in the stove.

"What are you doing now?" she asked.

"I'm looking for holes. Anything to explain how the rat got in here."

"Finding anything?"

"No."

She set the video recorder on the side counter and pulled one of the kitchen chairs out to sit.

"Are you still mad at me?" she asked.

"I'm not mad at you. I'm just mad."

She nodded even though he wasn't looking at her. "Do you think we made a mistake with this house?"

"No."

She started playing with her hair, rolling it in her fingers and then drawing it out to its full length.

"Me neither. Eric, are we going to be okay?"

"Why do you keep asking me questions? Can't you see I'm busy?"

"Sorry."

A sudden sadness fell on her like a rough blanket coating her soul.

For the next ten minutes, as the sun descended outside and evening rose in a cacophony of insect chorus, Tessa watched Eric work on the oven.

After inspecting the inside meticulously, he opened a box that sat on the counter beside the stove. With a small drill, he punched two holes in the stove, one at the top of the door and one above where the door shut.

While she sat at the kitchen table, not saying a word, she watched her husband affix a lock on the outside of their new stove.

When he was done, she asked, "What is that for?"

"When the door closes, it will lock automatically. You need to push these three small buttons in the order I tell you to so that it'll open. Only you and I will know the code. That means anything inside will never be able to get out, and if a stranger is taunting us in any way, he or she won't be able to get in."

"Why did you say he or she?" Tessa asked. "Are you alluding to me?"

He turned to look at her. "Feeling guilty about something? Want to come clean? Now's the time."

He waited, but she didn't respond. She was too shocked at the way he was talking to her. He'd never been like this before. Ever.

Eric finished with the lock and tested it. It held firm each time. He showed her the three-digit code and left the room.

Tessa sat at the kitchen table alone with her thoughts and her sorrow.

***

Later that night, Tessa lay in bed but couldn't sleep. Eric tossed and turned beside her.

They'd fought earlier. She had protested using the lock on the oven door because it wasn't about the oven. What had happened was more about the security of their home. Stop the intruder from entering, and then the oven becomes a non-issue. Eric argued that the intruder was attempting to send them a message and the oven acted as the messenger. Removing the oven from the equation meant no more messages.

This was so unlike them as a couple. They'd had arguments like any other couple, but never to this degree. The bed hadn't been put together because he was too tired and it was too hot. They lay on the box spring and mattress on the floor of their master bedroom.

He had time to hook locks up to our new oven and borrow a weapon from the local cop but not enough time to set up our bed like he'd promised.

The movers had delivered all their belongings two days before they'd arrived. Everything was where it was supposed to be. They had been prepared to spend the long weekend painting and cleaning the house, but instead, the weekend had started off with a fight.

She looked over at the window to see if it was open. The moon illuminated the sill with its soft white light. The sounds of the night had died off, leaving her with the soft cadence of Eric's breathing.

She had been lying in bed for at least two hours. The heat in the room seemed to be increasing. The back of her neck was slick with sweat. She eased off the mattress slowly, trying not to wake Eric.

She made no noise on the balls of her feet as she reached the window. As hard as she tugged, it wouldn't budge.

Sweat beaded down into her eyes. She wiped it away in frustration and headed out of the room. In the kitchen, the tape recorder still sat on the counter. She looked at it, opened the fridge, and pulled out the bottled water. She drank almost half of it. She used the towel by the sink to wipe off her face and neck sweat.

Why the hell is it so hot in here?

She thought of the rain and how it had sizzled upon contact with the house.

Why didn't I tell Eric about that?

Without thinking, she tilted the bottle of water until a fat drop left the lip and splattered on the floor, instantly bubbling up. The small bubbles danced on the surface of the wood and decreased in size until they disappeared. Heat radiated under her feet in the same second it took for the drop of water to disappear.

"What the fuck is going on?" she whispered.

Suddenly, it felt like she stood on hot pavement in the middle of a heat wave in August. She had to alternate feet as the heat in the floor rose in temperature.

She left the kitchen and grabbed her shoes at the door. After they were on, she walked back into the kitchen, her feet tucked in socks and shoes.

Should I wake Eric and tell him, or film it and prove there's a problem?

Without another thought, Tessa grabbed the recorder, hit the *record* button, and set the camera on the kitchen table with its back supported on a book to aim the camera down.

She brought the water bottle close, directly in front of the camera. Moving slowly, she tilted the open bottle and let a large drop of water escape.

She could still detect heat through her shoes, but not enough to make her hop on the spot.

The water hit the wooden floor and dissolved in front of the camera just as it had the moment before.

"Holy fuck. I've got that on camera, too."

She turned to lift the camera up, but her feet were stuck to the floor like she'd stepped in gum. The floor had heated up so much that the bottom of her rubber soles had melted. She would be standing on the burning floor in her sock feet within seconds.

She lifted her legs hard, dislodging each shoe, but with every step, they stuck and burned again.

The floor made her think of something like hot quicksand.

There was a burning in this house, and it was coming from the basement.

But we don't have a basement.

Then, at that moment, from under the house, a massive amount of heat rose up and grabbed hold of her. In a panic, she tried to run from the kitchen but lost her balance. They made contact with the floor when she thrust both hands out to break her fall. The pain was instant and intense. Tessa screamed as the flesh on each fingertip, and the base of her hand melted off.

Something grabbed her from behind and lifted her.

Eric shouted from upstairs. In her panic, she thought she heard him yell for her to be quiet, that he was trying to sleep.

The pain grew, the heat rose, and all she could think about was escaping. She struggled, but her limbs were held firm.

The oven door sat open. Someone had punched in the code on the lock.

This is Eric's doing somehow. Only the two of us know the code.

That was her last thought as her mind slipped and her eyes rolled back in her head. Consciousness wavered. She struggled hard to stay alert.

Whatever held her seared its imprints on her skin as if she were being branded. Her eyes bulged as the pressure in her head increased.

Paralyzed, she could do nothing as, one by one, each foot was lifted into the oven. Her mind raged at her limbs in protest, but whatever held her held firm and manipulated her to its will.

Her waist entered the open maw of the oven. Her whole body would not fit in the small square cavern. At the point where she could go no farther, she was shoved in hard, both hips breaking under the pressure until her upper body cleared the door, her arms crushing in around her chest.

Near her shoulders, as her head got forced down and in, she felt a subtle shift in her spine, and then the pain below the waist disappeared.

The invisible hands let go the second the oven's door closed. She gasped and took in a deep breath. She could barely move in the cramped space. Pain accompanied every breath as her body played a game of *Twister* with itself. In the confined space, she could only move her eyes. Her left hand lay jammed against the oven door. She pushed hard, but to no avail. The door simply wouldn't budge.

The new lock. It locks the instant the door closes.

She screamed, her eyes watering, her mouth stuck open.

Through the little window in the oven door, she saw her video recorder on the kitchen table aimed at the stove, the red light indicating it was still recording.

The kitchen floor had burned her hands badly, and whatever picked her up and lifted her into the oven had been strong and remained unseen.

Haunted?

A surreal, intense fear gripped her at the soft clicking sound.

The elements had been turned on.

"No!" she shouted and screamed again as she redoubled her efforts on the oven's door. Her hands ached to the point of numbness.

The element below her heated up, glowing red. Whatever put her in the oven intended to burn her alive just like the rat, and there was nothing she could do to stop it.

With every ounce of strength she still possessed, Tessa struggled inside the tight confines of the oven as the elements heated to their maximum, beginning the process of burning her where she crouched.

Before her mind gave way and her heart stopped, she could feel her skin cooking, sizzling, melting. Blood poured but cauterized where it met the burners, which seared deeper through her skin until bones met the heat directly.

Her last vision was of the tape recorder. The once rosy skin of her cheeks melted against the oven window, and both her eyes dried up and decreased in size as the water content of her body evaporated.

Tessa died, knowing it wasn't just the elements of an oven that killed her. Something else was in there with her. Something much hotter and angrier.

She knew she was just another victim of *the burning*, and Eric would be next.

***

Friday, June 1, 2012 ...

Clayton's screen flickered after the image of Tessa in the oven door's window melted and faded into a mash of skin and blood, cooking to a blackness he would never forget.

He had watched as she videotaped the water drop out and sizzle on the floor. He'd seen how she almost floated into the oven and how, on its own, the door slammed closed, engaging the external lock. As morbid as the sight was, Clayton watched while young Tessa cooked in her own oven.

He'd suspected something had been happening in the house for years, but he'd never known for sure. There were many years of disappearances. People who lived in the area refused to go near the house.

He'd always figured it was the natives driving people away. Many years ago, the Indians claimed that area as theirs.

He sat and watched the tape until nothing but white noise filled his screen. Then he decided what he must do.

Giving the gun to Eric was a precaution. If it really was the natives, then that couple needed protection. Since no one had seen Eric or Tessa except for him, he'd figured they'd returned to where they came from. Tessa's family had reported them missing, so he needed to do something about that. Now he had proof that Tessa was forced into the oven and burned alive.

He made one phone call and set his backup plan in place.

He grabbed two large boxes of black gunpowder and carried them out to his trunk. Inside the trunk, a little box sat on the right. From it, he grabbed an electric match that would ignite the powder. He held it up in front of his face and examined the small piece of thin resistance wire coated with a flammable substance. A small current through it and the wire would heat up, igniting the powder. He had done his research and bought the e-match at the local hobby shop where they sold rocket supplies.

If everything went to shit, he had decided last year after the disappearance of Jared Tavallo, his brother-in-law, that whatever was in that house would have to deal with his homemade car bomb.

He set everything up in his trunk, jumped in the cruiser, flicked the lights on, and raced away with the VHS tape in the passenger seat beside him.

***

Clayton arrived at *The Burning Chalet* before anyone else. He sat in his cruiser and stared at the house's windows, trying to imagine all the terrors that had gone on inside its walls. It felt like the house watched him, too, like it was alive.

The sun had moved toward the horizon, the sky darkening in the east first. It would be dark soon, and he wouldn't set foot inside the house after that, so he opened his door and got out, determined to get the answers he needed.

After adjusting his gun belt, he started for the front steps. There were no sounds in the wilderness surrounding the property. No insects, frogs, or mating calls. Nothing. The silence would normally be welcoming, but this close to the house where Tessa had been murdered two weeks ago, the lack of noise only caused unease.

He set one boot on the steps, pushed down, and then lifted his foot off again. The rubber sole remained intact.

He walked up the porch steps and stood in front of the door. One more check of his boots. They weren't melting.

Conscious of his duty and responsibilities, Clayton knocked on the door and waited. After waiting a full minute, he knocked again and turned to examine the woods behind him. Thick trees separated pockets of black. He was running out of daylight and time.

He tried the doorknob. It turned without a key. One shove, and the door opened all the way.

The inside looked nice and clean. Everything had its place. Furniture sat in a comfortable arrangement, surrounding a marble coffee table in the center of the living room.

Maybe he was wrong. Perhaps he saw someone's amateur attempt at a horror movie on the tape—something to be uploaded onto YouTube. A prank. Maybe someone got punked.

On the other hand, if it was real, it was his job to do what he had to do.

He pulled a flashlight from his belt and stepped inside the house. The distinctive odor of something burned hit Clayton's nose. Not like bread left too long in the toaster. More like flesh and hair. He almost turned around and walked out, but he knew if he did, it would take a long time to build up enough nerve to return.

The dim light outside barely made an impression in the living room. In the gloom of the living room, his flashlight lacked any real power.

I'll have to check the batteries on this thing tomorrow.

He made it to the door of the kitchen and saw the lock on the stove. The oven door was shut, and the lock engaged. There was a good chance that Tessa's body would still be inside.

He took one last look at his boots.

All okay. So far.

After a long, deep breath, he strode across the kitchen floor and shone his flashlight into the little window on the door of the oven.

There was nothing to see. The window was covered in a black film like someone had overcooked steaks, and grease had bubbled up to seal any view from the outside.

He tried the handle. It didn't budge. The lock held the oven door firm.

Now or never, he said to himself as he pulled out his sidearm. He resolved never to enter this house again, but before he left, he had to look inside the oven.

Off in the distance, a siren approached.

Backup's arriving.

His arm outstretched, face turned away, Clayton fired a bullet at the lock, shattering it into tiny metal fragments.

After holstering his weapon, he gripped the handle and counted to three. Then he eased the oven door down.

Inside, the tell-tale signs of what was once a human body were now melted and burned to a misshapen lump of blackened flesh and bone.

He averted his eyes to keep what little he had in his stomach right where it was. He opened the door farther and examined the oven's contents more closely.

The body was a mass of black juices and black flakes of skin. The bottom of the oven was covered in dark goo.

The elements didn't get everything.

A charred Medic-Alert bracelet stuck out of the lump of burned meat, like the one Eric had worn in the two times Clayton had met him.

How did Eric get in here, too?

He let go of the oven door and stepped away. Maybe Eric found Tessa's body and watched the tape. Then, whatever forced Tessa into the oven did the same to Eric.

It was time to leave this place for good. He'd found the missing couple. They'd been burned alive. The murderer was the house. He was sure of it. He wondered how that would look on the reports.

He felt heat rising through his boots. He'd forgotten to keep checking them. Clayton started walking, and with each step, he left behind rubber pieces.

The siren outside grew louder as the fire truck pulled up to the front.

He ran, stumbled once, but kept his balance and charged out the front door.

"Hank," he shouted. "Cover this place with every hose you have," he called.

Hank, the head firefighter in the area for the past dozen years, looked back at him, his eyebrows knitted in confusion.

"Where's the fire, Clayton? I can't empty my trucks on a dry house."

Clayton ran across the gravel driveway toward him. "Oh yes, you can, and you're going to."

"No, I'm not. I don't see a fire. Show me the fire, and I'll put it out."

Hank's men stood around and watched their boss argue with Clayton. He could still feel the heat rising from his boots.

"Okay, give me a hose, and I'll show you the fire."

Clayton waited in awkward silence until Hank nodded to his men. They unhooked a hose and dragged it over to Clayton. He grabbed it and pulled it to the front porch. He struggled with the end of it for a moment, and then water poured out.

After a look over his shoulder at Hank, Clayton aimed the nozzle and began shooting water in through the front door. A roar of steam billowed wherever the water hit the wooden floor, most of the water evaporating upon contact. In a weird way, it reminded him of placing a hot frying pan under the water in the kitchen sink.

"What's causing that?" Hank asked over the sound of the rushing water.

"I don't know, but what I can tell you is that this house is burning on the inside."

Hank looked at him with a hard stare. "How's that?"

"No idea—"

A shift in the house cut him off. Something moved behind the front wall.

"What the fuck was that?" Hank asked, stepping back a few feet.

"Get more men up here," Clayton said, completely ignoring Hank's question. "I need more water."

Hank waved at his men, and they grabbed hoses and hit valves.

Clayton saw it first. It was as if flames levitated in the living room. From where he stood on the front porch, he would swear the flames were walking. They edged along the front window and then disappeared on their way to the door.

Clayton stepped back two paces. Hank watched, mouth agape, as the flames now filled the doorway. It was an unnatural red flame, sections shooting out like sunspots off the sun. Hank's hose didn't have enough power to quench the flames. As the water hit the red flames, it seemed to fuel them like throwing grease on a kitchen fire.

Clayton stepped back even farther, increasingly concerned about leaving the property alive. He knew Hank was too trained to turn away. He now held a fireman's hose, shooting water onto a fire no bigger than a seven-foot-tall man.

The flames spun in a circle like the eye of a tornado and then rushed at the water. In the next moment, Hank was consumed by flames, screaming and wailing as he fell to the ground. But stop, drop, and roll wouldn't slow the ferocity of the red flames.

The fire lifted from Hank's blackened remains and shot across the gravel drive at the fire truck. Hank's men scattered in all directions as their truck began to burn. Men shouted and ran for the trees. If Clayton's car wasn't trapped behind the firetruck, he would've run for his cruiser and raced out of there, but as it was, he would need to run past the red flames to get to safety. Instead, he could only watch as man after man was cut down and burned alive as they fled.

Clayton's mind couldn't take in what was happening. It defied all sense of reason. His eyes saw the spectacle, but his mind refused to accept it.

In less than a minute, the last man fell silent.

The red flames hovered near the front of the burning fire truck. It watched Clayton, studying him.

Then the length of conflagration moved forward, easing its way to Clayton. It stopped five feet from him.

Clayton felt the heat but didn't retreat. He understood that running meant death by fire. He blinked to dislodge the sight—but the flames remained.

The heat burned his face like it was the middle of the day in the hottest part of the Sahara desert. Should he pull his weapon, turn and run, or simply wait to be burned alive?

The fire decided for him.

It backed away, circled him, and moved to the house's front door.

Clayton watched as it moved by the living room window again.

Every man present was a fireman. All of them died because he thought the house needed to be dowsed in water.

Clayton headed for his car. It was time to deal with the burning once and for all. He got in the cruiser, turned it on, and started around the ruined fire truck. He glanced through the windshield toward the house. The flames had extinguished.

He stopped the car. Whatever that thing was, he couldn't allow anyone else to enter. However, it came to be didn't matter to Clayton. What mattered was that Hank and all of his men were dead because of him.

He took his foot off the brake and hit the gas, the rear tires spinning in the gravel. The police cruiser raced at the house, hit the front steps, and mounted them without losing much speed. The front bumper smashed open the front door and the wall to the right, stopping the car half in, half out of the chalet.

Instantly the flames resurrected themselves and raced at him.

Clayton hit the button to pop the trunk and dove from the car. He ran for the back and grabbed the e-match. The moving flames were almost on him.

Clayton ignited the e-match. "Fuck you," he shouted.

The levitating flames hit him hard. The pain was intense. His mouth opened to scream. In the next moment, the e-match had done its job. Both boxes of gunpowder ignited simultaneously, knocking Clayton's burning body away from the house with a shock wave. The car's propane tank added to the explosion.

The last image his mind registered was the four walls of the house shattering as it collapsed, completely destroyed. He heard screaming and knew it wasn't his.

He had fought fire with fire.

As his soul left his burned carcass, RCMP Officer Clayton Green understood that the burning died with him.

The Numbers Game

I NEVER THOUGHT I'D be up on first-degree murder charges. The proof is in the numbers. It's all a numbers game. I know this. But they don't.

I'm a vacuum cleaner salesman. I used to sell shoes, but now I sell vacuums. I run door-to-door and try to sell my uprights. The murders have nothing to do with me, but one of the people I had just done a presentation for was murdered minutes after I left their house.

I'm innocent.

This is my story. Call it a diary. I won't lock it. Besides, I don't have a lock or anything metal in my prison cell. They don't allow those things. So I will write my tale and let everyone know what I do and how I do it so they can see that I'm not a murderer. I can't afford a lawyer from the money I make selling vacuums, but I've got legal aid, although that's worth nothing. Maybe the judge will read this.

It's lights out, so I'll write in the dim glow I get from the corridor. It's a short story, so I'll be brief, but there are two things you need to know upfront.

I only got caught because I had the murdered woman's shoes in my apartment. Also, someone saw my car in front of her home and wrote down my license plate number. That makes sense, as I was there doing a vacuum demonstration.

I'm innocent. Remember that as you read on.

It's important.

***

Tuesday morning

On the morning of the murder.

I'm off to a great start today. I've hit twenty-two houses. Ten doors weren't answered, and twelve were rejections. The rule is, for every one-hundred doors, you get into two. That means I should get in one door by the time I hit fifty. Once I show them how good the vacuum is, they'll want one for themselves. Although that's not always true because I only sell one for every four demonstrations. To break it down, I need to hit two-hundred doors to sell one vacuum on average.

See what I mean about the proof being in the numbers? I live by that. It allows me to finance myself properly, as selling vacuum cleaners is a one-hundred-percent commission. If I want a raise, all I have to do is hit another fifty houses per day for a week, and I'll, on average, probably sell an extra vacuum per week. At four hundred dollars a hit in commission, selling three to five per week, I'd say I'm doing all right. I'm not rich, but these are just the numbers. I know the proof's there, and that's how I get by, but in the end, they're just numbers.

I'm on Maple Street. It's still before lunch. Let's see how many rejections I can get. You see, that's the fun part. The more rejections I receive only means I'm one door closer to an *open* door. An open door is a potential sale. And any open door is a chance for me to add a nice pair of shoes to my collection.

What people don't know is that I collect shoes. Mostly, ladies' shoes. I don't wear them. I'm not creepy. I just collect them. I have over two-hundred pairs from different cities in the States. Today, I'm itching to add to that.

It's like a calling. I *need* them. I *have* to have them.

The next house coming up is a Victorian. Very nice white trimming with a manicured lawn. I'm sure the owners could use a new vacuum, and I could use a new pair of ladies' shoes.

I ran up the walkway and rang their bell.

No answer.

I rang it again.

Footsteps approached. The door opened.

"Hello?" A woman in her fifties stood in the doorway (I should say here that this is Mrs. Gavin).

"Hi! My name is Trevor Ashton, and we're in the area today offering free carpet shampoos to you and your neighbors." I thrusted out a bottle of Carpet Fresh and held it high in my hand. This always made me feel like those girls on *The Price Is Right* waving their hands in front of the items people were to bid on. "There's no obligation, ma'am. You get a free bottle of Carpet Fresh for letting us clean your carpet. Doesn't that sound great?"

The woman seemed stunned. She looked at me a moment longer, evaluating my smile, and then shook her head. She started to close the door.

"Excuse me, ma'am." I touched the door before it closed. "Is there a reason you wouldn't like a free carpet shampoo? There's nothing to buy and no obligation. It's completely free." I said this last part with an, *I'm so excited I just can't hide it* flourish.

She attempted a half smile. "I'm not feeling well. I've had hip surgery recently, and I'm not up to the company. But thank you, anyway."

She started to shut the door again.

"But, ma'am, you're the perfect candidate. Don't you see?"

The door is almost closed. It stopped at the frame. I waited. It opened again, almost defiantly.

"I already get my carpets cleaned by a company that does a great job. I pay them often to come and do it. They were here about two weeks ago, so the carpets are fine."

"That's perfect. I love a challenge. Do you realize how much they miss? In under five minutes, my vacuum would show you how bad they're doing."

She looked me up and down, showing her displeasure at my intrusion. In the end, I told myself I'd run to the next house and try again if I lost her. Eventually, I'd get in somewhere. That's a fact. It's in the numbers.

"The carpet cleaners that do my home are very good, and they're so cheap that I barely pay them a tip, and you want to know why?" She paused like the drama queen I could tell she was. "Because my son owns the company."

Okay, here's a challenge. I just told her the company she uses sucks. It's her son's company. To her, I've disrespected her family. I've got to talk fast and think faster.

"Let me ask you a question, and then I'll leave. Is that fair?"

She held the door firm. It looked like she was getting ready to slam it in my face. I didn't wait for her to tell me to go ahead.

"Let's say you just went to the doctor, who told you your cholesterol was off the charts. Arteries were clogging, and he required you to be hospitalized. He tells you to go home and pack your things and report back to the hospital by that afternoon. He also tells you to eat nothing until you return. Especially don't eat any fast food like greasy burgers because it could be what kills you." I use my hands a lot when I talk, so I dropped the bottle of Carpet Fresh on her doorstep and emphasized my next point about hunger. "Now, you haven't eaten all morning. Your nerves were jangling because you were worried about what your doctor would tell you. As you walk out the front doors of his clinic—"

"Are you going anywhere with this? I have to get off my hip. Please hurry."

"Yes, ma'am. Almost done. As you walk out the front doors of his clinic, you see a beautiful diner across the street. You can smell whatever it is they're cooking. The sign out front says *All you can eat bacon==> FREE!* You know the trick. Buy some eggs and get all the bacon you want. Your stomach turns with the smell. You're going to be hospitalized that afternoon. This is your last chance to splurge, to dazzle yourself with the second love of your life—bacon."

"Is there a question in there somewhere?"

I continued as if she hadn't interrupted. "Even though it's free and you know it's not good for you, would you still eat that bacon? Even though it could kill you? The parallel is, even though they clean your carpet for basically free, after the damage I show you they're doing to your home, would you still have them over, son or not?"

I waited. Sometimes direct questions like this get a slammed door in the face. Other times you've intrigued them enough to take the bait and let you in to see what you're made of.

This was that case. I had her. I saw a subtle change in her eyes.

The woman stepped back.

"Okay, you win," she said. "Get your vacuum, and let's see what happens, but I promise you, I won't be buying one. Just do the carpet and show me the results. We'll go from there. I'll leave the door open because I must sit down now."

She limped away from the open door. I turned and ran down Maple Street to my Pontiac, drove to the front of her house, and retrieved the boxed vacuum from the trunk. After carrying it to her door, I stepped in, closed the door behind me, and quietly locked it. I always lock the doors for our protection. You never know what psychos might walk in while I'm doing a presentation.

I took off my shoes and placed them neatly beside a beautiful pair of red Jimmy Choos. They sat up so pretty. A small heel and a lovely strap with little diamonds on it. Wow, the woman had class. These shoes also got me charged with murder, even though I didn't do it. Mrs. Gavin had less than two hours before she would be bludgeoned to death with a rolling pin and a meat tenderizer.

Although I couldn't know that at the time.

***

I entered her living room, got my vacuum out of the box, and set everything up. The display model, or as we call it, *our partner*, has an added piece that the customer's models don't have. It's a little circular window on the right by the air intake. It has small clasps to undo the top. I opened it and placed one of my hundred black cloths in it so we could see what my machine would pull from her carpet.

"What are you doing?" Mrs. Gavin asked. "It was just vacuumed yesterday."

"I must vacuum the carpet first to ensure no grit or sand is in it. Otherwise, when I'm shampooing, the sand will cut the fibers of your carpet. My goal is to clean the carpet, not damage it." I said this with my best car-salesman smile. "After I've gone over it and nothing else comes up, we can go right to shampooing."

She nodded and waved her hand to say, *carry on.*

What they don't understand is that I'm a Master Closer. Nobody gets it. No one understands me. I'm not a traditional salesman. I'm a Master Closer. Everything I do is to close the sale. Getting in the door is step one. Show the dirt is step two. Steps three and four get convoluted because, in each house, it's different, but eventually, I get the shoes. Then I leave. Whether they buy the vacuum or not, I get the shoes.

No one denies me the shoes. Ever.

I began vacuuming. Mrs. Gavin sat in the middle of her couch watching, her eyes brimming with suspicion.

The black cloth filled with dirt immediately. I stopped, unclipped the lid, and laid it flat on her carpet. I put a new cloth in the glass, clipped it, and resumed vacuuming. I repeated this process ten times and then stopped and looked at her.

Mrs. Gavin's eyes widened. "That's a lot of dirt," was all she could say.

I nodded. "Yeah, sorry about that. When did you say this carpet was vacuumed last?"

"Yesterday," she said, a dazed expression on her face.

"And when did your son's company clean it?"

"A few weeks ago."

"What kind of a vacuum do you own?"

She looked at me. This is where the sale turns my way. Crucial moment. Time stopper. Egg popper. Head cracker, kill her and stack her. Here we go.

"I use the Luxor Elite model, why?"

I shook my head and stared at the dirt as if she had just told me she was an addicted gambler and a thief. "Oh, my," I whispered. "That's why you have all this dirt."

I turned away and flipped my vacuum on. After a moment, I stopped to change the black cloth again.

"I don't understand," she said. "What's wrong with my vacuum?"

I turned to her. "You see the unit I'm using. It's an upright. No suction is lost with long hoses. The mouth where all the dirt comes in is right beside the powerful engine. The filter is in front of the engine. Not a single piece of junk gets near the motor in my unit. In the Luxor, the engine isn't filtered properly, so performance is jeopardized, and it's not an upright. You have a long hose. Think of it like this: a fire will destroy a home better than ten men outside trying to blow it down."

She frowned.

"The fire is this unit. Your Luxor is just blowing wind. This brings me to my next point." I started vacuuming again. "Do you have fire insurance on your home?" I raised my voice to be heard over the vacuum.

I turned the unit off and unclipped another black cloth, placing it next to the others.

"Of course I do. Why do you ask?"

I stopped and turned to her. "Really?" I sounded surprised. "Well, have you ever collected? I mean, have you ever had a house burn down?"

She looked away, obviously unsure where I was going with this. They never do. "That's an odd question."

I continued as if she had said nothing. "So you pay a monthly or a yearly charge for insurance against a fire, and yet you've never had one. If you added up all the money you've spent insuring against fire, I'd be surprised if it wasn't in the thousands over the years. Possibly more."

Mrs. Gavin was biting on her index finger. Something troubled her, and it wasn't where I was going with this. Maybe it was the twitching in my right eye. It gets like that when I'm about to steal a pair of shoes. Or perhaps it was my voice. In the moments of closing, I can get as passionate as a preacher on a Sunday morning tirade.

"My point is this. You're spending so much on something that has never happened and probably never will happen, yet *dirt* happens. It's right there." I pointed at the square black cloths covered in the dirt from her carpet. "And yet you're not paying for the right equipment.

You own a Luxor and get deals on carpet shampooing."

I turned away to let her think about it and started my last bit of vacuuming.

"How much does yours cost?" she asked.

And that was the last question Mrs. Gavin asked.

I gazed back at her and turned off the vacuum. "I have a question for you," I said, my finger raised for emphasis. "If you received a check in the mail for three dollars every day, would you be rich? Could you go out and buy a Benz or a new Porsche?"

She shook her head, biting away at her middle finger now. The sun shone through her living room window at an odd angle casting an ugly light on her wrinkles.

"Let's flip it. Would you be poor if you got a bill in the mail for three dollars a day? Would you have to declare bankruptcy? Would it all be over?"

She shook her head again and started in on the other hand, biting at her fingernails like they were enemies worthy of her teeth alone.

"That's what this baby costs; three dollars a day. On our plan, they're only ninety dollars a month."

Really, they're actually $1899.00, but when you reduce it to the ridiculous, the numbers say that more people buy.

The proof is in the numbers, and it's all a numbers game.

She seemed stunned. Something was wrong. I could feel it. Now was the time to deal with the rest of my business.

"Ma'am, with all this dirt, could I go and wash my hands?"

She nodded, and I stepped into the kitchen. She was quite the decorator. Everything in this room had colorful items placed on it. The fridge was a mirage of pictures and drawings from her grandchildren, no doubt. Knickknacks littered the top of the microwave and parts of the countertop. I pay close attention to kitchens. They say a lot about the people I vacuum for.

Beside the stove, I saw what I was looking for. A pottery-like container that held cooking utensils. I found a nice chopping blade, a whisk, two wooden spoons, and many other items. Who knew the meat tenderizer would be used in such a horrible manner in such a short time from then?

I turned on the kitchen sink to mask the sound of the drawers I was about to open.

I write this freely because any law enforcement officer reading it could only charge me with theft and snooping.

(*Drop the first-degree murder charge, please. I'm innocent.*)

The second drawer contained baking tools. The rolling pin lay there, innocent and not very threatening by itself. (*It wasn't covered in blood and matted hair yet.*)

I pulled it out to look at it. I touched other things, along with the meat tenderizer. (*That's why they have my fingerprints. Is there any law against touching things? Fuck!*)

I washed my hands and stepped back into the living room. Mrs. Gavin was compliant. She didn't ask any more questions. She sat on the couch and stared at me. I finished masturbating and then cleaned up the carpet with the shampoo attachment on the vacuum.

Afterward, I took my display vacuum to the door and began packing things.

"Mrs. Gavin, thank you for allowing me to demonstrate my vacuum's power to you today. It's been a pleasure to show you its prowess."

I always talk to the client in their hallway to judge how far they are from me as I'm slipping their shoes into my vacuum box. The nice pair of Jimmy Choos fit comfortably around the neck of the vacuum. The box's lid went on, and I was ready to leave.

"You have a nice day now, Mrs. Gavin."

I could smell something off. Something is coming from the living room. Maybe she ate beans yesterday. How could I know?

I opened her front door and peeked out at the street. It was empty. I took a moment to step back and look at Mrs. Gavin before leaving her home. She hadn't been too talkative during the last part of my demonstration.

She was still on the couch, although she was leaning to the right a lot more now. It must've been her bad hip. The sun was higher. It touched her below the knees, showing off her varicose veins nicely. They were so prominent that it almost looked like the blood was on the outside of her body.

I shook my head. Maybe I had a premonition about her death. Maybe I was looking at death.

I turned away, not caring for the smell coming from her.

The street remained empty. I stepped out and shut the door behind me. I was clean as I'd washed my hands in the bathroom after masturbating on the carpet in front of her. No one could tell what went on in that house. There were no witnesses whatsoever.

I offered her a carpet shampoo for free. She took it. I gave her a bottle of Carpet Fresh. She allowed me in. I did everything right. I stole her shoes, but is that a crime worthy of a death sentence?

I put the vacuum in the trunk of my car and drove home.

Later that night, at about 3:15 a.m., someone knocked incessantly on my apartment door. I remember it was exactly 3:15 a.m.

"What the fuck?" I yelled through the door. "Who the hell's out there?"

"Police. Open up."

My heart sank, and my stomach dropped. How's that? Why would they be here? What could I have done?

Realizing I had no choice, I opened the door, even though I was still in my underwear.

Four police officers stood behind two men in business suits. One of the suits looked like David Caruso on that television police show. The other cop looked like an asshole with his goatee perfectly trimmed and his earring dangling down like a faggot. I would later find out he was. An asshole and a faggot.

"Trevor Ashton?" Asshole asked.

"Yeah, that's me. What's up?"

Asshole motioned with his hands to the four uniforms behind him, and they rushed me, grabbing my arms and handcuffing me.

"Hey," I protested.

"You're under arrest for the murder of Eleanor Gavin. You have the right to remain silent. You have the right to an attorney …"

"I know my Miranda rights. Shut the fuck up and tell me why you're arresting me. What do I have to do with this woman?"

They pushed me against a wall so hard that I lost my balance and fell into the carpeted hallway of my apartment building. I could tell the superintendent wasn't using the kind of vacuum I sell.

Asshole leaned down and whispered his evidence in my ear like he was asking to fuck me.

"We found her body bludgeoned with a meat tenderizer and a rolling pin. She was torn apart on her living room couch. It was so bad that her abdomen was literally shredded, evacuating her bowels on the carpet. One of her neighbors spotted your car out front. It took us over a dozen hours to track you down through your license plate number, but we did. And guess what?"

He stopped and smiled at me. My heart was pounding so fast I thought he could hear its drum roll as well as I could.

"We found the killer's DNA all over the house. Hairs in the bathroom and kitchen sink. Fingerprints are still being lifted in her kitchen, but you wanna know what the best part is? The killer's semen is still on her carpet, and some dripped on her corpse. We retrieved a fresh sample from her right breast an hour after she was killed. Well, what was left of her breast. My guess is we'll find out that semen is yours."

I panicked. Of course, I panicked. Some of the demonstrations I do can turn kinky. As I said previously, I stole her shoes. For me, it's all about shoes. Sure I masturbate, but is that against the law? I asked Mrs. Gavin for permission. She had nodded yes. She even allowed me to finish anywhere I wanted in the house or on her body. Now, tell me, with that kind of consent, where does a courtroom get the right to question mature adults?

I waited until they got me to my feet and flipped out.

"You got the wrong guy!" I screamed. I turned to the wall and pulled the fire alarm with my front teeth.

"I didn't do anything—"

It was probably getting close to four in the morning. The cops were super pissed that I had caused so much raucous. They jumped on me and threw a couple of punches in, too. Then their combined weight left my back.

Something poked me in the ass cheek. I have never felt anything quite as horrifying and exhilarating as being tased. I flopped and bounced on the floor like a dying cockroach. I pissed myself and begged for it to stop.

They hit me again.

One of my neighbors opened their door at the sound of the fire alarm.

Within minutes the cops had me on my feet and were escorting me —carrying me, actually—to the waiting prisoner van.

I felt special. A whole van just for me. Yippie.

Assholes.

I was booked and placed in a holding cell. The next morning they brought me in front of a judge who felt, based on what they had already found at the crime scene, that I was a flight risk. I was ordered held until trial.

That was eight months ago. Since then, I have festered in this rat hole. I can't sell vacuums, and I can't collect shoes.

I've often seen a prison guard with a great pair of Reeboks, but the bars hold me back. I still masturbate, but it's not as much fun.

In my eight months awaiting trial, I've written to shoe companies to receive their mail-order catalogs, but my mail is inspected before it gets to me. I asked what harm there was in perusing picture catalogs. I went so far as to explain that they were my form of pornography. But still, the guards won't let me have them.

There's one more part I must cover before leaving this note for whoever finds it.

They gave me legal aid. I got a lawyer to talk to me two days after being incarcerated. His name was Delroy Conrad. He said he could get me off. I remember saying some half-assed comment like, 'Oh *really*.' He didn't like my attitude or sense of humor.

Another asshole.

Anyway, he's arriving here in ten minutes, so I will sum this up.

I didn't kill Mrs. Gavin. I touched her rolling pin and meat tenderizer. I touched her kitchen and bathroom. I even touched her, but that was because she offered consent. I stole her shoes. I have broken the law. But I didn't kill her.

Someone was in the house with me at the time and murdered her moments after my departure, or someone entered the house as soon as I left.

It wasn't me.

I love shoes. They're my religion. They're what drive me. But not just any shoes. They can't be store-bought. They have to have been worn by a woman. I love men's shoes, but not in the same way.

That is what it's all about.

Shoes.

***

Trevor set the pen down and massaged his aching fingers. He had just over five minutes left until the lawyer showed.

He piled the papers together and folded them in half, and then placed them under his mattress. A door opened down the corridor. Footsteps approached. A guard stepped up to his bars.

"Open on eight," the guard shouted.

There was an audible click as the lock disengaged, and then the bars began to roll.

"You have a visitor, Ashton. Let's go."

Another guard stepped into view. Both of them escorted Trevor along the corridor. They didn't handcuff him. They weren't rough. There was nowhere to go, even if he decided to run.

The gray walls enhanced how he felt on the inside. He hated being here. He was in his late forties. It was time to think about the latter years of his life. Beating this murder charge was all that mattered, and his legal aid lawyer said he could do it seven months ago.

Today would be the day Trevor found out how the investigation was going. He had looked forward to this day with a sense of trepidation and elation. He remained hopeful that he could be released later in the day.

Wouldn't that be something? The first thing I'd do when I walk out of here would be buying a celebratory drink and steal some shoes.

He entered the dank room where his lawyer waited. Delroy's briefcase sat open on the long table. Papers were strewn about in front of him.

He gestured for Trevor to take a seat. Then he turned toward the guards and said, "It's okay. I've got it from here."

Trevor turned back and watched the two guards leave. He glanced down at their shoes and wondered if he'd ever get his hands on a good pair of Reeboks.

"Please, sit," Delroy said.

"You got good news for me?" Trevor asked.

"I've got news, but I think you need to be sitting to deal with it."

That didn't sound like *you're going home* or *I got the charges dropped*. That sounded more like *you're fucked*.

He decided that sitting may be better. He had wallowed for eight months in prison, and they had no witnesses to the murder. All they had was him at the scene and a valid explanation of why. How could that be murder one?

He pulled out the chair and turned it around to straddle it, his arms on the backrest. This way, if things got shitty fast, he could find comfort in looking under the table at his lawyer's leather shoes.

"We have problems with your defense," the lawyer stated.

"What problems? It's cut and dried. I didn't do it."

Delroy held up his hand. "Fair enough. But we still have problems. The prosecutor has decided to profile this case and make a name for himself."

Trevor shot up from the chair fast, almost knocking it over. "Whoa! Profile the case? What the fuck does that mean?"

The door behind him opened with a bang. Three guards entered.

"Everything okay here?" the lead guard asked, a baton in his hand.

Delroy nodded. "Everything's fine. We're okay. You can leave us."

The guards filed out slowly and shut the door behind them.

"You have to remain calm. Remember, you're being held on first-degree murder charges. Those guys out there," he motioned toward the door, "are on edge when you jump around like that. Now sit down and stay seated. We have to get through this."

Trevor's hands shook as he reclaimed his seat. This time he sat in the chair the way it was supposed to be used and pushed it up to the table, resting his elbows on the cold metal surface.

Fuck him and his shoes. I don't want to see them anymore. If I'm really going down for murder, he'll be my next victim if he fucks up my case.

"The prosecution is saying you're the next James Lloyd or Jerome Brudos. That's going to be an easy sell with the jury after what they found in your apartment."

"What did they find in my apartment?" Trevor asked.

"Shoes. Women's shoes, mostly. Some were defiled and covered in old semen. They're still looking for the original owners of the shoes found in your apartment."

"Those two names you mentioned, James and Jerome, who are they?" Trevor asked, completely ignoring the comment about shoes.

Delroy shuffled papers around. He opened a folder and then set it in front of him.

"James Lloyd was arrested in 2006. He was known as the Thurnscoe Shoe Rapist. Thurnscoe is a small village in England. He was arrested twenty years after his first rape. He was found to have over two hundred pairs of women's stiletto shoes that he kept at his workplace as trophies."

"That's not me," Trevor said as he shifted in his seat.

"Jerome Brudos was an American serial killer. They called him *'The Shoe Fetish Slayer.'* After killing his female victims, he'd amputate their feet and dress them up in his vast collection of ladies' shoes. I mean, we're talking some pretty fucked-up people here."

A rage built inside Trevor that he'd only ever felt when dealing with his mother. He wasn't like those idiots. He wasn't going to make it in a trial. He would never be able to sit still while some dickhead prosecutor inferred that he was the same as those other assholes. He'd rather be dead.

Delroy had stopped talking and just stared at Trevor.

"You okay?" he asked.

Trevor nodded.

"You want me to go on?"

Trevor nodded again, struggling to control himself.

"Okay," Delroy said. "They're going to argue that a shoe fetish is an attraction to shoes, or other footwear, on a sexual level, and that when you steal the shoes, it's like a trophy. Certain serial killers will often take a trophy from their conquests. They're also going to say it's a psychosexual disorder and refer to it as *retifism* because of what some French novelist did with shoes in the late 1700s."

"I can see we have a problem," Trevor said, his teeth clenching so hard he felt his jaw cracking.

"What do you see the problem is?" Delroy asked, raising his pen to his lips, where he began to chew on the tip.

"You say *because of some French novelist* blah, blah, blah. That tells me you haven't even researched it. You have no details about it. The problem is, how can you be my defense if you don't have a defense? You aren't working hard enough. I have a right to a fair trial, for fuck sake."

Delroy set the pen on the table. "Trevor. Look me in the eye and tell me, did you murder Eleanor Gavin, or did you not murder her?"

Trevor couldn't believe it. His own lawyer was questioning his guilt. He wasn't on trial yet. This asshole was supposed to defend him. Innocent until proven guilty. What happened to The Pursuit of Happiness, the American Way, white picket fences, and shit?

"I'm innocent. I did nothing wrong. Yes, I'll admit, I love shoes. That's not creepy. What about people who tie each other up or men dressed as babies in submissive role-playing bullshit? That's not me. I just like shoes. I'm the normal one here, and if you can't provide me with a good defense, I'll have to retain another lawyer. I mean, seriously!"

Delroy gathered up the papers on the table. He tossed everything into his briefcase and then slammed it shut.

"Tell me one more thing," Delroy said.

Trevor tapped his foot incessantly. It was all he could do to hold himself back from Delroy's throat.

"What does the key unlock?"

Warning bells triggered in Trevor's head. Pinging noises resounded between his ears. He thought he heard a fire truck somewhere, but that was impossible. Too much concrete in this building.

He collected himself and tried to drown out the noise in his head.

"What. Key. Are. You. Asking. About?" He stopped on each word. It was time for Delroy to learn that he wasn't dealing with a psycho. This legal aid bastard was dealing with a professional. An innocent one.

"Investigating officers found a key to a storage unit or a warehouse of some kind when they searched your apartment. After eight months, they're stumped as to what it opens. It would go a long way in your defense to cooperate. You could do that by telling me what that key opens."

"I have zero idea what you are talking about."

Trevor leaned back in his chair and crossed his arms. They'd never figure out where the key goes. He used an alias when he rented the storage unit. The original key was thrown away after he had it remade so that the storage unit name wouldn't be on it. Things would get very interesting if they found what was in that unit.

"Well, I guess that's it," Delroy said as he stood up.

"What's it?"

"I'll give everything I have to your new lawyer when he's appointed."

Trevor turned his head sideways and unclasped his arms.

"What?"

"I quit the case. I'll ask the judge to release me as I can't properly defend you."

Delroy motioned for the guards.

"Why can't you *properly* defend me?" *Properly* came out sounding like a whiny little girl's voice.

"Because, Mr. Ashton, I don't feel you're innocent. They found your semen on the woman's breast. From what we know of Eleanor Gavin, she wouldn't allow that while alive. There's no way she would've consented."

Trevor heard keys going into and unlocking the doors behind him. He couldn't believe what Delroy was saying. There were no witnesses. How could anyone suppose what Eleanor would like and would not like?

"She was a regular church member," Delroy continued. "She fought for women's rights. She broke her hip when she tripped while helping an eighty-year-old woman move a piece of furniture. Eleanor never married. As far as investigators could tell, she was a lesbian. So why would she give consent for a vacuum cleaner salesman to ejaculate on her person? The jury won't buy it. I'm done with this case and—"

Trevor dove, hands outstretched. He had heard enough. He clamped onto Delroy's throat before his body hit the table between them. He tightened his grip and held on tight. Then he rolled sideways, causing the lawyer to bend over and roll with him.

Hands grabbed at his feet but were denied purchase. In under three seconds, the lawyer had hit the ground with Trevor on top of him, digging deep into Delroy's trachea.

It felt like a wall had caved in when one of the guard's bodies checked him off the lawyer. Trevor took the impact on his right, throwing him four feet into the steel wall of the room. His head spun for a moment, eyes blurred.

Then they hit him again.

After that hit, he saw nothing else as his vision faded to black.

***

Trevor woke in the infirmary. A doctor was dressing a wound near his eye.

The sharp pain of the doctor touching the injury made Trevor jump and try to knock the doctor's hand away. He came up short as his wrists were handcuffed to a gurney.

"Leave me the fuck alone!" he shouted at the doctor.

"Afraid I can't do that. Gotta fix you up."

"What'd they do to me?" Trevor asked as he mentally did an inventory of his aches and pains.

"Nothing I can't fix."

"Anything broken?"

"Nope. Massive bruising on the face and arms, but nothing was broken. You got off easy."

"Hmmph."

Trevor eased back in the bed and let the doctor do his work. He spent his time plotting and evaluating.

After a while, the doctor left and shut the lights out.

Trevor slept.

When he woke, he was back in his cell. The letter he wrote was exactly where he had left it. He held it up to the light and read every single word. Nothing implicated him. He lay back on his mattress, although tenderly, and got ready to fall asleep with a smile on his face.

Things could be worse, he thought. *I'm going to beat this, and then I'll add to my shoe collection. The proof is in the numbers. Trust the process. Follow and respect.*

I will walk.
One day, I will walk.

***

It took three months for a new lawyer to be appointed and brought up to speed on Trevor's case. They were set to meet in the same room he met Delroy, his previous lawyer. When Trevor entered, he had shackles on his wrists and ankles.

"Ah, guards, that won't be necessary," the lawyer said, pointing at the restraints.

"Sorry, boss, but they stay on. Didn't you hear what happened the last time he met with his lawyer?"

"Okay fine. Leave us. Trevor, why don't you waddle over here and have a seat?"

Trevor liked his new lawyer immediately. Slicked back hair, wire-rimmed glasses pointed up on each side like they held more purpose than just corrective lenses and a confident, don't-fuck-with-me way about him. He remained on his feet until Trevor could *waddle* over and sit. Trevor didn't turn the chair around this time. He didn't want to look at the new lawyer's shoes. He was done with that for now. Prison had weakened his resolve over the last three months.

What more could another lawyer do for him anyway?

At least the table was clean of papers. The attorney's briefcase sat on the floor, unopened.

"Good news," the lawyer said as he pulled his chair in and sat down.

"Okay," Trevor nodded for him to go on. "Let's hear it."

"I'd offer to shake your hand, but you kinda can't right now, so we'll dispense with the formalities. My name is Vincenzo Marconi. I was assigned to your case two months ago. I read the previous lawyer's files and almost got *my* gun to shoot him."

This made Trevor giggle. He tried to catch himself, but it was too late.

"It's okay, laugh. If I was in your shoes, I'd … oh, sorry, I didn't mean to talk about shoes. Anyway, his files were all fucked. Once I wrapped my head around everything, I asked questions, and guess what I found out?"

"I have zero idea what you found out," Trevor said. "I've been kinda busy lately with dinner parties and functions."

"Okay, I get it. Tough being locked up. No problem because today is your lucky day."

"How's that?"

Suspicion peppered Trevor's thoughts. He'd spent almost a year waiting in prison for a trial that kept getting put off. A new lawyer sat before him, saying there was good news. What could possibly be that good? What could make this lawyer smile like he was?

"I requestioned the witness."

Trevor shot forward. "There were no witnesses!"

"Calm down, calm down. Yes, there was. One witness. Eleanor Gavin's neighbor who called in your plate number."

"Oh, okay, sorry. What'd they say?"

"The neighbor couldn't be sure of the time of day. You see, they're placing the time of death somewhere between 12:30 p.m. and 2:30 p.m. We have you entering the house before lunch. I can prove that your vacuum demonstration was less than an hour. You weren't present at the time of the murder."

Trevor leaned forward. "You know something?"

"What?"

"You sound like a lawyer. I like that. The other guy didn't. He sounded like a jackass."

Vincenzo ignored his comment. "That's all the prosecution has.

Check this out," the lawyer said, using his hands in the air like he was playing a saxophone.

What is it with the Italians and hands?

"I requested to see the original search warrant and found a problem. It's something that happens a lot. Pretty common, actually."

"What happens a lot? What are you talking about?"

"It's a technical problem that got the search warrant voided."

"Voided? How's that possible?" Trevor allowed hope to permeate his thoughts.

The lawyer set both elbows on the table and tented his fingers. "Pieces of the warrant were copied and pasted from a different case. *'The suspect confessed to the crime'* part wasn't deleted from the warrant. You didn't confess. Therefore, the warrant the judge signed was false. Ultimately, the judge was tricked, making the warrant null and void. This results in suppressing all the evidence from your apartment. The prosecution only has a neighbor with your license plate, but that's explained away. You were there doing a vacuum demonstration." Vincenzo leaned back and set his hands on his thighs. He shook his head back and forth. "Your previous defense attorney was a shit. This kind of thing can be easily overlooked when there are thousands of pages of police reports, but a good lawyer will find it. This means they have nothing on you. You're free to go as soon as we do the paperwork."

Trevor's eyes shot wide. "So the warrant thing is that important?"

"You bet your five-dollar shoes it is. It's called a search violation."

Why all the jokes about shoes? What the fuck is up with this guy?

"It's important enough to get you out of here," Vincenzo added.

"You serious? This isn't a joke?"

"No joke. They have to drop all the charges on the technicality and release you. This case is over. It's done. In two hours, they're doing the paperwork. You'll be free to go. And you'll never see the inside of a courtroom. How's that for important enough?"

"Holy shit, fuck a goose and see if she's loose. That's great news. But what about my other lawyer?"

"What about him?"

"I attacked him in here. I assaulted him."

Vincenzo waved his hand. "Nothing to worry about. I showed the judge how bad his files were and how you weren't being given a fair trial. Of course, you'd be angry about that. Especially an innocent guy being wrongly accused. Delroy isn't pressing charges. He could if he wanted to, but he knows I would embarrass his ass."

"Wow."

"This is your first step forward in a brand new pair of shoes. How does it feel?"

Another reference to shoes ... I think I just figured out your game. I got you, motherfucker. I know what you're doing. How could I have been so stupid?

"It feels great," Trevor said.

Sweat beaded on his forehead. He looked around to see who was watching. A camera sat in the corner near the roof, red light blinking.

I'm being duped.

"Oh, don't worry about that camera. We get privacy in here. It's part of the rules."

Vincenzo set his briefcase on the metal table and opened it. He presented documents for Trevor to sign.

Two hours later, Trevor Ashton was released from prison. His lawyer had brought Trevor's car around for him.

They shook hands, and Trevor drove away as the sun dropped toward dusk.

He knew what they were doing. You can't sell a salesman.

And he knew how he would get them for it.

He would make them all pay.

No one fucks with Trevor Ashton and gets away with it.

***

Trevor sat in his Pontiac and waited for the streetlights to come on. Freedom was to be had tonight. He knew their plan. He'd figured it out. But his plan was better, and it had taken all four days since his release to set it up.

Nobody pulls the wool over my eyes. Nobody.

He checked his mirrors. A few vehicles drove past his car, but nothing looked untoward. As far as Trevor could tell, no one was watching him.

He looked down at the passenger seat. The Louisville Slugger sat smiling up at him. He could almost hear it talking to him, caressing his ear with words of duty and honor. It would do what it was made for. It would serve him. It would be loyal. But most of all, it wouldn't judge him.

He looked in the rearview mirror again and saw someone sitting in his back seat.

"Hello, Mrs. Gavin." Trevor didn't jump or get startled. It was a common event when the owners of the shoes he had recently stolen would pay him a visit. They often hung around for days on end. She hadn't visited him in prison, but it was hard to get in there. After stealing another pair of shoes, he'd get a new visitor. They always watched when he would masturbate on their shoes. He knew they enjoyed watching him, so he let them.

"Trevor," she said.

"Lovely evening," he said.

She nodded at him. "Why are you going to do it? You don't have to."

"I do have to. I need my freedom."

"But those women are innocent."

"Isn't everyone?" he asked. "I'm innocent."

"Trevor, walk away. The lawyer wasn't playing you. You're too smart for that. Let it go."

Trevor looked across the street at the shoe store. It was 9:21 p.m. They would be closing in nine minutes. He had to leave in seven.

"They played me. I know their kind. But tonight, they pay for it."

"You used to work at a shoe store," Mrs. Gavin said. "Over ten years until you got fired. All those women you sold shoes to and then looked their names up off their credit cards. Following them home and taking the shoes they'd bought." Mrs. Gavin looked down at her lap. "Trevor, how many women have you killed?"

"I'm smart. They will never catch me."

"Trevor, how many?"

"I lost count after I'd collected 120 pairs of shoes. Sometimes I'd killed them but didn't get the shoes in time. Only two had been unconscious and walked away, but they didn't report it to the police. I got them both days later. Don't worry, Mrs. Gavin, I clean up my mistakes."

"Is that why you started selling vacuums? To clean up after and have a plausible reason to be in the victim's house?"

"What is this? Why are you so curious? You're dead. Fuck off."

He looked at the clock: 9:26 p.m.

Almost time to go.

Trevor eased out of the driver's seat and walked around to his trunk. He opened it and retrieved two red cans filled with gasoline. After slamming the trunk, he opened the passenger side door and grabbed his partner, Louisville.

A distant pair of headlights were coming toward him. They were too far to see him yet. He hustled across the street to the little strip mall and opened the shoe store's front door.

A young female clerk walked toward him, key in hand.

"Oh, sorry, sir, but we're just about to close. Could you come back tomorrow?"

He set the gas cans down and looked to the right. Another clerk was helping a woman in her forties try on a pair of black heels. He counted three women in total.

"I'm sorry. I was on my way home from the baseball game," he said, then pointed at the gas cans. "I ran out of gas. My car is a block away, and then I remembered my wife said she needed a pair of red pumps. I cannot go home without a red pair of pumps, size eight."

He smiled in his best car salesman role.

The clerk with the key couldn't be over twenty-five years old. She looked at the other clerk with a question on her face. The other clerk nodded.

"Let me lock the door, so no one else comes in, and then we'll set you up."

"Oh, thank you so much. Thank you."

Trevor glanced at the display on the far wall looking for the pumps. They were behind the older clerk who was still helping her customer. He saw Mrs. Gavin standing in the corner, shaking her head. He almost shouted for her to leave. These women were his. He was already getting an erection, and Mrs. Gavin would ruin it all for him.

After locking the door, the young clerk pulled down the blinds on the two large front windows and yanked the chain on the OPEN neon sign to turn it off.

He leaned on Louisville and waited for her.

She pocketed the store key and said, "What you're looking for is right over there."

She didn't see it coming. He leaned down as if to set the bat on the floor, but he was winding up. Louisville came around in a smooth arc and connected with the side of the clerk's head. It hit her so hard that he heard the audible crack of her skull. She didn't make a sound as she crumpled to the floor at his feet.

He couldn't believe his luck. A home run on the first hit.

He turned to the other women. Both their faces were masks of shock. They were paralyzed with fear. Neither one moved.

He jumped around a square floor display of sandals. His wooden partner hit the back of the customer's head as she tried to duck, knocking her to the floor.

"Now, if that isn't a sack of potatoes, I don't know what is," he yelled. "I should've tried out for the majors."

The older clerk was screaming now. She bolted for the back room. Trevor gave chase.

Damn is she fast, he thought.

Behind the counter, around a corner, into the small doorway, and into the back room, he chased her. She tossed shoe boxes down behind her. He tripped over a couple and lost ground as she ran for the back door.

"Fuck!"

He righted himself and continued to run, hopping over boxes and dodging the others.

She was five feet from the back door. She would disappear in seconds.

He stopped, wound up, and threw the baseball bat. The bat raced across the open air, pinwheeling as it went.

It was a perfect throw, but at the moment, it would have hit her head, she made the door and dropped from view as she turned the corner.

The bat hit the outside stairwell railing and clanged down the stairs behind the fleeing clerk.

"Fuck, fuck, fuuucckkk!"

"She's going to call the police," Mrs. Gavin whispered in his ear.

"I know."

He ran to the back door and looked outside. She was gone. Nothing moved at all. He grabbed his partner off the stairs, locked the door, and bolted the three locks along its frame.

Then he ran back to the front and retrieved one gas can. He opened it and soaked the front of the store in gasoline. He grabbed the other can, coughed a few times at the fumes, and ran for the stockroom. He started near the back door and began soaking everything around it. With all the shoes and cardboard boxes, he knew the shoe store would burn fast.

He had done it before. When they almost caught him at his previous job selling shoes, he had to burn the store down. Almost didn't get out that time, but he had a better plan tonight.

After emptying both cans of their burden, he tossed them aside and returned to the two women lying dead or unconscious on the carpeted floor.

The fumes were fast becoming overwhelming.

"You should've done this first and then poured out the gas," Mrs. Gavin said.

"Fuck off, Mrs. Gavin. Don't need you, bitch."

The young clerk wore running shoes. Nothing very sexy about that. He turned to the customer. Her feet were bare because she was about to try on a pair of shoes. He glanced around and found the boots in which she had come to the store. They were worn and ugly, with a small zipper on the side.

"Motherfucker. I hate when they aren't sexy shoes. Now I can't even finish on these women. Ugly fucking whores."

He grabbed the bat and pounded it on the wall two feet in front of the counter. He knew exactly where to make contact. Yesterday, he played the role of a comic book store owner from Los Angeles. He was in the area scouting locations for the next big store. The landlord of the strip mall had given him a tour of the empty unit beside the shoe store.

There was no alarm system currently monitoring the empty unit. Yesterday he saw that the lock was a thumb latch on the inside. It would work perfectly.

After ten hits with his loyal partner, he had broken through the drywall. The hole was big enough to crawl through.

He brought out a pack of matches, lit one, and tossed it toward the back room. Instantly the gas caught, flames rising like a witch-burning in Salem. A second match produced the same result at the front of the small shoe store.

He waited and watched. It was good to burn. He loved the heat.

Mrs. Gavin stared at him from the far corner. She was shaking her head in disgust.

He flipped her the bird.

The young clerk's hair caught. He waited a moment more to watch her skin start to melt and bubble up near her neck.

Trevor smiled wide. He was free. This is what freedom meant. Freewill. To do as he pleased. At all times.

He slid a leg through the hole and bent to pass into the empty unit. Then someone started screaming.

He looked back into the store. The customer had woken up. The hit must not have been as hard as he figured. She got to her feet and scurried around, her hair and face aflame.

The wail that came out of those melting lips caused Trevor to almost tear up in pleasure. A light fixture popped from the heat, making him jump.

He laughed.

"My job is only half done tonight. Gotta go. Bye, ladies."

He slipped the rest of the way through the hole and ran to the back of the empty unit. It was an L-shaped unit with a back door on the side of the complex. This meant that if someone was watching the front of the shoe store or the back, they couldn't see him exit.

He opened the side door slowly. No one was around.

Trevor slipped out, closed the door, and ran along the building toward a side street where, two blocks up, he'd parked a rented van.

He walked slowly so as not to attract unnecessary attention. A siren wailed in the distance. A woman screamed. It had to be the older clerk that had gotten away. She had probably called the authorities and was now watching the flames burn her co-worker.

All in a day's work for Trevor.

Mrs. Gavin was gone.

Maybe that young clerk will come to talk to me now. Or maybe not. I didn't steal her shoes, after all.

He got to the van, started it, and raced away from the burning shoe store, intent on finishing the evening properly.

***

They were obligated to give him back his key when they'd released him from prison. The one that nobody could figure out what it opened.

He thought about that as he pulled up in front of his storage unit. No one had followed him, and he was sure the storage unit premises were empty as he hadn't seen anyone.

He opened the unit and stared at all the boxes of shoes and mementos from the whores he had killed. He was amazed at what he had amassed over the last fifteen years.

A cool evening breeze picked up and brushed across his face as he felt emotions rising in him. It brought him back to when his mother dressed him up in high heels at age five. She'd always wanted a girl. She even called him girl's names until he was ten years old. He demanded to be called Trevor, as that was his real name, but his mother never cared.

She'd beat him and humiliate him for being male, but he got used to it. He wanted to be a girl so that he could please his mother. But nothing pleased her. Nothing ever could.

He recalled the day he killed her. He was nineteen. She was sitting alone in the living room, knitting another pair of pink winter gloves because he always lost his.

Of course, I lost them, you fucking whore. I'd never wear that shit.

The thought brought his smile to a solid line. Whenever he recalled memories of his mother, he brooded. She got off too easy. He should have hacked her to pieces instead of using the pillow on her face to suffocate her. He should have torn her vagina out to make her a man.

Just to see how it feels, bitch, just to see how it feels.

After all the times she kicked or punched him in the groin, she'd explain that it wouldn't hurt that much if he didn't have that fucking stuff. He couldn't remember a week where she didn't kick him in the balls or try to tear them off. He was surprised when he grew up that everything still worked.

"Yeah, well, fuck you, Mom. You're dead, and I'm sending as many whores as possible to hell with you. I'm sure you need the company."

He began to unload the storage unit, filling the back of the van.

Halfway through, he thought he heard footsteps. He stopped and listened.

Nothing.

He started loading the van again.

A firecracker went off somewhere. He felt pain in his left leg. The boxes in his hands fell from his grip.

"What the …?"

Trevor lost his balance and dropped to the concrete. He looked down and saw blood coming out of his jeans below the knee.

I've been shot?

"Good evening, Mr. Ashton."

That asshole faggot with the dangling earring stepped out of the shadows. It was the same asshole who arrested him at his apartment almost a year ago.

"You know, I knew that key was for a storage unit. All the guys back at the station kept trying to figure out where the secret compartment was at your place. But I thought for sure that you'd store everything off-site. Wait until they hear I was right."

"How did … how did you find me?" Trevor asked, the pain creeping to intolerable levels.

The cop stepped closer, the gun extended in his right hand. "Before your release, I canvassed every storage facility in the greater metro area. Do you realize just how many there are? Man, it took me almost two months to get to this one. The owner, a nice German fellow, said you come and go at night. He recognized your photo, but I couldn't get the exact unit number without a warrant. No judge would give me a warrant with you being released and the charges dropped. No way this side of Sunday."

"Released? Charges dropped?" Trevor moved up against the brick wall. "My lawyer, Vincenzo. What he said was true? You guys weren't playing me? I was released for real?"

The cop laughed.

What an asshole.

"Of course. He's your lawyer. We don't play games. People could be killed if we released potential murderers without proper documentation. There really was a technical problem. You were free to go. But not now. Look at this warehouse. You could open a shoe store with all these, and my guess is that I will find fingerprints on dozens of these shoes that'll point to persons missing or deceased. Am I right?"

"Fuck you." Trevor looked off into space. "I can't believe Mrs. Gavin was right," he whispered to himself.

"What? Mrs. Gavin? What the hell are you talking about?"

"Nothing." Trevor averted his eyes and refocused his attention on the asshole.

The cop raised his weapon and fired from four feet away. The bullet tore into Trevor's right knee.

Trevor screamed and breathed in and out in fits and starts.

"Holy shit! What are you doing?"

"Killing you because you don't deserve to live."

"You're a cop. You can't do that. You have to read me my rights."

The cop shook his head. "Nope. Tried that once. Didn't work. The justice system sucks for guys like you. This is the only way to cure you. Think of it like I'm doing you a favor."

"*This* is a favor?"

"Yeah, watch."

The cop closed one eye and aimed slowly in circles.

"No. Wait." Trevor begged.

The gun went off. He felt a punch in his groin. Trevor looked down. The bullet ripped a hole in his crotch, severing his penis and ripping the skin off the edge of his scrotum.

"There, all cured. See ya around."

Trevor screamed. The cop walked away.

"You can't leave me here. I'll bleed to death. I can't walk."

"That's the idea."

"They'll catch you. You can't kill people and get away with it."

"You did." The cop kept talking as he walked away. "The gun I used is untraceable. This will go down like a simple robbery. I'll write the report and ensure the judge hears about what's inside your little storage unit. I'll be back in an hour in my cruiser after I receive the call that there's gunfire in the area …"

The pain rose to excruciating. He couldn't hear the cop anymore.

His life source slowly ebbed from the three new holes in his body.

He looked up at the stars but couldn't find God.

Mrs. Gavin sat beside him, smiling. He looked away, his strength diminishing.

His mother stood in front of the van now.

He forced his eyes open to stare at his mother.

"Fuck you, Mom. Fuck you. It's all your fault. Every woman I killed was for you."

His eyes shut. The pain ceased.

Then nothing.

Trapped

A restaurant appeared out of the dense fog, murky and shimmering. The darkness had begun to work on her nerves, causing her to second-guess the existence of the building. Melissa Walkens eased off the gas and flipped her blinker. The neon *Open* sign flashed on and off, beckoning her to a restroom and a coffee. Maybe directions, too.

I've probably taken a wrong turn along the way.

She pulled up close to the building and turned off her Cadillac. The silence was deafening after the prolonged din of the road, the engine ticking as it cooled. She took a brief look around the outside of her vehicle and then cracked the door.

Something about the café bothered her. The large windows offered no reassurance, no comforting light. No smiling waitresses were beckoning her to enter. Only darkness waited on the other side of the panes. She wondered if someone had left the OPEN sign on by mistake.

In the corner window, she spied upon a woman and a child sipping a beverage each. That was enough to convince Melissa that everything was fine.

She eased the car door open all the way and stepped from the vehicle. The cool, moist air filled her nose. She took a deep breath and stretched her arms high to wake the cramped back muscles since she had left her sister's place.

The light from the restaurant only went as far as the edge of the road. The other side of the two-lane highway remained obscured in darkness. The thought of being alone in that darkness when she should be home was enough to unsettle her.

A fly got caught in an electric zapper hanging to the door's right. She jumped at the sudden sound and turned toward the building. Her bladder screamed for release, and she needed caffeine more than an addict required a fix.

Once inside the restaurant, she saw how modern it was as far as roadside coffee shops go. Beautiful wooden tables were lined perfectly down the left side by the windows, and padded chairs sat empty by each table. A long silver bar-like counter stretched the length of the restaurant with a row of fifties-era circular stools lined in front of it. An old jukebox sat quietly at the far end of the café, lights flashing on and off, waiting for another music lover to deposit a coin and choose a classic.

"Can I help you?"

Melissa jumped and raised a hand to her chest. "Oh my," she said. "You scared me." She took a deep breath. "I'm sorry. I don't usually spook so easily."

The woman looked to be in her fifties. A gray batch of hair tied into a bun, wrapped in a net, sat atop her head. She had the skin of a smoker and the longest earrings Melissa had ever seen.

"It's late," the woman said. "We're closing in about fifteen minutes, but I still have coffee if you need some."

"Coffee would be great." Melissa pointed to the restroom sign and said, "I'll be back."

"I'll set your coffee on the counter over there." The woman pointed halfway down the length of the counter.

Melissa nodded and started past the tables toward the jukebox where the restroom sign hung.

Why am I so nervous? It's just a roadside restaurant. I'll be in and out in ten minutes.

Once seated on the toilet, a young male voice shouted from the other side of the wall. He said something about the fryer being turned off and the grease already replaced for tomorrow's shift. He continued talking about the dishes, but she lost the clarity of his voice as he moved away.

She washed her hands and used a brown paper towel to open the door so as not to touch the door handle. While walking the length of the tables, she looked past the main counter and saw just enough room for two more tables on the other side of the front door. One of the tables was occupied by the woman and the young girl she had seen from the outside. The woman was facing her. Her eyes locked on Melissa's for a brief moment. Melissa offered a slight nod, smiled, then looked away and sat on the stool where her coffee awaited. The clock on the wall said it was ten minutes to midnight.

A young boy walked by the square hole in the wall where waitresses clipped orders to a circular wheel. Most of the lights in the back of the restaurant had been turned off, so she only saw his profile. The side view of his face was enough to spike her radar again.

Something's wrong here.

Even though the boy wasn't looking at her, she felt his eyes on her somehow.

Melissa stole a glance to her right. The woman with the little girl hadn't stopped staring at her. She quickly averted her eyes and took another sip of coffee. It was hot and tasted like dishwater.

After a few heartbeats, Melissa turned just enough to the right to catch the woman in her peripheral vision. The woman was looking out the front window now. Melissa turned around to see what had caught the woman's eye. A black van pulled in beside her Cadillac. The headlights turned off, and both the front doors opened. The driver ran to the passenger side to help the other occupant. Not to be caught staring, Melissa turned back in her seat. As she did, her eyes snatched a glimpse of the boy in the back disappearing from the corner of the rectangular hole in the wall.

He had been watching her.

A shiver coursed through her. Goose bumps formed on her arms.

What the hell is going on?

It was time to leave. But she had to pay for her coffee and wanted advice on getting back to the main highway.

Should I just get up, leave money on the counter and walk out?

Once she was back on the road with the doors locked, she'd feel much better.

She placed enough bills on the counter to cover the coffee.

The door opened behind her, and the van's occupants entered the restaurant. She rationalized that with more people around, she'd be fine. Safety in numbers.

The men who entered wouldn't be a problem. The driver who had run around to help the passenger had done so because the passenger was blind. He wore thick black sunglasses. His white cane had a red tip. It was difficult to peg an age because of the glasses, but Melissa guessed him to be in his mid-thirties. The driver was a clean-cut military type in his forties. He nodded at her, then smiled. Then he looked over his shoulder at the woman and the girl. They also nodded, but it was different somehow. Like they knew each other, or they'd seen one another before.

Maybe they're all regulars.

The driver smacked the bell on the counter to get the employee's attention.

I'll wait until the woman emerges from the back, pay, get directions, and get out.

But the woman who served Melissa coffee didn't come to the counter. Instead, the young male from the back did, and he looked worried, his eyes furtive, his hands shaking.

Something is definitely wrong.

The driver of the van asked the kid for two coffees. As he did, the blind man turned to face her. As much as she could tell he was blind and couldn't see her, it felt as if he was staring a hole through her chest.

Then he turned to the kid and raised his hand. He put his index finger to his neck as if to scratch an itch, and then his hand shot forward and opened.

Melissa jolted in her chair.

Sign language.

The driver glanced at her now. She stared down at her coffee, avoiding his eyes.

Her cell phone was in the car. Her purse was in the car. She had spent the weekend at her sister's house. Eva lost her hearing when she was five years old. Melissa learned sign language alongside her sister all those years ago. Sometimes, when not using signs often, she failed to remember certain things. But after an entire weekend of it, she was right back in and honed on the acronym HOLME. She recited it to herself while the kid poured coffees for the men from the van.

Hand shape. Orientation. Location. Movement. Facial Expression.

For the last seventy-two hours, she had been signing. That's why she easily recognized the word the blind man who just walked into the restaurant signed. It was a word that scared her, making her legs shake.

Kill.

But it couldn't be. There had to be a mistake.

She glanced up in time to see him brush his cheek with his index finger twice.

The sign for *woman*.

Then he held his palm up, aimed at his face. He twisted it around to face outward and moved it away slowly.

The sign for *attitude*.

What's he saying? *Kill the woman if she gives you any attitude?*

"Can I help you?" the driver of the van asked.

Melissa felt like her nerves were made of confetti as she almost slipped off the stool. The driver had caught her staring at his blind companion.

"I'm sorry," she muttered. "I meant no disrespect."

"It's okay," the driver said. "Not many people see a blind man in these parts." He leaned closer to her as he placed a hand beside his mouth. "Stare all you want," he whispered. "He can't tell."

The driver stood back to his full height and smiled. Then he turned around to face the kid behind the counter who was placing two coffees down.

The clock above the kid's head now read three minutes to midnight.

When the driver picked up the coffees, his jacket lifted enough for something to reflect light off his belt. The butt of a large gun rested just under his jacket.

Is it legal to carry a concealed weapon in this state?

She tried to pay attention to her coffee, cradling it in both hands.

Stop looking at them, she scolded herself.

They were going to rob the place. She was sure of it now. They would kill anyone who gave them attitude. And only she was privy to this information because she knew sign language.

How can I get out of here? How do I get the woman and her kid to safety without anyone realizing what I'm doing?

The boy behind the counter was looking at her again. Melissa put on a bold face. "Where's the woman who got me the coffee earlier? Or do I just pay you? And I need directions back to the main highway."

Only half his mouth moved in some kind of stupid smirk. "She punched out. She has left for the evening."

Melissa gripped her now-cooling coffee cup with both hands.

Everything's fine, she told herself. *Everything's going to be okay.*

The blind man and his driver edged past her and sat at the table by the door. As they ambled by, the boy ran around to make sure the table was clean, and they were seated comfortably.

"Okay, you're all set then?" the boy asked loud enough for everyone to hear.

No one responded audibly. With her back to them, she had no idea what they were up to.

Melissa got to her feet, made sure there was enough money to cover her beverage, and turned for the door. The boy moved in front of it.

"Excuse me," Melissa said, attempting to move around the boy. "I'm trying to leave."

"I don't think so," the boy said, a stern look replacing his earlier creepy smile.

Her stomach dropped. "Pardon me? What did you say?" She was surprised her voice didn't match the shaking of her hands.

"I can't let you leave at this hour, in that darkness." He pointed at the window. "Without giving you proper directions, now could I? My boss told me that every customer needs to leave satisfied. How else is a restaurant like this, out in the middle of nowhere, going to make a name for itself?"

Melissa's eyes moved to the woman with the little girl. She glared back. A sidelong glance at the clock said it was just past midnight now.

"Aren't you closing?"

"Sure, but we never ask a customer who is already here to leave. People ought to be allowed to finish what they ordered."

"Just tell me which way to drive, and I'll go. The money for the coffee is on the counter."

"Well then, be on your way, but first—" the boy reached into a large pocket in his apron. Melissa stepped back. To her relief, he pulled out a folded map. "Let me take thirty seconds of your time to set you on the right path."

There's nothing to worry about here. No one knows what I've got in the trunk of my car or how important it is. Get it together, Melissa.

These people were just being kind, and she acted like they were trying to kill her. As if a blind guy would be using sign language to communicate with a sixteen-year-old dishwasher. She would be worried if they knew who she was and what she had in her trunk.

She looked down at the map the boy had unfolded a foot from where she had been sitting. A chair slid across the floor behind her. She looked over her shoulder and saw the blind man getting up.

"It's okay," he said to his driver. "I will find my own way."

Melissa looked back at the map as the boy pointed out where they were. She was over twenty miles off the highway she needed. Back on Interstate 90, construction signs had said she needed to take a five-mile detour off the main road as it had been flooded out. The detour had gone longer than five miles until she ended up here.

"When was the last time you had rain in this area?" she asked the boy.

He rubbed his chin, his face lost in thought. "I don't seem to recall any rain. Why do you ask?"

"When I was on Interstate 90, I came upon an area where I had to make a detour due to flooding."

A light chuckle escaped the boy's lips. "You must've imagined it. Interstate 90 never floods. Not out here, anyway. It's too dry—"

A lock clicked behind them, cutting the boy off in mid-sentence. Melissa turned. The blind man had just locked the restaurant's main door. He didn't need a toilet after all. Nor was he blind as he removed his dark glasses to reveal alert eyes.

"Sit the fuck down, and maybe you will get out of this alive," he said.

A long barrel edged out from his waist as he produced a weapon. Melissa had no problem with the sitting down part because her legs were already thinking along those lines.

The boy knocked the map off the counter and stood back, grinning like he'd just solved Rubik's Cube when no one else could.

"Now," the formerly blind man said. "You have some explaining to do."

What the hell is he talking about?

She held her stomach, hoping it would contain itself.

"You have ruined people's lives for too long, Melissa Walkens."

They know my name.

"It's past midnight," he continued. "We are over twenty miles from help, and there's no one here but us cats. It's payback time. Wouldn't you agree, Vicky?" He gestured at the woman sitting with the little girl.

Melissa contemplated what he was saying as her mind raced through escape options.

They're all in on it? But in on what? Revenge? Murder? Theft? Am I supposed to be killed? How have I ruined other people's lives? How do they know me? Could this be about what's in my trunk?

"Go ahead, Vicky," he said, the gun in his hand raising high enough to be even with her eyes. "Tell this bitch whore who you are."

Vicky got up from her seat and walked maddeningly slowly. She sat on a stool beside Melissa, hip to hip. She wondered if Vicky could feel her body shaking this close.

"I am Layton's lover," she whispered. "Soon to be new wife."

A hole opened up in Melissa's heart as she leaned forward and pressed a hand on her stomach. She moaned in pain even though no one had touched her and no weapons had fired.

It can't be true.

"That girl is our daughter. Isn't she beautiful?"

The little girl had turned in her seat. Their eyes met. She looked sad, forlorn. Her hair was obviously cut at home, as no hairdresser would ever do that bad a job. She didn't appear to have been bathed recently. But the oddest feature of all was she looked exactly like a female version of Layton. DNA tests be damned. There was no doubt those freckles and red hair could be anything but Layton's.

Pain shot through Melissa's head like a searing rod had just branded her. Vicky held a clump of her hair and brought her back up to a full sitting position. She couldn't help the tiny scream that escaped her lips.

"Go ahead, scream all you want," Vicky taunted. "No one will hear you. Here, I'll scream with you—AHHHHHHHHH!"

The hand released. The pain subsided quickly, but a throbbing remained. Vicky got up and walked over to comfort the little girl as she started to cry.

"It's okay, pumpkin. That there is a bad woman." Vicky pointed at Melissa. "She done some bad things like steal your daddy away. Your daddy is rich. He promised us a great life, but that woman stole it. Mommy just needs to teach her a lesson, okay baby?"

The little girl wiped her eyes and nodded.

"Okay, baby?" Vicky repeated.

The little girl nodded again.

"Say okay, dammit," Vicky shouted. "I wanna hear you're okay with this."

The little girl looked up at Vicky with red, puffy eyes. In a soft trembling voice, she said, "Okay, Mommy." Then she looked away and rubbed her eyes as if trying to remove an offending image.

Is my husband in on this?

Could Layton really have a mistress? This was orchestrated in detail. Someone went to a lot of trouble to set this up.

It had to be the guy holding the gun. His blind-man ruse and sign language bit. He had to know stuff about Melissa. Stuff only Layton knew. He had a gun. He had the brains. Diffuse him, and this could all fall apart and go away.

The driver of the van got up from his chair. Everyone seemed to stop what they were doing to watch him. He adjusted his pants and walked to the door.

"Mark, did you take care of the bodies like I asked you to?"

What?

"Yes. They're in the cooler."

"What bodies?" Melissa asked. Now her voice cracked.

"The truck stop closes at nine in the evening. The owners wanted us to leave, but we couldn't as we had to wait for you. May they rest in peace." He said the last part with so much sarcasm it dripped off it. "Their customer service was exemplary. They offered us their establishment to set a trap for the fly." He made a buzzing sound. "That's you, caught in the fly trap."

Vicky grabbed the little girl's hand and walked her to the door, where she unlocked it and stepped outside. The driver followed but stopped before the door closed.

"Mark, clean the joint up. Leave no traces that we were here. Then, follow us to the cabin." He looked at Melissa. "Get up. You're coming with me."

Melissa crossed her arms and leaned on the counter. She had never considered what looking tough was supposed to be like. The last fight she had was in grade school. But leaving this restaurant and going to some remote cabin meant certain death. She'd seen their faces. The owners of this establishment were dead. She had no choice but to refuse to go.

"I would rather clean my ears with an ice pick," she said.

The driver stared at her, frowning.

Clearly, you didn't expect that, eh, asshole? Actually, I didn't expect that.

The gunman moved his weapon up and down. The boy stepped back out of the way.

"What did you say to me? Repeat it because sometimes I don't hear things right?"

"I said, fuck you," Melissa said, feeling emboldened now. "I'm not going anywhere with you." Melissa remained seated, arms crossed, trying for a look on her face that would've defied Medusa.

"So you wanna play?" the driver said as he closed the door. "Mark, go start the cleanup. Trent, go wait in the van."

"Do I have to?" Trent said. "I want to watch."

The driver looked back at him. "You did your part perfectly. Your share is as good as in the bank. Don't fuck that up by not listening to me now. Go wait in the van."

Trent lowered his weapon and holstered it. He turned to the table they had been sitting at and retrieved his white cane. With only one backward glance, Trent left the restaurant, the door clanging behind him.

She realized how wrong she had been. The blind man wasn't in charge. The mastermind was the driver.

But what was she supposed to do now? She didn't even know how to throw a proper punch. The alternative of going to a random cabin somewhere or facing the consequences here was her only option. She had no choice. The cornered animal had to strike out even though it knew it would die. She would be no one's fly in a fly trap. No one owned her. They never had.

Make the first move. That's the only way. There's no turning back now.

The driver edged closer. "Last chance to comply."

The best way to attack him would be when standing. Melissa uncrossed her arms, leaned forward, and made to get up.

"Too late," he whispered.

She felt something strike her left cheek. She had no idea the pain would be so intense. Her face felt like it was broken. She fell to the tiled floor and writhed there, moaning, held under the grip of unbearable pain.

She caught movement above. Her brain took over, and reflex attempted to move her head away, but she wasn't fast enough. The driver's boot hit her in the forehead, whipping her skull back like she was on a roller coaster ride from hell. Stars filled her vision, pain her mind. She lay moaning and crying, waiting for the next blow.

When it didn't come, she opened her eyes and peered through the tears.

The driver was gone.

She moved her head to look at the counter, but her neck protested too much. She kneaded her fingers into her neck muscles. Nothing protruded from the skin or felt broken.

Then the driver reappeared from the back room. Light from the moon came through the window and glinted off something in his hand.

A butcher knife.

He smiled down at her like a clown at a circus before he was about to give her a big balloon.

"Now we're going to have some fun. Reach in slowly and give me your car keys, or I'll remove a finger. You've got five seconds."

A simple carjacking? No one knows what's in the trunk.

I will never give up my keys.

In her precious seconds, Melissa rolled to her back and slowly reached for her pocket, attempting to stall as long as she could.

"Come on," he said. The knife edged closer to her hand. He held it just above her stomach as he kneeled over her.

The loop of the keyring wrapped around her index finger inside her pocket. She pulled the keys out and then threw them at his face. He reflexively turned away. Melissa used her other hand to grab his wrist, spin the knife around and jab at him, using the floor for leverage.

She was surprised at how easily the knife entered his chest. It all seemed surreal as it slipped between the bones of his rib cage and effortlessly carved a slit inside his body all the way to the hilt. The knife was long enough that the tip would be close to protruding out of his back.

The look on his face was a mix of shock, anger, and surprise. He looked down at the handle sticking out of him. His balance was lost, and the driver fell back onto the floor, where blood seeped out of his wound. Now blood bubbled up on his lips.

He was dying. She had killed him, yet she felt nothing.

The boy was still in the back. The rest of them were outside. She had to deal with the boy, then she could run out the back and escape.

Melissa snatched her car keys off the floor, pocketed them, and stepped over the dying driver. He moaned and rested his head back. Resignation covered his face. He, too, knew this was the end for him.

Melissa quietly tiptoed to the front door and turned the thumb lock to secure it. She peeked outside. Trent was in the van with the woman and the little girl. Trent had a gun, she reminded herself. First, the boy in the back.

She returned to the driver on the floor and hunched over him low enough so no one could see her from the outside. He wasn't moving. She looked up at the counter to ensure the boy wasn't watching and then rifled through the driver's pockets in search of a weapon. He had a gun in a holster under his left armpit. She unclipped the holster and yanked the gun free.

"Get up and turn around slowly."

Judging by how close the voice was, the boy had to be directly behind her.

"How did you do it?" It sounded like the boy was sobbing. "How could you?"

She eased the gun toward her waist, out of sight of the boy, and started to stand.

"Hands where I can see 'em," he said.

"Listen," Melissa whispered. She was surprised at how much talking hurt her face after being punched. Using as little of her mouth as she could, Melissa continued. "We don't have to do this. It was all a misunderstanding."

Blood seeped into her vision from the kick she received to the forehead.

"No, bitch. No misunderstanding. You just killed the only man who ever loved me. He took me in when my dad threw me out. He got me this job."

"He got you a job so that you could hurt people?"

"No, Kevin was all about righting the world's wrongs. He told me about you. He said … wait a second. Turn around. Look at me when I'm talking to you!"

"Do you have a weapon?" Melissa asked. "Are you going to hurt me?"

"Damn right. Turn around, or you get it in the back."

Melissa turned slowly, rolling the gun around by her side,

protected from his view. The boy held a hammer in his right hand. It was high, over his head, as if he was going to throw it like a baseball.

"Is that the best you've got?" she asked. "There's a whole restaurant in the back, and you come out with a hammer."

The boy was visibly shaking. She couldn't tell if he shook in fear or glee. The business end of the hammer vibrated in the air. His eyes were wild, darting from her to the dead man on the floor. At that moment, she felt sorry for him. His age hurt him as he wasn't mature enough to make better decisions about whom to associate with. The lack of maturity made this scene even more difficult to deal with. She had to disarm him, but the wild look on his face made things that much more difficult.

"Let's talk about this," Melissa said. "Maybe we can work something out. I know you're frightened."

"There's nothing to work out. There's me alive and you dead. Once that's done, you and I have worked out everything we're supposed to deal with. Do not mistake my appearance for fear. I am absolutely fucking angry. I may need to murder Trent out there for leaving you two alone. Now," he took a deep breath. "Step to me, bitch. Come closer so I can look at what a whore looks like. Come on." He gestured with his free hand.

A loud bang erupted at the front door, roughly four feet behind the boy. As Melissa jumped, her hand holding the gun popped out of hiding. The boy had also jumped and spun around to see what had caused the noise. Melissa brought the weapon up in that two-second window to aim at the boy. He turned back to her.

"Let me in," Trent yelled from outside.

Melissa squeezed the trigger back. The bullet's impact shocked the boy as much as the weapon's recoil in her hand surprised Melissa. He looked down. The hammer lowered. Melissa held the gun ready should she need to use it again. She caught a look of absolute surprise on Trent's face.

Blood spread slowly across the floor outward from the boy's foot. The wound had been a lucky shot. The bullet entered the front part of the ankle. His right leg shook and then buckled. The hammer fell free from his hand and smacked hard onto the restaurant's floor, bouncing once. The boy crumpled to the floor beside it.

Melissa ran past the fallen boy to the back. White aprons hung on the wall just inside the door. She grabbed two and ran back to him.

"Here, wrap your lower leg with the apron's straps, or you could die from blood loss."

Trent yanked hard on the door behind them. Melissa quickly aimed the gun at his head through the window. He stepped back at least two feet.

"Do not fuck with me!" she shouted. She had no idea where this side of her came from, only now that it had escaped, she was quite happy to have it. Losing control in a situation like this felt better than trying to maintain it.

"You're just another dead whore whose corpse I'll fuck for days after." He pulled out his own weapon.

As fast as he produced the gun, he fired it. Glass from the front doors sprayed toward her. She screamed and ducked her head, raising her arms to cover herself. Trent reached through the broken window to unlock the bolt when she looked back up. An audible click told her he was in.

It all happened too fast. Things were spiraling out of control. She bolted for the back of the restaurant. Two more bullets rang out behind her. One came so close she heard the wind parting as it passed her head. Once she entered the back room, Melissa scanned her body for holes or blood. Her hands came up dry.

She ran past the fryer and a well-used wooden table and ducked beside the walk-in freezer door. The large silver handle was cold to the touch. Melissa pulled on the handle and eased the door open to conceal herself behind it, the wall to her back. When they came into the back, they'd figure she was hiding in the freezer. She peeked around the edge of the door. No one had followed her into the kitchen yet.

She swiveled her head toward the hole in the wall where waitresses passed orders back to the cooks. Trent was there, grinning like a creepy pervert. His arm rested on the small shelf, his weapon aimed directly at her. In an instant, his hand twitched. She ducked down as far as she could, screamed, and yanked on the freezer door, hoping it would move another foot to conceal her. Her gun was eerily quiet as it spit a bullet into the freezer door roughly six inches above her head.

She screamed again, sprawled out on the floor, and pushed off the wall with her legs in a desperate attempt to distance herself from Trent. She raised her gun, extended it above her head, and yanked on the trigger repeatedly, firing in Trent's general direction. A moment later, she lay under the edge of a long metal table that sat like an island in the middle of the restaurant's kitchen. Trent's face had disappeared from the waitress's hole in the wall. There had been no chance to see if she had hit him or not.

A buzzing in her ears accompanied the firing of the weapons. It began to subside, but not fast enough for her to hear if anyone was coming. A cool sweat had broken out and beaded on her forehead as her breath came out in fits and starts.

She wondered if the woman and the girl had driven away in the van yet. Melissa looked around for another weapon without knowing how to check the gun to see if there were any bullets left. The only option was knives, which wouldn't work against a man with a gun.

The freezer door remained wide open. She could see to the back from where she lay under the table. She blinked, wiped blood and sweat out of her eyes, and took a second look. The head and part of a shoulder of a woman lying on a freezer rack. It was the same woman who had served her coffee when Melissa had shown up at the restaurant just before midnight. Now she knew what they did with the owners.

She detected someone moaning from the front of the restaurant. It sounded like the boy.

"Call an ambulance," he shouted.

"Is Trent dead?" she asked.

"Yes. You shot him in the forehead. It's over. Please help me."

Was he telling the truth? Or did they just want her to reveal her position?

"How do I know you're telling me the truth?" she asked.

"You don't. But it'll be on your conscience if I die because you did nothing."

Whether Trent was dead or not, she couldn't remain under the table all night. She moved her head out of hiding. No one stared through the waitress's hole. With a last glance around the back room, she edged out farther. She was alone.

It took her a full minute to get to a standing position. The beating of her heart seemed louder in her ears than the boy's moans from the other room. It was hard to believe what had happened in such a short time. It was like a dream or a nightmare. She also had no idea how her husband would explain the woman, Vicky. Or the child.

Could it be true?

Melissa understood that what happened tonight would completely change her life. The only way to find out how much things would change was to walk out of this restaurant alive; she had every intention of doing that. This was a game humans have played since the beginning of time. The Mayans beheaded the losing team, the gladiators died in the Coliseum. On this evening, in this restaurant, people had died. The victor wouldn't be the most agile or the most physically fit. Tonight's successor would be the smartest one. Melissa knew her best weapon was her mind. Right now, it was honed and alert, ready to outwit her opponent.

She knew Trent wasn't dead. No way. Her random shots went wild. She would've been seriously lucky to have had a direct hit.

Now standing in the kitchen, a perfect target, she only had seconds to accomplish her task before Trent laid down another barrage of deadly projectiles.

Inching for the rear of the restaurant, she shouted to the front, "Is there a phone out there I could use to call an ambulance for you?"

"Yes," the boy shouted back. "It's right by the cash register. Please hurry."

"Okay, but you're sure Trent's dead? I don't want to come out there and get a nasty surprise."

"Yes, please hurry. I can't seem to stop the bleeding. I'm feeling faint like I'm about to pass out."

She grabbed a cloth that lay across one of the back sinks. After balling it up, she got into position.

"Okay, I coming out."

Melissa tossed the cloth through the opening to the front of the restaurant, then turned and ran for the back door. She was three steps from the back when a hail of bullets rained down on the cloth, embedding into the wall behind it. Before her assailant could realize that he'd been duped, Melissa was already yanking on the metal bar of the back door. It opened without protest, and she burst into the night, stopping and staring.

A single vehicle sat parked in the far corner of the lot in the darkest area, unlit by any of the building's lights. The car was a Lincoln Navigator with twenty-four-inch silver rims. She would recognize it anywhere. The exact vehicle and rims that her husband drove. Her husband, Layton Walkens.

Everything came to her in a rush, like a magnet picking up its prize. Layton had orchestrated the attack on her. He was the brainchild. He hired the thugs to kill her. She had to assume he knew what was in her trunk. Which meant he had plans to take it. After nine years of marriage, how could she not see who he really was in all that time?

Scuffling noises from behind brought her out of her reverie. Without turning to look, Melissa ran for the side of the building and jumped around the corner. A quick sprint brought her to the front of the restaurant, where she saw her Cadillac and the van still idling beside it.

The trunk of the Cadillac was open. Her husband was responsible. He had stolen what was rightfully hers and wanted to kill her for it. The feeling of being so unwanted that the person she loved would rather have her dead was debilitating. A paralysis of loneliness swept over her as she stood in the dark and stared at the open trunk of her car.

Then the night lit up in front of her, a ball of fire pushing her backward until she stumbled to remain standing. It all happened so fast. She only caught a glimpse before her eyes closed out of reflex.

The idling van had exploded into a large fireball. Her Cadillac rocked beside it as its windows all shattered inward. The force of the explosion knocked the wind out of her. She gasped and held her stomach. The gun fell from her hand as she stumbled again, then fell. She landed in a small bush, rolled backward, and ended up on her stomach. After a moment, she got her breathing back under control.

The van was completely engulfed in flames now, a roaring fire. No one could have survived that. Her car was catching the fingers of flame now.

The immense loneliness she felt a moment before the explosion was replaced by a deep sadness that a bottomless well paled in comparison to it. Vicky and the little girl had been in the van. Unless, by some stroke of luck, they had gotten out before it exploded, which seemed unlikely.

Melissa rolled into a ball and hugged herself.

How could this be? What had really happened tonight? Could this all be about her mother's jewelry?

It had been eight years since her mother's ring was last seen. Her mother had been diagnosed with Alzheimer's nine years ago and lost the ring shortly thereafter. It remained a mystery until she died. Melissa's sister found the ring in an old jewelry box packed with photo albums and trinkets from another era. The ring was apparently purchased during World War II and given to her mother, but the story was that it had gotten removed from the hand of a rich woman who had died during a raid on Nazi Germany. An appraisal had pegged the ring's value at a quarter of a million dollars back in 1955. It had been willed to Melissa. She had placed the ring in a waterproof, fireproof safe for the trip home, keeping it in the trunk where no prying eyes would see it.

The only person who knew about the ring was her sister. And now her husband, Layton.

Maybe they had set it up to look like a robbery gone bad, or perhaps this was all about having the insurance payout on the theft of the ring. Whatever the reasons, Melissa knew it wasn't over. Layton had gone too far. He wouldn't allow her to just walk away.

She eased out of her scrunched-up position and turned around to get up.

Footsteps approached over the sound of the flames. Trent stood fifteen feet away, his arm extended, the gun barrel aimed at her. She looked at her hands, but they were empty. The gun had fallen somewhere after the explosion. With nothing to defend herself with,

Melissa looked into the eyes of her murderer.

Trent closed one eye in an exaggerated expression of taking careful aim. Melissa closed both of hers and waited.

The gun fired. She jolted, stumbled, and almost fell backward again. There was no pain yet, but she was sure it was on its way.

When she opened her eyes, she understood why there was no pain.

She hadn't been shot.

Trent was on his knees. Blood surged out of his mouth in spurts. The gun that had fired was held by her husband, who stood directly behind Trent.

"How the fuck could you have screwed this up?" Layton asked.

Melissa wondered if he was talking to Trent or her.

"Seriously. I cannot believe you had this kind of ability to stay alive. You are one brave fuck, you know that?"

He was talking to her.

"I hired these guys to do one simple fucking task in the middle of nowhere. But no, you gotta fuck that up."

He advanced on her. As Layton walked past Trent, he lowered his weapon and fired two more quick rounds into Trent's corpse.

Vicky stood back by the Lincoln with the ten-year-old girl. Relief at seeing the little girl alive coursed through Melissa. No one had died in the van explosion.

"If you wanted a divorce," Melissa said. "There are better ways to go about it."

Layton closed the four-foot gap between them and backhanded her so hard she hit the ground with almost as much force as the blow. Blood flowed freely from a new wound on her face. She wondered if having a baby was more painful because the pain she felt at that moment was like a burning piece of metal being applied to her cheek.

Layton's rough hands grabbed her and lifted her to a sitting position.

"Stand up!" Layton shouted.

Melissa used a tree to get to her feet.

"All this," she paused to catch her breath. "All this for the ring? Are you for real?"

"Not just the ring. Life insurance, you stupid bitch. One-million dollars on your life. But the only clauses are, I can't kill you, and it can't be suicide. That's what these inbreeds were for. I gave them everything. All the tools they'd need. The planning, the restaurant, and even the detour idea. Everything, but they're too stupid to fucking do it right. And now they're all dead."

"Why is my trunk open then?" Melissa asked. "If it was just life insurance, why take my mother's ring?"

"The ring was extra. Knowing you were retrieving the ring from your sister this weekend was the catalyst. When I'd decided to have you killed, I needed to nail down a time. After the good news of the ring, I knew this was my opportunity."

"So what now?" Melissa asked. She needed to attack him. Since *he* couldn't kill her, she could try to kill him. But her energy was gone, depleted.

"What now, you ask? There is no, *what now*. You die here tonight. I will leave this place, collect the insurance, cry fake tears at your funeral, and go golfing. That's what now, you piece of shit." He grabbed her shoulder. "I fucking hate you." He was brute strength against her weakened adrenaline-depleted body. She was no match for him.

Layton dragged her out of the bush and onto the gravel clearing toward the Lincoln Navigator.

"I'll get that stupid Vicky to do it for me. You can be killed by my new bitch, and then I'll rat her out ..."

The gun she had dropped sat two feet from her. She twisted, turned, and thrust her body toward it. Layton's grip was lost as she landed beside the weapon. Continuing into a roll, Melissa snatched it, slid her finger past the trigger guard, and brought it up to shoot. Layton was about to reach for her again when his eyes widened at seeing what she had in her hand.

"What the fuck?" he asked.

She pulled the trigger.

Nothing happened.

She pulled again and again.

Layton smiled. "You are a dangerous one. I had no idea. Where did that come from, I wonder?"

It riled her to hear him talk like that. He always did it. *I wonder where my wallet is. I wonder why our neighbor does that.* All the time, pondering out loud, driving her crazy.

Layton grabbed the front of her shirt. He pulled hard and started dragging her across the gravel again.

"You actually scared me for a moment there." He puffed out audibly. "You're going to love what I have planned for you—"

A gun fired in the parking lot behind them. Layton stopped. He let go of Melissa. She hit the gravel and rolled onto her side. A moment later, Layton's gun dropped from his hand. The weapon fell one foot from Melissa's right hand, as fortune would have it. She snatched it up and gripped it tight, aiming it at Layton.

Shooting her husband was pointless, though, as he was already shot. He dropped to his knees and fell forward onto his face, where he lay motionless.

From the ground, Melissa spun toward Vicky.

Then someone spoke from behind her.

"Nobody talks about Kevin that way," the boy said. "He was the only one who mattered to me. He took me in when my dad threw me out. He was not stupid, and he was not a fucking idiot."

The boy sat on the back step of the restaurant, a gun in hand, his foot wrapped in the white apron that was now completely red. He dropped his head and sobbed.

Melissa swiveled around as she heard the pitter-patter of feet running toward her. Vicky had left the little girl by the Lincoln and was running to the boy's aid. Ten feet from the boy was as far as she got. The boy lifted his gun and shot her in the face. Her forward momentum made her look like she had done a funky dance as she jiggled her way to the ground. Vicky landed on the gravel and slid to a stop, a large chunk of her face landed a foot from her body.

"Don't you come running to me like you're on my side, bitch. You were going to blow up the van with us in it and run away with all the money and that asshole. Fuck you, Vicky." The boy pointed in Layton's direction. "And fuck you, too."

Melissa couldn't believe it. Everyone was dead but the boy, the little girl, and herself. Inch by inch, she moved her hands to aim Layton's gun at the boy to ensure she didn't get a bullet after all her efforts to stay alive.

The boy saw her intentions and recognized them for what they were.

"I got one bullet left, and it ain't for you," he said. "Kevin is gone. My parents are dead. I killed the owners of this restaurant. There's nothing left to live for. I won't spend the next thirty years in prison."

He lifted his gun and placed the barrel in his mouth. Before she could shout in protest, he pulled the trigger. The back of his head lifted off and smacked into the doorframe. His body slumped and made a slow motion fall to the ground.

Melissa tried to collect herself. She did her best to stand on wobbly legs. She half limped, and half walked toward the Lincoln Navigator and the ten-year-old girl beside it.

"Are you going to be my mother now?" the little girl asked.

"Yes, I am. Would you like that?"

"Yes, ma'am. But I might be sad for a while. I loved her, but she was mean to me every day. I prayed for her to go away. I said that if she ever did, I would be a good girl after that. She always told me I was a bad girl. I'll still be sad, though."

"I understand. I might be sad, too. Do you think we could be sad together?"

The girl shrugged and seemed to think about it. "I guess so." Then she said. "Can we leave here now? I don't like this restaurant anymore."

"See, you're already being a good girl."

Melissa got in the Lincoln Navigator, made sure her small passenger was buckled up, and drove away from the carnage. Later that morning, she dropped the little girl off with her deaf sister and drove to the police station, where she gave them her statement. Her mother's ring was in the back of the Navigator, right where Layton had placed it.

In the end, Melissa collected one million dollars in life insurance money on the death of her husband. She cried fake tears at his funeral.

She didn't go golfing.

About Jonas Saul

Jonas Saul is the bestselling author of the Sarah Roberts Series—more than two million sold!—and has written and published over sixty thrillers. After acquiring an agent, he signed several deals in Los Angeles, with MadRiver Pictures optioning his Sarah Roberts Series —over forty books!—(currently in development).

Jonas has often outranked Stephen King and Dean Koontz on Amazon over the past decade. He's regularly invited to be a guest speaker, teacher, or workshop presenter at international writing conferences and film festivals worldwide. He hosts an annual writer's retreat in Greece, where he currently lives. He focuses his teaching on how to get tension and emotion in every scene, on every page, how he made it as a creator/writer, the path to success in this business, and the pitfalls to avoid. He also hosts a reading retreat in Greece with guest authors, yoga retreats, and hiking retreats. Visit the Imagine Greece Retreats website at www.imaginegreeceretreats.com, or email him directly to discuss an opportunity to join one of the retreats at jonas@imaginegreeceretreats.com.

Jonas is also a professional freelance editor. He works for several publishers and does private editing for clients, with many testimonials on his website at www.imaginepress.org, which details each author's response to Jonas's editing skills. Email Jonas directly for an editing quote at editor@imaginepress.org.

To book Jonas for a speaking engagement at a writer's conference/festival, to have him on your jury at a film festival, or even to say hello, email Jonas directly at jonassaul@icloud.com.

For updates on releases, hit the "Follow" button on Amazon or Bookbub, and join Jonas on Facebook, where he's most active.

Contact Jonas Saul

Linktree: Find me here

Email: jonassaul@icloud.com

www.ingramcontent.com/pod-product-compliance
Lightning Source LLC
Chambersburg PA
CBHW021413010826
48972CB00014B/2054